THE
KEY

J.B. PRICE

 FriesenPress

One Printers Way
Altona, MB R0G 0B0
Canada

www.friesenpress.com

Copyright © 2024 by J.B. Price
First Edition — 2024

All rights reserved.

No part of this publication may be reproduced in any form, or by any means, electronic or mechanical, including photocopying, recording, or any information browsing, storage, or retrieval system, without permission in writing from FriesenPress.

ISBN
978-1-03-919550-9 (Hardcover)
978-1-03-919549-3 (Paperback)
978-1-03-919551-6 (eBook)

1. FICTION, DYSTOPIAN

Distributed to the trade by The Ingram Book Company

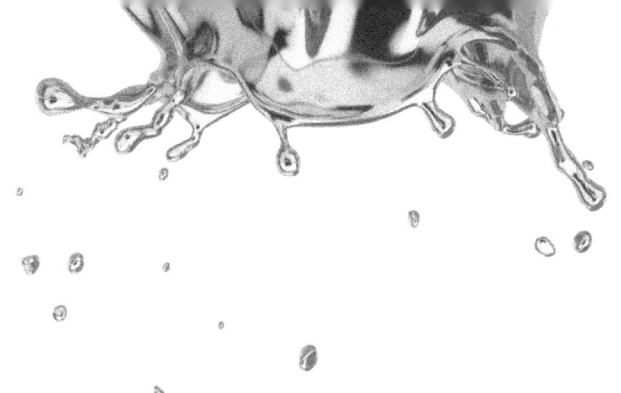

CHAPTER 1

Something was terribly wrong—and Darcy did not like when things went wrong. She was usually the one on the receiving end of some scathing lecture, disappointing the lecturer even if she hadn't been involved. Darcy could tell by the way in which the man across from her was sitting that something had sent his nerves on edge. The small sneer to his face and the glint in his eyes sent her pulse racing and she twisted her fingers between her knees. He sucked his teeth disapprovingly and let out a tremendous sigh.

He was nervous, and her father was very rarely nervous.

A business man, Charles Newton prided himself on being a man of action and results, not someone who waited for others to act. He was one of the biggest business moguls in all of the world and the leader of Faction 2. He had practice and skill at forcing people to bend to his will. But Charles bending to another's will? Never—that was completely foreign to him.

Darcy knew that her father's uneasy demeanor would only lead to a more ruthless attack on whomever he was expecting to walk through that door. Darcy tucked one of her dark curls behind her ear and tried to swallow.

Her father drummed his fingers against the thick glass top of the desk between them and unbuttoned the center of his crisp, gray suit jacket. His silver hair was just a shade darker than the fabric, and his clear blue eyes, as cold as crystal, darted from side to side as he worked the knot of his navy tie.

It struck Darcy, then, how different the pair truly were. From their contradicting dispositions down to the stark contrast in their physical features, it was a wonder they shared blood. Where her father was commanding—even hostile at times—Darcy was demure and apprehensive.

Darcy's features were of a darker variety, while her father's seemed to radiate light. Her chocolate-colored curls had been the focal point of her sister's teasing for the majority of their youth—her brother and sister were both fair and slight, much like their parents. Darcy's curls landed just between her shoulder blades, but it wasn't often she let them hang free, choosing instead to tie them back and hope they disappeared. Her dark eyes were almond shaped and almost too large for her round face. Darcy had inherited her mother's height, coming just under the chin of all their other family members. It seemed the only thing the young woman shared with her brother and sister was the strong, straight nose that ended in a button just above her full lips. She was a parody of the effortless perfection her family exuded.

Her father checked his gold pocket watch for the fifth time since they had entered his office, yanking the thing from his pocket and squinting at the ticking hands. He shoved the offending item back into the pocket of his jacket, the gold chain attached to the end of it tapping against his lapel lightly.

"It shouldn't be taking this long," he muttered to himself, and stood abruptly from his leather chair. He paced for a second before his eyes landed once again on Darcy. She curled into herself at his inspection. His eye was a discerning one, and she always seemed to come up short of his expectations while pinned beneath it. "For God's sakes, Darcy," he boomed in the empty space surrounding them. "Don't look so frightened."

"I'm sorry, Father," she responded, and lowered her gaze. It was never a good idea for her to keep eye contact with him long. She wished one of her siblings were here with her. She always fell into the shadows when Shane and Krista, who were considered the superior siblings by far, were around. Darcy despised being in the spotlight within range of her father, especially when he was feeling particularly heinous.

CHAPTER 1

He continued, fiddling with his tie, "I need you looking sharp. We have to sell this as a family—a unit—and I can't afford for this deal to go south."

"Yes, sir," she replied, and tried her best to harden her expression. She had a lot of practice with fixing her face. She felt like a marionette doll more than she felt like an actual human. The press functions her father was a part of required finesse and supreme acting skills to pull off. They couldn't look anything less than the perfect family, or all of the power he had acquired would be snatched from his precarious grip. Her father had clawed his way to the top, but there were always those who wanted to pull him from his throne.

Darcy jumped about a half a foot in the air when the office door crashed against the opposite wall. Two men the size of redwood trees framed the door way, and between them was a thrashing mess of ink and denim. Black boots kicked in all directions, and curses flew from a split lip. The leather of his jacket creaked as he jerked his arms in all directions.

"Get your fucking hands off of me! I swear I'll rip both of you to shreds! I'll melt your asses with lasers from my eyeballs! You fucking pricks!" the irate form was yelling, thrusting his body back and forth in a futile attempt to break free.

"Let him go," her father instructed, sounding bored by the whole scenario. Darcy found his tone curious, considering just a second ago he was practically jumping out of his skin at the thought of this mysterious man arriving in the office.

The two men dumped the figure unceremoniously on the hard tile of the floor. The man leapt to his feet, his tattooed fists lifted and ready to fight. He struck out with a fist and the man on the right dropped like a sack of potatoes. Darcy let out a small shriek and jumped from her chair, circling the desk and putting some space between herself and the danger. The man was lean and clearly muscular, but the currently unconscious form he had just knocked to the ground was easily three times his size. Darcy was amazed that the leather-bound figure was capable of taking on the enormous man at all, let alone knocking him out with a single hit.

"Mr. Riggs!" her father bellowed, coming around the desk to glare at the leather-clad maniac. The man in question turned suddenly, his bright-blue eyes wild. "That is quite enough!"

THE KEY

The figure that had captured everyone's attention seemed to have trouble registering where he was—and what it meant to be standing in this office. He snarled at Charles, baring silver caps on his molars. Darcy shifted back further and pressed herself against the window that framed the back of the office. She was wringing her hands so tightly, the blood had long since drained from her appendages. She could feel her heart thumping in her throat, and sweat broke out along the nape of her neck. The familiar prickle of panic crawled its way up the back of her skull. Who was this man, and what in God's name was he doing in her father's office?

Her father commanded again, "Get control of yourself, Mr. Riggs. I only wish to speak to you. We mean you no harm."

The man—Mr. Riggs—leaned back slightly from his defensive stance, but Darcy was smart enough to know that this didn't mean he wasn't just as dangerous as he had been just moments before. She stayed back against the window as far as she could but made sure to fix her face and clasp her fingers together in front of her to keep from wringing them wildly. She knew her father would not approve.

"Who the fuck are you, and what do you want with me?" Mr. Riggs snarled. He hadn't taken his eyes off of the older man. Her father looked calm, but she could see the rosy tint to his cheeks and the rapid rise and fall of his chest. He was feeling the rush of the moment, and this only worked to amplify her own anxiety. She had never seen her father so bothered.

"I am Charles Newton, founder and CEO of Newton Industries, the largest manufacturing company of modified human prosthetics and leader of Faction 2. I'm sure you've heard of me." His face curled into a sinister smirk, knowing full well the man across the room had to have heard of him. There wasn't a person in all of the Factions that hadn't heard of her father.

Reality finally seemed to hit the man square in the face, and he stood stalk-still, blinking a few times in shock. He then let out an incredulous laugh and turned in a circle, eyeing the opulent office surrounding him. He whistled low and shook a tattooed hand in faux amazement. "Nice place you got here, Charlie." He continued his appraisal of the space by walking around, his tattered boots falling hard against the white tiled floor.

Darcy finally allowed herself to move away from the cool glass pressed

CHAPTER 1

against her back. The giant man that had been lying in a heap on the floor slowly stirred from his position and pushed himself upright. He shook his head slightly and rubbed at the purple mark on his jaw. Darcy swallowed thickly as she thought of the thudding sound he had made as he hit the floor, and she wondered if she would make the same noise if he felt so inclined to attack her. She didn't think anyone in this room had the ability to stop him. Not even her father.

The man picked up a decanter from the credenza and tossed it from palm to palm as though it were worth nothing more than the jacket on his back. "That real crystal?" he asked, tossing the delicate glass unceremoniously into the air before he started to walk around again as though already bored by it. Darcy watched as the remaining security officer practically leaped into the air in an attempt to save the poor crystal from its doomed fate. His sausage fingers gripped it only a second before it touched the floor, and Darcy let out a deep sigh.

"Welcome to Newton Industries," her father began again. "I would tell you to make yourself at home, but it appears you already have."

The tattooed man continued his circle through the office, around the cream-colored chaise and sleek end table. He took a grease-smudged finger and dragged it along the mantle of the built-in fireplace, then inspected the digit for dust before wiping it on his leather jacket. He seemed so at ease, almost comfortable in the unfamiliar space, and Darcy couldn't tear her gaze away from him. She wondered if all of his bravado was a show or if he really was so carefree. She also couldn't help but wonder what her father could want with a man that appeared so feral. She had never seen anyone in her life so raw.

For all of his confidence, false or not, Darcy found herself his opposite in equal measure. She was terrified. Not only of the man that had been circling the office like a shark closing in on its prey, but of the man standing on the opposite side of the desk from her. Her father had summoned her without any explanation, and she had known better than to question his motives. She had arrived at exactly the time he had demanded and waited to receive his orders. Never in any of her musings about their meeting had this scene played out so bizarrely.

Mr. Riggs, for all of his circling, had not made eye contact with her until that moment. His clear blue stare penetrated her skin and made her squirm under his inspection. His eyes seemed to be looking deep into her bones, and she felt exposed, a feeling she was not familiar with and did not appreciate. She wished there were some way for her to cover the flaws he must be seeing within her, the same flaws her father saw whenever he looked at her. She wrapped her arms over her chest and looked down at the floor. One of her curls sprang forward into her eyes and she swatted at the swaying strand. She heard her father clear his throat and was thankful for the distraction.

"Please have a seat," Charles interrupted. "Both of you."

Darcy gulped and waited as the figure that had been the center of her undivided attention paused, rubbed a hand along the blonde stubble of his chin, and finally slouched into one of the chairs across from her father's desk. Her father smiled and began circling around to return to his own chair. He gave Darcy a meaningful look on his revolution and nodded his head to the chair sitting beside the slumped figure. She paused for only a second before she forced her feet to move.

She slowly lowered herself into the chair and sat as far away from her neighbor as possible. She didn't want to make it obvious that she was avoiding his presence, but she couldn't quell the uneasy feeling in her stomach. She wished her father would reveal his motives soon. She was beginning to feel queasy and lightheaded from all of the excitement. She longed for the comfort and sameness of her own home. She couldn't possibly guess what her father had in store for her, and all of the unknown was pressing against her nerves.

When the trio was settled, her father smiled and began, "I'm guessing you're both wondering what you're doing here."

Darcy smiled a little unevenly and nodded quickly. She didn't trust her voice in a moment like this.

"What I want to know is, what does a guy like you want with a Mod like me?" her neighbor drawled, picking at his nails. Darcy gasped and pushed herself farther away from him. He was a Mod? How could that be? What would her father want with a Mod? They were dangerous, vile creatures that would just as soon look at a human as kill one. And now she was sitting next to one. After she registered the small smirk playing at Mr.

CHAPTER 1

Riggs's scarred lip at her gasp, her eyes darted briefly to her father's, but he only continued to focus solely on his guest.

"Very clever, Mr. Riggs," her father said, deadpanned. "Very clever indeed."

The Mod pulled a loose cigarette from his jacket pocket and stuck it between his teeth. Darcy's anxiety had reached an all-time high, and she could feel her sweat dampen the curls at the back of her neck. She wanted to swipe the beads away with her shaking hand, but she was afraid to move. She had heard that even the slightest movement could trigger a Mod into a fit of rage. She had seen it as clear as day when he had been brought in. He was dangerous, and she needed to watch her every breath.

Her father grinned as he tented his fingers and leaned his elbows on the glass table between them. "I've heard rumors, Mr. Riggs, that if someone is in the market for something that another already owns, you are the man to call."

The Mod lit the cigarette with a match he had pulled from the same pocket and puffed the smoke into his lungs. Darcy was waiting for her father to snap at the man and tell him to put it out immediately, but the scolding never came. He just watched as the red ember glowed between them. "Nasty rumor, that," Mr. Riggs murmured around the tobacco between his lips.

Her father continued as though the Mod hadn't spoken. "The job I am hiring for would be the most dangerous and challenging you have yet to encounter in your line of work. I need the very best, Jesse, and the very best is, unfortunately, you. This item has been rumored to not exist. I have spent over half my life searching for it and have never come as close as I have today to possessing it. I just received confirmation that this item has been spotted in a lab not too far from my greatest competitor. If he got his hands on it, I would be ruined. But if I had this item in my possession, it would unlock the door to my greatest desires. You understand why this is so important?"

"This all sounds great, but I still don't get why you asked me here. What do I give a shit about some mysterious item that could give some rich guy more power?"

"If you can deliver this to me, the world will be yours. You'll be renowned in your field, an icon, even."

"What field would that be? I'm just a lowly Mod, living a modest life as a factory worker."

Charles smiled and tapped the tips of his fingers together. "I know all about your drug-smuggling ring, Jesse. You have a very clean operation, almost impossible to detect. Your techniques are almost flawless, and your ability to work around security systems is beyond anything I have ever witnessed. Your operation is truly remarkable, though a despicable way to make a living. I would applaud you if I didn't find your practice so vile. It took my team months of questioning and infiltration to finally track you down. I have to say, you are a hard man to find."

Jesse smiled at the compliment and took another long pull on the cigarette. "A hard man to find but not impossible. You found me."

Charles nodded slowly, seeming to let the Mod beside Darcy stir before continuing, "As true as that is, you will need to be impossible to find because your survival depends upon it. Make no mistake, they are using the highest level of security clearance available in any of the Factions. Heat sensors, DNA detections, weight scans, retinal scans, infra-red camera systems—if you can dream it, they are utilizing it for security. You'll need to bypass all of these obstacles to be successful in your mission, and that's only in the lab itself. The Border guards are another issue: once my rival realizes it's missing, there's no telling what he might do to return it to his possession.

"This is beyond anything you've seen to date, Mr. Riggs. If you're discovered, you will be eliminated on sight. I need the most experienced criminal—the best of the best of the underworld—to realize my dream."

The Mod grinned again and watched as Charles grimaced at him. "Looks like you're barking up the wrong tree, Charlie. You might think I'm the best of the best, but only a ghost can do what you're asking. Better luck next time."

"No one can be a ghost, Mr. Riggs."

"How about an apparition?"

Her father scolded, "Again with the wit,"

"What can I say, I'm a funny man." The Mod clearly was not understanding the power her father held. He could have this man killed in an instant if he wasn't careful. She wasn't sure if the man before her was really that dense or just that brave, but her heart climbed into her throat as she

CHAPTER 1

watched the security officers behind her lift their hands to their holsters.

Though Darcy's nervousness seemed to be taking center stage; her confusion still rattled on behind her eyes. This meeting was clearly meant for her father and the Mod sitting next to her. Why involve another person in the meeting if the scheme was supposed to be top secret? She hadn't ever been involved in her father's business—she had barely had a conversation with the man in her twenty-three years of life—so why she was here now remained a mystery. Maybe he was trying to expose her to the goings on of his daily life? Or show her that Mods could be hiding in plain sight without her even knowing? Clearly, she knew. She had Mods that ran her household—her maids and cooks were all Mods—but Adam dealt with the help while she dealt with their societal expectations. She had never been this close to a Mod before. She looked more closely at his profile under the cover of her lashes.

And he was a sight to behold.

Jesse Riggs was tall and lean. Tattoos covered his knuckles and around his wrists. Roses bloomed along twisting vines around his neck and across his throat. His Adam's apple bobbed as he took another puff of the cigarette between his fingers. His jaw was covered in a light dusting of flaxen beard that was mirrored in the tousled hair on top of his head. It was buzzed down short on the sides and longer on top, pushed back away from his eyes. His silver-blue eyes shone with mischief, the left intersected by a crooked scar that ran a jagged line from his temple down to his chin, creating a slash of brown across his blue iris.

"Your humor is not what I am in the market for, Mr. Riggs—"

"I know, I know, you want me to get you something. Still haven't told me why you called me. Why don't you get one of your goons to do it?"

Her father leaned back in his chair and eyed Jesse ominously. "Like I previously stated, I need the best of the best for this job, and it's of the utmost importance that no one knows about any of this. If anyone were to find out about what we were attempting to pull off—before I had the object in my possession, that is—I could be ruined. I could be jailed and my empire would crumble."

Jesse smirked, tipping the cigarette back between his lips. "Why tell me all of this, then?"

"Because if we're working together, we need to be able to trust one another."

Jesse responded, "I never said I would work for you. All of this sounds a whole lot like not my problem. Sorry, Chuck, but I think I'm going to sit this one out." He gave a sarcastic grin and lifted himself from the seat.

Darcy felt a weight lift from her chest as the Mod put some much-needed distance between the two of them. The tension in her shoulders was causing pressure to build in her neck and skull. She would be happy when this whole interaction was finished.

"I'll let myself out," Jesse called over his shoulder and began sauntering toward the door.

Darcy's father merely smiled knowingly and pulled one of his desk drawers open. He pulled a file from the drawer and thwacked it onto the glass table. Jesse turned only slightly but continued his trek toward the exit. "I know where she is, Jesse," her father informed, sitting back in his chair as though he had pulled an ace from his pocket.

Darcy looked to Jesse, only to find that he had, in fact, stopped dead in his tracks. His shoulders tensed and his fingers curled into fists as his cigarette fell unceremoniously onto the white floor, leaving a trail of ash in its wake. The room was completely still, even the security officers standing at the door didn't dare to breathe. It was as though everything was sitting at the top of a precipice, waiting for Jesse to tip them all down into the deep end.

"You're lying," he ground out, still not moving.

Her father replied, "It took me a while to put the pieces together, but I was able to do some digging. You've been looking for her for what? Ten years? It took me less than six months to track her down with my connections. You Mods have a way of slipping through the cracks, but the power of connection has a way of bringing things into the light."

Jesse finally turned, and Darcy could feel the anticipation rolling off of him. He stood to his full height, looking every bit of the lethal, killing machine the government had raised him to be. However, they had no doubt hoped his skills would have benefited them on the battlefield, not in the office of a billionaire.

"Where?" he asked, the one word booming through the office like a bomb had been dropped.

CHAPTER 1

"I'll tell you"—her father slid the file back into the drawer, locking it—"when the job is done."

Jesse scoffed, "Bullshit. You don't know where she is."

"Harper Riggs, right? Split from her brother at the Modification Site Hospital ten years ago? You were promised to be reunited when it was all over, but that promise was broken and you never found one another. You were sent to the front lines in the Second Civil War, and she was never to be seen again. Like I said before, no one can be a ghost and having connections in all of the Factions has its advantages. I have her location; all you have to do is agree to my terms."

Jesse's face turned a queasy sort of green. He slowly made his way back to the chair and collapsed into it like all of the life had been drained from him. He looked worn, not like the sarcastic playboy that had swaggered in here only moments before. "What do I have to do?"

Her father beamed at his response and straightened his tie. "I knew you would see things my way!" He pulled some papers from another drawer in his desk.

Darcy could see some ID cards, Border paperwork, and some documents with her father's signature on them. She immediately felt her stomach turn. Nothing good could come from this.

"I am looking for a substance called Element Five. This element is very rare—so rare in fact that it is rumored to not exist. I have found the only sample of Element Five stored in a lab in Faction 8."

"Wait," Jesse interrupted, leaning forward so his elbows rested on his knees. "Let me get this straight: You want me to get some top-secret substance from a lab in Faction 8 and bring it all the way back here without anyone noticing? That's bigger than I can—"

"Are you telling me that the knowledge I have to offer you isn't enough to motivate you to successfully complete this mission? Why, you surprise me, Mr. Riggs. I was told that you were a man of action, much like myself, and that risk was in your nature."

Jesse didn't respond to his goading, only glared in his direction. Her father smiled menacingly. Darcy noted that he was enjoying pushing the Mod to his limit, torturing him with knowledge she wasn't even sure he had. Darcy was beginning to have a bad feeling about all of this.

Her father continued, "This element is dangerous and will require skill with smuggling back into Faction 2, but I trust you can handle that. Being the best of the best and all that." Charles gave Jesse a secret smile as though they now shared some sort of inside joke. "You will act as Darcy's companion on her trip to Faction 8 for the wedding of the leader of Faction 8's youngest daughter and the son of the Faction 6 leader. She's going to be married in a week, and Darcy will go as our representative. She will attend the wedding while you go to the lab and do whatever you need to do to acquire the element.

"Once you have it, you'll need to transport it back to Faction 2 without being detected and hand deliver it to me, here. Once Element Five is in my possession, I will then give you the location of your sister and five million dollars for your trouble."

Jesse inhaled sharply in surprise when Charles had announced the number. "Five million dollars?" he repeated, and ran a hand over his hair. "And what happens if I get caught?"

"Well . . ." Her father coyly grinned. "Then, I suggest you don't bother trying to come back. If you so much as breathe a word of this to anyone outside of this room, you will find yourself staring at the end of a gun very quickly. I have eyes and ears throughout all the Factions. There is nothing that will get by my people, and if I hear one rumor about what we've discussed here, I will end your life before you have time to blink."

Darcy could tell by the way her father said it that he was serious, and her blood ran cold. She had always known that her father played by a different set of rules—no one since the Second Civil War had come into power playing it safe—but hearing him say the words made her skin crawl. Mod or not, she didn't want Jesse's blood on her hands.

"And me?" she finally spoke, her voice thick with fear. "What is my role in all of this?"

Jesse and her father both turned to her with shocked expressions, as though they had forgotten she was even there. She gulped and wished the floor would swallow her. She hated having so many eyes on her at once.

"You're the alibi, my dear," her father answered. "You will cross the Border by car with the Mod acting as your companion and attend Sasha's wedding. There will be no need for you to be involved in any piece of the

CHAPTER 1

smuggling; you are only there to act as the distraction while Mr. Riggs completes the assignment." His answer should have made her happy, but her insides quivered. She would have to be alone, on the road, with this Mod for over a week.

"Can't Krista or Shane go? Shouldn't they represent our Faction?" They, after all, were the ones that her father had pulled into his inner circle. She was still considered an outsider by all accounts.

She watched as her father's eyes grew stormy. He didn't like being questioned, and Darcy immediately regretted her words. "Krista is newly married, and Shane is a man. Neither would need a companion to go to another Faction, which defeats the purpose of the entire plan."

Darcy felt her cheeks warm at her own stupidity and wanted to crawl under a rock once again. Her heart was hammering in her chest, and she felt like a trapped animal. She wanted to gnaw her own leg off to be out of this trap she had been led into. She could be killed by the Mod sitting next to her at any moment, and her father seemed to care very little about that fact. His singular focus was on this Element Five, and her heart plummeted at the thought. She had hoped that one day she would be important to him—or at least important enough to care for.

"Do we have a deal?" he asked Jesse, and held his hand out to shake. Jesse seemed to ponder this for some time.

"What the hell," he muttered in agreement, and shook Charles's hand. Her father clapped his hands together once in excitement and motioned to the two men in the doorway behind them.

"Excellent!" he cheered and stood from his chair. "You both will set out this afternoon. I will send for a car for you. Jesse, you will drive to Darcy's home and escort her from there. I will give Darcy the company card so that you can get whatever you may require on your way, but I have also taken the liberty of packing supplies for you with everything you may need. Darcy will need to go home to pack, but, Mr. Riggs, you have a supply of suits that you will be required to wear during the entire trip waiting in a bag in the car. You are posing as a companion, so you'll need to dress and act the part. I'm assuming Darcy can handle showing you the motions." He eyed her meaningfully, and she nodded shakily. Her thoughts were spiraling, and she felt as though she was suffocating.

"Before I forget," Charles continued as he walked around the crystalline desk. Darcy's hands were slick against the arms of the chair she was currently sitting in. Her face felt as though it were three shades too bright, and her stomach was churning. If her father dropped another bomb on her, she might actually explode. "As I need to know your whereabouts at every point in time—to ensure you don't decide to double-cross me, of course—I am having my personal medical staff attach trackers to you both."

Two men in white coats entered the room, pushing silver carts with needles and pliers. Darcy felt a wave of nausea hit her, and the blood drain from her face, the sudden contrast making her woozy. "Father!" she gasped out as one of the men pushed the cart to her and began sterilizing the items.

"Woah," Jesse complained, and stood up suddenly from his chair. "Back the fuck up!" he threatened the medical staff. The man in the white coat simply blinked at Jesse and continued to sterilize his own items.

"This is just a precaution," her father soothed, placing his hands in his pockets. "This is only to ensure that you continue to honor our agreement. I will be able to ping your locations in order to make certain you are continuing on our path. If something were to happen to either one of you, the tracker will alert me and I will be made aware. If you are captured, there is a failsafe option as well."

The man next to Darcy lifted her hair from her neck and applied a strong-smelling liquid to the base of her spine. Chills ran across her arms, and she jumped at the cool contact. "A failsafe?" she asked, her voice many octaves too high.

"Don't worry, my dear." Her father approached her and placed a hand against her bare arm. She wasn't sure she had ever remembered a time when her father had ever offered her physical comfort. "The failsafe is for him. I know I can trust your loyalty to this family."

His reassurance worked to soothe her frayed nerves just as she felt the pinch of a needle and the cool rush of liquid injecting into her. The area around her neck immediately faded to numb, and she felt a deep pressure as the medical staff began working to apply her tracker. She was bending her neck, so she could only see the navy fabric of her pantsuit in her view. She heard Jesse cursing as she assumed the staff had started their assault on him.

CHAPTER 1

"Two weeks, Mr. Riggs," Charles continued their earlier conversation. "This should take no longer than two weeks to complete. I expect you to follow my timeline to the second, and if that does not happen, you will not be coming back home. I will keep in close contact via phone with Darcy, and she will keep me abreast of all of the events of your trip. You will be booked into the most exclusive accommodations across the country and will be allowed to enjoy the luxuries offered during this trip. Do not allow these luxuries to cloud your memory. You are on this trip to complete a job, and I expect it to be done."

"Yeah, yeah," Jesse mumbled, and Darcy lifted her head just as the medical staff were weaving their carts back out the office door. "And how do I know you'll hold up your end? How do I know you won't blow my brains out with this little trick the second I give you what you want?"

Charles chuckled. "There's a level of trust we must have for one another if this is going to work, Jesse. You need to trust me to keep my word."

"Kind of like how you're trusting me to keep mine?"

Charles glared at the Mod for only a second before he cleared his throat and sat back behind his desk once again. "You will be required to pick Darcy up in two hours at her home. My men will take you down to the car and escort you to your"—he made a noncommittal hand gesture before his eyes—"hovel and allow you to grab any necessities you require. The GPS will be set to Darcy's home, and I will be tracking to make sure you arrive on time."

"Does Adam know?" Darcy asked, her voice small.

Charles sighed as though she was a chore to answer. "Yes, Darcy, Adam is aware that you will be traveling to Faction 8 for Sasha's wedding. He knows nothing more, and he will know nothing more. Your discretion in this matter is vital to our operation."

"Yes, Father."

"Now, if you both are ready, you are dismissed," her father said as though he had just checked an item off of his to-do list.

Jesse didn't say anything. Darcy wasn't sure if she expected a scathing remark or a sarcastic reply, but he gave neither. There was a set to his jaw that told Darcy he had resigned himself to his fate. She wasn't sure why, but that scared her more than the task that had been set before her.

She allowed one of the security officers to walk her out of the office to the private elevator. She was sure that Jesse would take the public elevator to the garage, so she was saved, for the moment, from any awkward encounter with him. His brash, impulsive attitude was jarring, but the thought that she would be spending almost two weeks with a being that had been transformed from a human to a soulless, killing machine was beyond terrifying.

As Darcy slid into the warm leather of the SUV that had been waiting for her, she realized that this would be the first time she would ever be away from home on her own. And it very well may be her last.

CHAPTER 2

"How did it go?" Adam asked as she walked into his luscious home office. Her father had instructed him to work from home so they could have some privacy for their meeting this morning. Darcy now had the sneaking suspicion that he had asked Adam to stay home so his presence wouldn't interfere with their guest's arrival. Adam definitely would not have approved.

The high ceilings of the enormous room were accented by towering dark oak bookshelves filled to the brim with authors she had never had the opportunity to read. Being intelligent was not something the men in her life found attractive, so schooling had been more about learning how to care for a home and keep a busy schedule. These were things that men found attractive in a wife—especially her fiancé.

"It went well," she lied, and hoped her face looked less pinched than it had when she had practiced her lines in the bathroom mirror moments ago. "I'll be leaving in just a few short hours."

"Oh?" Adam asked, his eyes still trained on the screen in front of him, working through some algorithm that her father had assigned to him, no doubt. "Leaving?"

She turned her head slightly in curiosity as she answered, "I'm going to Faction 8 for Sasha's wedding."

"Faction 8?" This time his dark-brown eyes did rise from the screen, and he pulled his thick-framed glasses from his nose. A lock of blonde hair escaped the confines of the ample layer of gel Adam had applied and tickled his brow. He pushed it back in frustration and tapped his fingers erratically on the desk before him. "Why are you going to a wedding in Faction 8?"

Irritation bloomed in her chest from his ignorance. Her father had indicated that he was already aware of their plan, but it seemed that Adam only gave minimal attention to matters that included her. Something rotten and hurt soured in her belly.

"My father is demanding I go as a representative."

"Who's going with you?"

"I'll be taking a companion." She could tell her voice was too tight when she pushed the words from between her lips. Her nervousness was beginning to show, and she tried to gulp it down quickly. If Adam suspected anything at all was odd about this trip, she knew he would bring the issue to her father. If he brought this to her father, she was sure his disappointment in her would only grow ten-fold.

"You're going *alone*?" The only reason for Darcy to bring a companion would be in lieu of bringing an *actual* person with her on the long journey. She could tell immediately that Adam did not approve of this.

"Is that a problem?" She was surprised by his snap. She wondered if maybe he was worried for her safety. Maybe he felt some urge to protect her?

"Who is going to run my social calendar in your absence?" His tone hardened, and he shuffled the errant hair once again. "Who will take over our events?"

Darcy really wished he was being sarcastic or that he was joking, but she could tell by the crease that had formed between his eyes that he was deadly serious. He had no idea how he would make it without her, not because he would miss her, but because he was afraid of how their social schedule would play out in her absence. Her heart sunk into her stomach, and she pulled her arms over it to try to quell the ache.

"I'll have Krista take over while I'm away."

This seemed to soothe his worries momentarily. He nodded, placed his glasses over his nose once again, and continued to stare at his screen. "I'll see you to the door before you leave."

She nodded once, then was about to ask him to come hold her before

CHAPTER 2

she thought better of it. She and Adam had never been really physically affectionate toward one another, but today felt like an exception. She wanted someone to run their hands over her hair and tell her everything would be fine. She felt better with the knowledge that her father had built in a failsafe to Jesse's tracker, but it still sent her nerves on fire when she thought about all of the things that thing could do before her father found out.

She needed to be brave all on her own, but she didn't know how to do that. She knew she needed to make her father proud, but she wasn't sure she knew how to do that either. Everything Darcy had ever done in her short life had been to please her family and make her father proud, but his shrill stare had always made her acutely aware of her failings. She couldn't be trusted to make the right choices. She never could. And that's why it was so surprising that her father was trusting her with such an important mission.

Though, he did bring about a good point that she was the only one that could pull this off with a companion without it rousing suspicion. She could use this opportunity to finally make her father see that she could be valuable to the family. If she were able to bring back his greatest desire and deliver it to him, he would have to see her worth. He would finally have to accept that she wasn't just the child born as a mistake—that she had a purpose.

With her resolve renewed, she climbed the thick oak staircase to her rooms and began to pack. She knew she would only be gone for two weeks, but she would also be attending a wedding. She needed to make sure she brought all of her supplies for travel and the black-tie event. She went through her closets and packed her finest jewels and silks. She made sure to pack her nicest wears suitable for travel. She had been taught—as all of the Elite women in the Factions had been—how to dress and pack for any occasion that might arise. A secret mission to collect a dangerous element for her father? That one hadn't been on the list.

Darcy had changed from her navy pantsuit into a cream-colored romper and stripy sandals. The mid-May air would be hot, but the humidity was still at bay. In a few weeks, it would be unbearable.

She finished her packing and had a staff member bring her bags down to the front door. She popped back into Adam's office to let him know she was leaving shortly, then stood by the front door, waiting for Jesse to pull down their mile-long drive. She had resigned herself to being the most professional traveler she possibly could be during their trip, only speaking to him when she absolutely had to. She also resigned herself to the fact that if he tried to rip her to shreds, she was going to have to use her limited fighting skills to get away and find a way to call her father. She just hoped it wouldn't come to that.

The sleek black SUV rolled to a stop before her window and she sighed. It was time, but she wasn't so sure she was ready for the next step.

"I still don't understand why you have to go," Adam pouted as he watched Jesse clamber out of the car and adjust the unfamiliar suit across his shoulders. He looked good, like really good in the suit, but Darcy knew better than to think this was something he had ever worn before. "What does your father care if you go to some wedding in Faction 8? He's never been concerned about showing up for them before. He despises them—especially Darien Blake."

Darcy simply shrugged and sighed again. "I'll be back in a few days. It'll be like I never left." She felt as though she was trying to convince herself more than Adam. What if Jesse killed her and went on the run? What if he kidnapped her and demanded a ransom from her father? She gently placed a hand on the back of her skull where the tracker had been placed. The only benefit of this whole ordeal was that her father would know where she was at all times.

"Just make sure that you stay alert out there. This world is full of people just waiting to take advantage of a naive girl like you. Mods are getting harder to spot, too, so be on the lookout. You can always tell a Mod by the dead look in their eye."

She nodded quickly and grabbed her bags from beside her. She could have asked a member of the staff to help her, but she decided it would be better to have less witnesses to this fiasco. Adam gave her a chaste peck to her lips and watched as she walked out to the idling vehicle. She dropped her bags before her companion on the curb, and he stared back at her over

CHAPTER 2

the rim of his dark sunglasses. Aside from the fair color of his hair and the pink of his scar, he was dressed from head to toe in black. Darcy thought it suited him as she appraised his figure.

Suited him? Get a grip, she chastised herself, and felt her cheeks flame.

He snorted, "What do you want me to do with those?" He nodded his head in the direction of the bags sitting before his feet.

"Put them in the trunk," she replied through her teeth, recognizing this was the first time they had ever acknowledged one another. It had been such a whirlwind at her father's office that neither one had been concerned with the other. Now, there was no avoiding it.

Jesse stared more incredulously over the glasses and leaned forward slightly. "What do I look like? You're fucking butler?"

"If you're going to pass as my companion," Darcy gritted out, "you need to start acting like one. As a companion, it's your job to do the heavy lifting."

Jesse rolled his eyes and pushed his glasses up his nose with his middle finger. Darcy balked at him and had half a mind to turn around and stomp her way back inside; the only thing keeping her rooted to her spot was the threat of disappointing her father. "Right away, Princess," Jesse sneered.

Darcy harrumphed and crossed her arms over her chest as she waited for her unwilling companion to complete his duty. Once the bags had been tossed—literally—into the trunk of the car with the two other black bags, which she assumed had been provided by her father, he jogged his way up to the driver's seat and slid in. She continued to stand on the sidewalk, tapping her foot and drumming her fingers impatiently against her arm. The longer she waited at the curb, the more her anger flared. He obviously had no clue what he was doing, and they were going to be found out the minute they crossed the Border.

He finally rolled down the back window and looked at her, arms spread wide in disbelief. "What now?"

"The door." She sighed and lifted a hand to the back door. He groaned and banged his head against the steering wheel a few times. Darcy really hoped that no one was watching them, otherwise they wouldn't even make it past her driveway.

Jesse pulled himself from the front seat and begrudgingly dragged his feet to where she stood. He plastered on the widest, falsest smile he could muster and pulled the door open. He bowed dramatically and put a hand out to indicate she should enter. She growled under her breath—surprised at her own boldness—and quickly slid into the backseat. She felt the whoosh of air rustle her loose curls before the hard slam of the door. He was obviously a hothead—from what she knew of Mods, they all were—and he would need to work on his demeanor if they were going to pull this off.

He finally made his way back around to the front of the car and put it in gear. Darcy watched through glassy eyes as her mansion began disappearing from the rearview mirror. She even turned her body slightly so she could watch the figure fall into the distance. This was her first time leaving home without her family, and she already felt the loss in her gut. She wanted to order the Mod to turn around, to take her back to where she was safe. But she had a point to prove, and she was going to prove it.

"It'll still be there when we get back, Princess," Jesse said from the front seat.

Darcy's head snapped back around, her dark hair swinging with the movement, and glared at her companion. "My name is Darcy," she corrected, "but you can call me Ms. Newton."

"Miss, huh? With a rock like that, I figured there'd be a mister at home."

She guffawed at his audaciousness. "Not that it is any of your business, but I'm only engaged."

He made a ticking sound with his tongue and nodded his head as though it all made sense. "Daddy needed to send you with an escort to make sure you're a good girl while you're gone. Can't afford any scandals that could put a black mark on his name."

"The nerve of you!" she practically shouted, and sprang forward in her seat. "I have never in my life met someone so bold. I could have you killed for implying what you're implying."

He chuckled—actually chuckled—at her and whistled low, much like he had earlier in her father's office. He lowered the dark glasses again so his icy blues could meet her caramel browns. "You're a feisty one. I can see why Daddy has to put a leash on you."

Her jaw practically hit the floor. No one had ever described her as feisty—mostly because this was the only time in her life that she had been

CHAPTER 2

so outwardly defiant—and no one in their right mind would ever dream of speaking to her the way he was currently. "You forget your place, Mod."

His blue eyes grew stormy, and she gulped at the dark clouds rolling in. Her heart was practically flying in her chest, and she could feel the heat blooming on her cheeks and throat. There was a stirring in her belly at the freedom she felt; something inside her liked the way he treated her. Not that she liked what he was saying, but that he wasn't afraid to say it. Everyone treated her like fine china, but Jesse Riggs apparently felt like a bull today.

"You better watch yourself, Princess," he threatened, low in his throat. "Your daddy might have a bomb set to blow my skull open, but it'll take less than a second for me to teach you a lesson."

She swallowed and sat back in her seat. The threat was as real as the glasses he pushed back over his blue eyes. She wanted more than anything for this to work in her favor, but the farther they traveled from home, the more she wanted to turn back. If they were going to be at odds for two weeks, she wasn't sure she would last. She needed to stick to her original plan and not engage with him.

She crossed her arms over her chest and pulled her phone from her black purse. She scrolled through the news pages and the gossip pages. She saw her sister's name mentioned a few times—*was she pregnant already?*—but nothing earth-shattering or life changing. Because her family was the most prominent in the Faction, the gossip pages always seemed to circle around them like vultures. When she and Adam had first gotten engaged, she had seen her face plastered along the pages for weeks. It was unfamiliar and uncomfortable for her, but Adam seemed to revel in the attention. He had always longed for the type of fame her family had been burdened with.

By the time she looked up from her scrolling, she noticed they were headed into the city and away from the Border. The sprawling mansions she had grown up around were nothing more than a speck on the horizon, and the looming towers of the rundown metropolis were coming into view. Her heart plummeted into her stomach and fear seized her vocal chords. They hadn't even made it out of the Faction and this Mod was already going against orders. This was the biggest mistake and her worst nightmare rolled into one.

"You're going the wrong way," she was finally able to grumble out.

Jesse didn't answer but kept driving down the dilapidated highway. The slums of the city were filled to the brim with tightly packed apartments held together by tattered shoelaces and bubble gum, and her father had always warned her to stay away. All of the Mods had been shoved into slums of similar value by the government. They couldn't be trusted around humans—at least, not in any civil way—so they were packed together like rats in a trap. Running water and electricity were said to be scarce; drugs and violence ran rampant through the streets. Few Mods were trusted with honest work in order to keep the line between human and Mod very clear.

It was a repulsive way to live, or it would be if the Mods were even close to being human. Most of them were more machine than man and had no real feelings. Those feelings had been erased long ago when they had been modified by the government. It was a widely known fact in the circles that she frequented that modified humans were not human at all.

Darcy shuddered at what might await them here where they all resided.

This was the closest she had ever come to a city, and she wanted to be no closer. "Stop the car! You're going the wrong way!"

"Don't get your panties in a wad," the Mod responded distractedly, barely glancing back at her through the mirror. "I forgot something in the city."

The nervous gnawing in her gut continued its ravenous chewing. She didn't like this one bit. What could he have possibly left in the city? Her father had already told them both that they would want for nothing; they both would be perfectly taken care of, and there would be no reason for them to return to this place.

"Absolutely not! I demand you turn this car around immediately."

"What? Afraid Daddy might blow your brains out right along with mine?"

She scoffed at the idea, though the comment twisted like a knife in her chest. "I'm afraid I'll have to find myself a new companion before I even get to the Border. If he so much as thinks we're doing anything untoward, we'll be finished."

"And being the good little solider you are, that shit doesn't sit right with you."

She didn't respond immediately, but only glared at him through the

CHAPTER 2

mirror. She couldn't tell if he was looking at her or not through the black frames over his eyes, and that only irritated her more.

"This won't take long, Princess," he reassured, sounding almost apologetic. "Just grabbing a few things, and no one will be the wiser."

"My father will be the wiser, and that's not a risk I'm willing to take. You need to turn the car around immediately."

"No can do, sweetheart. But I promise we'll still make it on your daddy's stupid fucking timeline. Scout's honor." He raised his right hand and gave her a shit-eating grin like he meant it.

She wanted to growl in frustration but worked to keep her face the picture of composure. "I said, turn the car around."

"And I said, I can't," he responded as he made a sharp turn into the outskirts of the city. It was a ghost town. There were no signs of life anywhere, just vacant buildings gaping at the black SUV as it bumped along the disheveled road. "I need this job just as badly as you do, Princess. I'm not going to do anything to jeopardize this."

Darcy harrumphed in the back seat and crossed her arms over her chest again. She highly doubted he needed this as much as she did, but there was nothing she could do—short of taking the wheel herself and sending them crashing into one of the grotesque facades surrounding them. She thought about calling her father, getting the jump on this betrayal before she could be implicated, but decided against it. If her father was in fact testing her, she didn't want him to have the impression that she couldn't handle it.

The ride was silent: Darcy not knowing how to persuade the Mod to abandon his belongings and continue their mission to the Border, and Jesse training his eyes solely on the rough terrain, trying to navigate without getting a flat tire. Darcy bounced along the backseat, holding onto the door for dear life as they trekked farther into the dangerous city.

The buildings seemed to sag as they pressed into one another, holding each other upright by the barest of scaffolding. Windows were blown out and boarded up with old signs and pieces of old billboards. Sheet metal replaced doors and sometimes acted as a ramp up the steps. Mods in all states of decomposition meandered down the broken roadside.

Some of the Mods Darcy watched from the safety of her tinted windows were very clearly modified—shining steel fused with scarred tissue or poked from raw eye sockets. Darcy noticed that most of the aging Mods had pieces that were more reddish than silver, while the younger models sported almost-new modifications. She was sure if she cared to do any further inspection, she would see her father's insignia branded into almost all of the metal pieces in her view.

What surprised her the most was that even among the poor and desolate, most of the Mods were still smiling. They acknowledged one another as old friends, and not the careless fiends she was told about. She expected to see muggings and the sound of gunfire, but instead, she saw men and women bustling through the street, making their way to their destination in relative peace.

Of all of the Mods she saw along their trip, she didn't notice any children. She thought it was odd that these beings didn't feel the need to procreate. Maybe it wasn't in their nature like it was for humans. Maybe they weren't programmed to fulfill such a carnal desire. She wondered if the other Mods—the genetically modified rather than physically modified—felt the same way.

Her cheeks warmed at the path her thoughts had taken. Why she would care about the goings on of these beings was beyond her. She blamed her nervously fluttering heart for her roaming thoughts. She held tightly to her phone, waiting for the second her father decided to call and scold her for their detour. She was frightened of what he would say, his words scalding her from the inside out, making her feel worthless and dumb. She wasn't sure she could handle his critique in front of her companion.

The SUV rolled to a stop at a street corner, and Darcy waited for Jesse to exit the vehicle. She was suddenly struck by the thought that he would leave her alone in the car. Who knew what could happen to her without him to protect her? Would he even protect her if he could? The fear she had been feeling began clawing its way up her throat and she felt as though she might start screaming.

"Excuse me," she frantically called, and pulled herself forward so she was face to face with the Mod, close enough to smell the light scent of smoke wafting from the jacket he was wearing. He smiled at her. "Would it be possible for me to go with you to get your things? I would feel much better if I were able to go too." She could tell her voice was rushed and

CHAPTER 2

breathy, her nerves getting the better of her, but she couldn't find it in her to care at the moment. She just wanted to live long enough to be embarrassed by it.

"No can do, Princess," he answered, and unlocked the doors with the button on the console. "But don't you worry because my things just arrived."

She shifted her head just in time to see two Mods open the doors aligned with the curb and throw themselves into the SUV. Darcy felt the scream she had been holding back bubble up through her chest and explode out her mouth. She flung her hands in the air to cover her face and pushed herself all the way to the back corner of the seat she was in. The Mod that now resided in the passenger seat threw a duffel back into their seat, and the Mod now sitting beside her tossed both of their bags into the trunk.

"No!" Darcy heard herself shouting. "Get out! Get out! Who are you? What do you want?"

"Relax, sweetheart." Jesse tried to soothe her, but Darcy couldn't seem to get a grip on her own emotions.

She continued to scream, "Get out of this car! Now! I demand you leave us be!"

Jesse pulled the car away from the curb and locked the doors just as Darcy tried to open her own. "Chill the fuck out, Princess! They're with me!"

"Absolutely not!" she yelled at him only glancing at the two beings now chuckling and pointing at her. "My father said nothing about bringing them along, and I will not allow them to stay! He will be furious when he finds out. They need to exit this car immediately!"

The female Mod sitting next to Darcy finally spoke. "Hey, it's okay. We aren't here to hurt you, we're here to help." Her voice sounded like chocolate-covered gravel, and something about the rasp of it made chills spread like wildfire along Darcy's skin. The female Mod was attractive. She had skin the color of desert sand, her wild blonde locks thrown back into a barely contained ponytail. Freckles lined her nose and cheeks, surrounding one green eye and one robotic. Darcy felt a slight jolt to her stomach as she watched the robotic eye scan her, and she swallowed hard.

Darcy repeated, more calmly this time, "My father did not say you could come, and you need to leave."

"Fucking Christ, Jess," the male Mod in the front seat groaned. "What is she, a fucking parrot?"

Jesse snickered and shook his head. "Listen, Princess—"

"It's Ms. Newton."

"Right, anyway—listen. What your father doesn't realize is that while my smuggling operation is top notch and my skills are fucking phenomenal, I can't do this alone. The only reason I'm the best in the business is because I have Tick and Jericho. That's it. So if you want to prove to Daddy that you can do this, then I suggest you keep your mouth shut on this. If you force them out, then we don't stand a chance."

Darcy was shaking her head before he had even finished his thought. "I can't just keep my mouth shut. If he finds out that we told anyone else about this, we'll both be in for it."

"Sounds like somebody has Daddy issues," the male Mod in the front grumbled.

"Shut it, Jer," the female scolded, and slapped the back of his shaved head. He ducked and made a yelping sound at the contact.

"Listen." The female turned to Darcy, her eyes sympathetic. "I understand your need to do this, I really do. I used to be in a situation just like yours. But, to get this done, you'll need all of us. Jesse told us the terms, and we aren't looking for any of the glory, but you know what that kind of money could do for this place?" She spread her arms, and Darcy took in the scene around her. She had just been thinking about how desolate the place had seemed. "There are people here that are in need of medical care but can't get it because they can't afford it. There are people that need food or water—or even just clothes on their backs. So, five million might seem like cake to you, but that's a lot of money that could do a lot of good here. We have a big stake in this, and we wouldn't do anything to fuck that up."

Darcy was silent for a moment. She knew what the woman was saying was true, but she wasn't so sure she could trust her. What would stop her from double-crossing them? She didn't know these two; they didn't have a chip in their heads set to explode, so what would keep them from ruining all of this?

"Darcy," Jesse pleaded from the front seat, and her eyes snapped up to meet his in the mirror. He had taken his glasses off, and his eyes looked

CHAPTER 2

soft, not the threatening storms he had cast her way earlier. "I have a lot to lose in this—a lot to fucking lose—and I need my team with me. I need you in on this too."

She opened her mouth to answer, ready to turn him down again, when her phone vibrated in her hand. Her father's name flashed across the screen, and she gulped hard. She knew this moment was coming, but she wasn't sure she was ready for it. How was she going to tell him she had already failed? Sure, they were headed back toward the Border at record-breaking speed, but that didn't mean she hadn't failed. She needed to tell him the truth, no matter the consequences.

"Hello." She answered in that small, insignificant voice that always seemed to slither between her lips around her father.

He replied, "What is the problem, Darcy? Why have you gone off course? I thought I made myself explicitly clear when I told you to keep to my plan. Have I made a mistake in choosing you for this mission?"

She hated to say it; she could feel the words forming a lump in her throat. The fallout from her admission would have lasting effects, no doubt. "Everything is fine, Father."

So she decided not to say it.

Three sets of eyes locked on her, every face in the range of shock and excitement. Jesse's smile bright enough to light the entire city.

"What was the cause for delay?"

"Mr. Riggs forgot some equipment needed to complete the job." The lie felt foreign on her tongue, and she felt an odd jumping in her bones at the mere thought of lying to her father. It was equal parts exhilarating and paralyzing.

He paused, long and hard, as if waiting for her to crack under the pressure.

She began wringing her free hand between her thighs, sweat dampening the fabric of her romper. A calming palm lay over her own and she jumped at the contact. The woman next to her gave her an encouraging smile, and she simply nodded.

"Make sure that this doesn't happen again" came her father's voice.

"Y-yes, sir," she stuttered, and the call ended. She hung up and tossed the phone in her lap with shaking hands.

She had never in her life even considered not telling her father the entire truth. If he found out that she lied to him, the consequences would be swift and harsher than anything she had ever known. She knew that he was ruthless in his pursuit of power, and he would not stop at punishing his daughter in his quest. She had just raised the stakes of this game, and she was hoping she could deliver.

"Holy shit!" Jesse whooped, and banged his palm against the steering wheel, pressing the accelerator harder, pushing the limits of vehicle. "I can't believe you just did that, Princess."

"It's Ms. Newton," she reminded him again, but even she knew her attempt was half-hearted.

The male in the front seat still remained nonplussed. "All she did was tell her dad a half-truth. My shits have done more."

"Jericho!" the woman beside Darcy chastised. "This is a big deal to her. Be nice."

"Tick, baby, if you don't know me well enough to know I'm not nice by now—"

"Enough you two," Jesse ordered, and they both immediately gave him their attention.

Darcy finally found her voice again, though it was still shaking. "What do you plan to do at the Border?"

"What do you mean?" Tick asked, pulling her hand back from Darcy's and settling in with some kind of makeshift computer on her lap.

"We're not going to make it through the Border like this."

"What's that supposed to mean?" Jericho sneered in her direction. His tanned skin looked just shy of a rusted color, his black eyebrows raising high into his shaved hairline.

"Well," Darcy began again and pushed her curls behind her ear. "No one is going to believe that I'm traveling with three Mod companions. This whole thing rings false, and they'll want to contact my father."

Jericho began to argue, "If we have the right paper—"

"She's right," Jesse interrupted. "I saw how fucking nuts these people are first hand; they aren't going to believe it without hearing from her father."

"So what's our play then?" Tick asked, sounding more resolute than Darcy felt. "How are we going to make this work. We have about a half an

CHAPTER 2

hour until we make it to the Border, and I'm going to need to have these IDs made."

Darcy looked sharply at the woman as she began tapping away on her computer. Jesse answered, "According to Newton's timeline, we have about an hour before he decides to introduce my brains with the concrete."

"We could make a stop and try to wire a car," Jericho suggested. "Tick and I could follow."

"They'll flag the car, and we won't make it through the next Faction," Jesse rebuked.

Tick snapped suddenly and looked up from her screen. "We could hide in the trunk and try to smuggle through. No need for IDs at all."

"What if they find us?" Jericho asked. "We'll be dead before we can say, 'Howdy, boys.'"

Darcy scratched at the fabric of her romper as an idea began to form in her brain. She knew it was a longshot, but it was the only way she could think to work it. "How legitimate are those IDs?" Darcy asked Tick.

The other woman smiled and flipped one side of her ponytail. "They are good enough to get us in and out of the Faction 2 prison without being caught."

Darcy nodded while Jericho said, "Why? You too good for Tick's work?"

"No," Darcy replied, narrowing her eyes at the Mod. "I think I know how we can pull this off, but it's going to be a risk."

Jesse smiled wide and seemed to consider her words. "Let's hear it."

CHAPTER 3

This was never going to work. Darcy wasn't even sure why she had suggested it in the first place, let alone why they all had agreed to it. Well, all of them except Jericho. She was getting the distinct feeling that this Mod in particular held a grudge against her, and she wasn't sure what she had done to incur such a fate. Or, if she even really cared.

Regardless of his feelings on her, the other two had persuaded him to their side, which had led them to this roadside gas station. Of course, a roadside gas station for the Elite of the Faction was much different than the roadside gas stations offered to the more middle-class humans of the Faction. This gas station was located on one of the many acres owned by a real estate tycoon. He lived close enough to the Border that he was able to profit from the needs of those traveling—those that he felt comfortable enough allowing on his land, that is.

The station was made of solid brick, painted white to resemble the larger estate that was located about ten miles down the road. It had four bathrooms in total: one for Elite women, one for Elite men, one for companion women, and one for companion men.

Tick and Darcy had been holed up in the bathroom for Elite women for close to ten minutes, Darcy working furiously to give Tick the appearance of someone of her equal. The men had taken to the bathroom on the opposite side of the building reserved for the companions. Jesse was trying to work some magic as well, but he knew far less about companions than Darcy did women of the upper echelon.

Sneaking Tick into the bathroom without alerting the guards watching the cameras had been a difficult task all its own. Darcy had reached in her bag and done her best to throw scarves and jewels over the woman to give her the appearance of Elite status, but nothing could detract from her cargo pants and white beater shirt. Both looked as though they had seen better days, and there really wasn't much Darcy could do about them at the moment. When they stopped, she had grabbed her makeup bag and a light sundress that would pass Tick off as Elite for now.

"Here, close your eyes—like this." Darcy imitated what she hoped Tick would do and heard the other woman sigh. She had already changed into the dress and sandals, but the makeup was taking a little longer to execute.

"This feels ridiculous," she complained, the first pessimistic word Darcy had heard from the woman since she met her.

Darcy replied, "It feels ridiculous because it is. If we manage to pull this off, it'll be a miracle."

Darcy continued applying the tinted mascara to the other woman's lashes. Her makeup was a few shades too light to really do Tick justice, but she thought, with the right colors and some more time, Tick could really knock the socks off of anyone looking. Even the metal glint in her robotic eye didn't detract from her good looks. She was hoping Tick's natural beauty would be enough to fool the guards by their deception. Even with her God-given looks, they would need to do some serious shopping when they crossed the Border . . . if they crossed the Border.

Two thunderous knocks came from the solid wood door, startling both women in their oversized chairs. Both sets of eyes looked toward the heavy door. At this point, either woman could answer and no one would be suspicious, but Darcy felt she still needed to take the lead in this situation. Darcy closed the palette in her hand quickly and moved toward the door, cracking it slightly so the cameras would only get a full view of her face.

"Yes," she answered, looking up into black lenses.

"It's now or never. If we don't hit the road, your pops is gonna get suspicious," Jesse informed her. She watched as he rubbed along the vines of his throat nervously, and she felt that emotion mirrored within her own skin.

CHAPTER 3

She answered, "Just give us a second." Darcy shut the door solidly and turned back to her awaiting canvas. Tick looked just about as terrified as Darcy felt. There would be no coming back once they fully committed to this charade. And, unfortunately, Tick would be taking the largest risk of them all. If she was caught in this lie, she would be executed on the spot. Impersonating an Elite member of any Faction was a crime punished by execution, without exception. A thought suddenly struck Darcy as she stood staring at the beautiful woman before her. She pulled the door open wide and called, "Jesse!"

He turned and watched as she made the space between them disappear in three long strides. "Let me have your glasses," she demanded.

"What?"

"Give me your glasses. We're more likely to pull this off if we have something to cover her face."

"You don't think they'll ask her to take them off?"

"If they believe the ID, then they shouldn't."

"And if they don't believe it?"

"It's a risk we'll have to take," she answered, and held her palm out. He pulled the lenses from his eyes and plopped them in her waiting hand. She smiled brightly at him in thanks and turned on her heel. When she returned to the room, she placed the glasses on Tick's face and smiled. "Perfect," she whispered.

Tick giggled and stood from her overly plush chair. "For all of our sakes, I hope you're right."

The two women stood and stared at one another for a moment. Darcy felt the sudden urge to reach out and embrace the woman before her, though she barely knew her. Adding the fact that she was a Mod and more likely to kill Darcy than to hug her, Darcy retreated fully into herself once again. The feeling was confusing, and unnatural, and Darcy chalked it up to the events of the day wearing on her emotions.

They collected Darcy's scattered cosmetics and made their way silently to the idling SUV. The twenty-minute ride to the Border was a silent one. All four members of this monumental deceit had become decidedly anxious as they waited for the cars before them to slowly make their way through the electrified gates.

Men with guns, wearing the black military uniform for Faction 2, walked up and back inspecting cars as more men waited at the plexiglass station to scan IDs and ask all of the usual questions of the bodies in the vehicles. Giant cinderblock towers stood looming over the cars below, housing more military personnel. Dogs sniffed and barked at tinted windows, and guns were held at the ready. In situations like this, Darcy was usually of such high status that they moved swiftly around this traffic and missed the more thorough investigations. This time, though, she didn't have her father to protect her. Her only shield was three Mods and a thinly veiled lie that she hoped would be enough to pass them through.

Jesse pulled slowly up to the plexiglass, and Darcy noticed that a cool mask slid over his face, his expression eerily similar to the one he had worn when they were seated in her father's office. He looked cold-blooded and ready to murder, but calm and dangerous. She felt a chill run up her spine and a cool sweat break out along the scar on the base of her skull. She now doubted her ability to form words, let alone make this lie sound anywhere near believable.

"I need to see some IDs," the man at the booth ordered. He barely looked up as he scanned each one into his system. He typed between scans, not paying a bit of attention to the four beings staring daggers at the side of his head. Darcy seemed to be the only one who felt as though she might explode at any moment. Tick inspected her nails while the men up front looked less than perturbed at the man in the booth. The images Tick had uploaded in her computer flashed across his screen with the names of each individual. "Ms. Darcy Newton?" he addressed, and finally looked into the SUV, his expression as dull and lifeless as his voice.

"That's m-me," she stuttered back, mentally chastising herself for being so obvious.

He looked down at her ID and back at her before handing it back. "Jesse Riggs?" he asked, and Jesse gave a quick nod of his head. "Paperwork says you're Charles Newton's daughter?"

"That'd be the brunette in the back," Jesse sarcastically replied, and gave a grin.

The attendant did not seem amused and only stared. "Cute," he said, voice monotone.

CHAPTER 3

Jesse couldn't resist the urge and blurted, "If you think that's cute, you should see my—"

"Yes!" Darcy interrupted before Jesse could make matters worse. "I'm Charles Newton's daughter."

"And I'm guessing the clown over here is supposed to be your companion?"

"Yes, he is," she answered sharply, and gave Jesse a meaningful look. He continued to grin—his scar hitching the left side of his top lip a little higher—like nothing was amiss.

"Elisha Harris?" the man asked, clicking through to the next set of names. A picture of Tick, a recent photo but with her eye still intact, pulsed onto the screen.

"Yes," she answered, her face trained just to the left of where the man was sitting. "That's me!" Her voice was bright, but there was a practiced formality to it that surprised Darcy.

"And it looks like Hector Fuentes is your companion?"

"In the flesh," Jericho answered the alias. Darcy gulped and started to feel the familiar prickle of panic across her skull. She didn't like lying, but it seemed that lying would be the name of the game she was playing for the next few weeks. Though, it didn't seem she was getting any better at it.

"Ms. Harris, I'm going to need you to remove your glasses for me," the attendant ordered, still sounding as bored as ever.

This was the moment they had been dreading. Every fiber in Darcy's being had told her that this was bound to happen; she had only hoped it would've been after they had crossed a few more Factions. Darcy held her breath and tried to harden her expression in the same way she had taught herself for so many years. She wasn't sure it was working. She saw Jericho fidget out of the corner of her eye, and Jesse was watching the guards in the rearview mirror like he was getting ready to bolt. This was not going as planned.

"Excuse me?" Tick responded, sounding as offended as if he had asked her to remove her shirt. "You would like me to do what?"

"Remove the glasses, ma'am."

"How dare you!" she blustered, bringing the attention of the surrounding guards to them. Darcy was fully sweating now and attempting to melt back into the smooth leather of her seat. Her father was sure to hear about this. "You must know who I am! What I have been through!" she shouted again as the guards began surrounding them.

The attendant finally seemed stirred from his permanent stupor and began fumbling on his computer. He must not have read through the entire profile of the woman Tick was pretending to be. Elisha Harris had been a girl Darcy had gone to boarding school with. They hadn't been friends, not really, but they had run in similar circles. Her dad was the chief board member of multiple modification hospitals throughout the Factions and made millions. She was a nice enough girl, if not a little too brash for Darcy's liking.

Elisha had been a part of a hazing prank that had gone wrong their senior year at the school. She ended up losing her sight and the hospital had to remove her left eye in order to keep the acid from spreading. She had gotten a prosthetic eye from Darcy's father free of charge, but her vision could never be restored. It had been easy enough for Tick to hack into Elisha's life and replace her own face with Darcy's long-lost acquaintance while also fudging the hospital records to reflect Tick's mechanical right eye.

Now, if Tick could only sell the lie to the end, they would be home free.

The man must have finally stumbled his way to the information they had hoped he would find, and his face went fully pale. "Oh, no," he whispered to himself, and slumped back into his seat. "I didn't—I mean, I'm so—"

"I should have your head for such an insult!" Tick continued to rave, really piling it on thick. Both men in the front seat were looking away, failing at hiding their smirks. Darcy, on the other hand, felt like she might be sick. She just wanted to be away from this horrifying encounter. "Asking me to remove my glasses after all I have been through. I just wanted to travel to a wedding with one of my oldest and dearest friends, and this is what I am met with!"

"Ma'am, if you would like—"

"I would very much like to speak with your supervisor. No one should have to endure what I have had to face today," she whined. The guards that surrounded the SUV began to pace nervously as their dogs yipped at the backseat of the car.

"Ma'am, I am so very sorry. If we could just talk. . . ."

CHAPTER 3

Tick finally ended his misery when she muttered, "I just want to leave. Please, let my party pass in peace."

The man shuffled the papers back as quickly as he could through the window to Jericho and hastily pressed the button to allow them to pass through the electrified gate. The gate jerked, then slowly slid open so the SUV could pass through, armed guards watching as they sped past the Border and into Faction 3.

When the gate was fully shut behind them, Darcy let out the breath she had been holding for ages, her heart still careening in her chest like a canary in a cage. Her stomach was rolling, threatening to unload the breakfast she had eaten in what felt like lifetimes ago. It felt odd that just this morning, she had been sitting across the long glass table from Adam as he watched his news broadcast on his phone, and now she was crossing the Border with three Mods she barely knew.

"Fucking hell!" Jesse whooped, and let out a relieved laugh. "I don't think it's ever been that close before."

Jericho countered, breathlessly laughing, "Not true. Remember the cocaine smuggle through Faction 12? That shit was wicked. I had some dudes finger up my—"

"Woah!" Tick interrupted, and clapped a hand over his mouth. "We remember but could live without the play-by-play." Her voice was also breathless with laughter.

Jesse and Jericho both laughed heartily, seeming to ride the high of making it through those gates. Darcy felt like death warmed over. She wanted a bed and some space. The deceit of the last twenty-four hours was making her limbs heavy and her head pound.

"You okay back there, sweetheart?" Jesse asked, genuine concern coming through despite the obnoxious nickname.

Tick and Jericho both looked in her direction as though they had forgotten she was there at all, something that seemed to be a common theme for her today. Tick's expression immediately turned soft, and she leaned back so they were at eye level. Jericho merely rolled his eyes and faced forward once again. "Daddy's Little Princess can't take the heat," he grumbled.

Jesse reminded, "She's not used to this shit like we are, Jer. It'll take some time for her to adjust."

"Life must be real hard," Jericho continued. "Not having to worry about a damn thing."

"Enough, Jer," Tick snapped. Jericho only crossed his arms and glared out at the rolling hills beside them.

They had made it through, but there was no way they would make it to the other side of the Faction by dark. The Borders shut down at night for security purposes. Sure, there were still guards looking out to make sure no one got through, but the gates were closed and no one was allowed in or out until the sun came up in the morning. It had been a long day, and Darcy was glad for the opportunity to rest.

"We won't make it much longer," Darcy reflected her thoughts out loud, her voice sounding tight. A lump had suddenly formed in her throat and she worked to loosen its hold. She definitely needed to be away from these Mods and on her own for a bit. "We need to stop for the night."

"Any suggestions?" Jesse asked, for the first time not sounding like he was making fun of her.

She responded, "My father has a connection just a few miles from here. He has a bungalow we can stay in. I'll send the address to the car's GPS and call his assistant to set it up."

Though she was exhausted, it felt nice to feel useful in this moment. And Jericho was, thankfully, silent in his assessment of her. His words were beginning to grate on her nerves, and she was sure she was going to snap at him at any moment. She wouldn't mind leaving him behind for the remainder of their trip, but if Jesse said he was vital to the operation, she would need to listen.

The call had been swift, and the bungalow was ready for them by the time they reached the property. The gate that separated Mr. Sweeney's land from the outside world was guarded, but it only took Darcy a quick conversation to grant them clearance. The SUV rolled down a sleek blacktop road lined with blooming cherry trees. The air was cool in the setting sun, and the grass was dewy with a recent rain. Tick looked on in awe as they rolled slowly toward their destination. Even Jesse and Jericho looked mildly impressed at what they observed.

CHAPTER 3

They rolled to a stop in front of a small cottage, just a short mile from the main house. The lights had already been turned on, and the cobblestone walk was illuminated by a small front porch light. A light breeze swayed the cherry trees on either side of the walkway, bringing in another round of rain no doubt. When Jesse finally threw the car in park, the men exited the vehicle and began pulling their luggage from the back. Tick began to follow suit before Darcy linked her arm around the Mod's and began leading her toward the small house.

"Come on, Elisha, let me help you to your room," Darcy said just loud enough for anyone to hear if they happened to be listening.

Tick seemed to get the idea and allowed Darcy to lead her up the steps and into the small foyer. The house was decorated modestly with solid wooden furniture and plush carpets. A fire roared in the hearth, and windows lined the back wall, allowing in the last rays of light before the sun completely set. There were two rooms and two bathrooms in the house, along with a modest kitchen with the latest appliances and a pool around back for anyone that fancied a swim.

Darcy just wanted a shower and a bed.

The men pulled all of the luggage into the room and silently appraised the space before them. "There are four of us and two showers. We'll need to shower in shifts," Darcy announced as though the people around her couldn't count.

Tick gaped at the woman before her, and her eye sparkled in pure joy. "A shower?" she asked, her voice quietly optimistic. "This place has a shower?"

"Uh," Darcy began, unsure of what she had expected. "Yeah, there is one in each bedroom."

Tick jumped up and down in glee and began squealing like a kid on Christmas. "I get to take a shower! An honest-to-God shower!" Off she ran into one of the closed doors, and the sound of running water hitting tile followed soon after.

"Guess I'm headed there too. Save some water, right?" Jericho cheekily grinned and followed Tick into the room, shutting the door behind him. Darcy's face flamed all the way up to her ears and she thought she might explode from embarrassment. He didn't even try to hide his intentions. If anything, he flaunted them. Feral beasts would be a good way to describe these savages.

THE KEY

"I guess," Jesse started, rubbing the back of his neck lightly. "You can take the other shower. I'll go in after Tweedle-dee and Tweedle-dumbass are done."

She watched as he walked toward the back window and opened the glass door that sat in the center of the enormous frames. He pulled a cigarette from his pocket, and a match soon lit in the dull light of the fading sun. She wondered what he was thinking, what he thought about all that they had done that day, but she was honestly too tired to ask. And she probably shouldn't care, anyway. What did she care what a Mod thought about anything?

She grabbed her bags from the doorway and hauled them into the bedroom. She wasted no time in grabbing her toiletries and locking herself in the bathroom. She had heard stories about Mods, and she didn't want to make herself vulnerable to the ones that were literally right outside her door. She knew it was a risk to let her guard down, and she wasn't willing to take it.

Once she melted into the hot spray of the water, she finally let herself break. All of the tension and worry of the day rushed forward and a sob escaped between her lips. This wasn't her. She had never been a liar or a con woman, and she wasn't sure if that's who she wanted to be after today. She knew that she wanted to make her father proud, but this? This all seemed too much.

The sobs wracked her body and she let them. She felt her shoulders heave with every deep breath, and her jaw ached with the effort to keep it from snapping in two. Her heart couldn't take the anxiety it was carrying, and she wanted to force it away. She needed a way to let it out and keep it at bay if she was going to survive this.

She was drowning, and there was no hope in sight.

Darcy finished with her shower, letting the water drain away the last of her tears in the process, and dressed modestly for the night. Normally, she would let herself relax in a loose-fitting shirt and shorts, but with her current company, she elected to wear a silk button-down chemise and matching pants that tied at the waist. She thought about heading straight

CHAPTER 3

for the bed but decided to bid her companions goodnight.

When she left her room, she saw the trio sprawled across the furniture like they had lived in this small space their entire lives. Tick was wearing the plush, white robe and matching slippers that Darcy had seen hanging in the bathroom for guests. She was perched on one of the couch cushions with her makeshift computer on her lap.

Jericho was shirtless, wearing a pair of pants that were loose fitting and had definitely seen better days. Darcy noticed thick, puffy scars that crisscrossed along most of the skin of his chest and upper arms. The sight made her queasy, and she worked not to look away from him. His black eyes appraised her every move, and she didn't want to give him more reason to berate her. Jesse was still wearing his suit, though his jacket had been tossed haphazardly on the floor and his tie loosened at the neck. He had unbuttoned the top button to let the tip of a tattooed star residing at the dip in his throat peek through. The sleeves of his black shirt were rolled to reveal splashes of color so vibrant across both arms that Darcy could have mistaken him for an expressionist painting.

He had a beer dangling from the tips of his inked fingers and was currently smiling at something Tick was saying; she was gesturing so wildly, her computer almost tumbled off of her lap. Darcy couldn't peel her eyes from Jesse—the Mod sitting across from her. He had a feral look in his eyes, like he had lived his life in the wild, and it struck something deep in her gut. She wanted to know him, and that fact scared her more than anything else she had encountered that day.

"Well, look what the cat dragged out," Jericho snickered, taking a swig from his own beer bottle. "I thought we'd seen the last of you for tonight."

Darcy immediately felt her cheeks warm. It had been a mistake to come out here. She started to turn back when she heard Jesse call, "Why don't you come settle a debate for us, Darcy?"

She looked back over her shoulder and tucked a damp curl around the shell of her ear. That was the second time he had ever called her by her given name, but this time it somehow seemed more intimate. The unnamed feeling fluttered more furiously in her gut. She resisted the urge to start wringing her hands again.

"Yeah," Tick chirped and turned to face her. "I need another perspective on this one. These two think they're right about everything."

"Because we are," Jericho stubbornly maintained.

Darcy couldn't help the small smile that touched her lips as she padded her way to sit on the couch, keeping a good distance between herself and Tick. She noticed a few beer bottles lying across the glass table between the four of them, and a glint in Tick's eye told her they had been indulging for a while.

"Tell us," Jesse began dramatically, "because we'll never agree on this one. Is it better to have running water or hot food?"

All eyes turned to her, eagerly awaiting her response. Darcy was startled by the question. Of all of the questions she thought they would ask her, this wasn't one of them. She had never needed to decide between two amenities she had come to expect every day in her own life. She hadn't dreamed that people would have to choose between the two. Or, maybe, she knew that they had to choose but made sure to keep her distance from the issue, blaming the fact that they were Mods and nothing more.

"Like, here in this place," Tick provided, noticing her hesitance. "It has everything you could ever want—food, clothes, running water, heat, air, couches, beds. It's all so amazing, but if you had to choose one thing to take back with you to have forever, what would it be?"

Darcy pondered for only a second longer, acutely aware of all the eyes on her, before answering, "Running water?"

"Bingo!" Tick cheered, and stood from her position on the couch to do a small victory dance. The men booed and hissed at her; Jesse even threw a pillow, hitting her midsection.

Jericho interjected, "Now, if we could just get one or the other all the time, we'd have it made."

Both Mods chuckled, and Jesse agreed, "Or at least get something eatable every once in a while—now that would really be the dream."

They continued their joking laughter, but Darcy was disturbed. She had known that conditions in the cities had been bad, but she hadn't found herself in a position to ever really care. She had never been up close and personal with a Mod before, she hadn't seen the softness of their eyes or the brightness of their smiles. In fact, the farther she traveled from home, the less she found herself afraid of the people before her, and the more she

CHAPTER 3

thought that the way they were treated wasn't entirely fair.

"You really don't have food or running water?" she asked in a small voice, ready for Jericho to pounce on her any second.

Jesse beat him to the punch. "Well, Princess, when the Elite thinks your usefulness has run out, they stop giving you things. That includes the shit you need to survive, like food and water."

"And clothes," Tick wearily supplied. "Don't forget about the clothes."

"And shelter," Jericho added.

Jesse made a noise of agreement and took a swig of his beer, his eyes finding Darcy's and pinning her to her spot in the chair. "When was the last time you had to pick a meal out of a garbage can, Princess?"

His words were scalding, almost as scalding as the fire she saw burning in the deep blue depths before her. When they had arrived, Tick had seemed elated at the chance to stay in a place so accommodating, but now it seemed that the opulence of the cottage was leaving a bad taste in their mouths. She wouldn't be surprised if she found Jesse sleeping on the porch tonight. The tears she thought had long since vanished began pricking the corners of her eyes while embarrassment choked her. "Never," she finally whispered out, annoyed at her own shame.

She shouldn't feel bad. They weren't human. They were practicality machines, and they had sealed their fate when they had signed up to be a part of the Second Civil War. That wasn't her fault. She hadn't forced anyone into joining anything they didn't want to be a part of.

Jesse continued, burning a hole in her soul with his gaze. "Life gets real, real quick when you don't have Daddy to protect you, huh, Princess?"

"Jesse, I found something," Jericho interrupted, saving Darcy from having to answer.

She quickly looked away and brushed her knuckles against the tears that had threatened to fall. She didn't want these Mods to think she was weak. They would exploit any weakness they saw in her, a fact that had become glaringly obvious in the last few minutes.

"It looks like there are some top-secret-type documents that mention Element Five."

Once she had composed herself enough to return to the conversation, Darcy stared at Jericho curiously. He was staring off into the distance, his eyes trained in a far off corner of the room where the ceiling met the wall, but as far as Darcy could see, only cream-colored paint adorned the space. Where was he pulling this from? Darcy looked between him and the wall a few more times, trying to assess the origin of his information.

"Got anything other than that?" Jesse asked, leaning forward and swigging his beer once again.

Jericho shook his head slightly. "Not yet. This is some top-notch, dark-evil-type shit I'm looking through, Jess."

Tick leaned into Darcy's ear and whispered, "They replaced his brain." Darcy practically jumped out of her skin at the closeness of the Mod, but the unexpected revelation made her insides squirm.

"They what?" she whispered back, horrified.

"They took parts of his brain out and replaced it with computer parts. He's basically a human computer; can research anything and everything you need to know. Top-of-the-line hacker and computer genius rolled into one." Her voice sounded dreamy as she described him, and Darcy could practically see cartoon hearts forming over Tick's eyes. She definitely had it bad for the Mod sitting across from them. Darcy wondered how someone so jaded could end up with someone that seemed so lighthearted.

Darcy asked, "So, how does he do it? How does it work?"

"Hell if I know. I just know that he can tell me anything and everything I need to know in the blink of an eye."

The men continued their conversation back and forth and seemed to be completely ignoring the women whispering on the couch across from them. Either they were of no consequence to them, or what they were talking about was really that important. Whichever way it landed, Darcy was happy for the insight into the group.

"Then why do you need that?" Darcy asked, and pointed to the computer sitting precariously across Tick's crossed legs.

"Oh." She smiled and patted the thing lovingly. "This baby is of my own making. I put it together from spare parts I found around the city and was able to get it up and running. I specialize in fraud, forgery, and falsification of documents. I am the woman to go to if you want a new identity or want your old one wiped clean. I can make people appear and disappear with just a few taps on this old screen. Uncle Sam thought they had me in a

CHAPTER 3

good spot when they forced me into who I am, but little did they know, they made me too good. They've been looking for me for close to eight years now." The pride in her voice was unmistakable, and Darcy began to wonder what they had done to make her hate them so much.

"And him?" she asked instead, pointing to Jesse as he paced with his beer in his hand. He had started to flip a cigarette across his knuckles, and Darcy watched with rapt attention at the dexterity in his fingers. Heat tickled her neck, and her throat ran dry.

"He's the brains of all of our operations," Tick informed. "He has the ideas and the means to execute them. The government wired him so he doesn't feel pain, which makes him almost impossible to beat in hand-to-hand combat. He doesn't give a shit about his life or anyone else's, which makes him completely fucking nuts and willing to try just about anything. He'll put a plan in place and make sure it gets done, no matter what the cost could be. He says that we make this operation run, but in all honesty, it's his fearlessness that gets us through. He doesn't think twice, he goes all in."

Darcy gulped as she watched his lips move over his words. She had seen it first hand in her father's office earlier that day. She had thought that the Mod didn't know the power her father possessed, or his willingness to enact harsh punishments, but the truth of the matter was, he just hadn't cared. He had cared so little for his own well-being, and possibly hers, that he had been willing to walk away from the offer on the table, no matter the price.

Until her father had mentioned the name Harper Riggs.

His sister was clearly the exception to his rule about caring for others. He cared for her. He wanted to find her. And he had been willing to risk not only himself, but his friends and Darcy to find her. This trip just became a lot more complicated.

"Keep looking," Jesse ordered, and stopped in his frantic pacing. "The more we know about this shit, the better chance we have at getting this done the right way."

"I'm on it," Jericho answered, and continued his search.

Tick had slid slightly away from Darcy and started tapping on her computer once again. She said, "I'm solidifying our identities so that way we won't run into any more issues as we cross the rest of the Borders. All of our documentation dating back twenty years will be updated."

"I want birth records in before the night is over," Jesse demanded.

"Make that twenty-seven years," she replied dully, and continued typing. It seemed that everyone had their place here in the living room, except Darcy, which felt wrong. She of all people should feel as though she had a space in this room, but she felt like she was merely an onlooker.

"Any word from the puppeteer?" Jesse asked, turning his stern gaze to her.

Darcy shook her head, wringing her hands in her lap, and said, "I don't expect to hear from him for a while. As long as we stay on course, we should be in the clear."

He nodded once, eyes far away once again as he continued his pacing. "You've done well so far, Princess. If we can keep him off our trail until we get back, we'll be some lucky sons of bitches."

Tick giggled and nodded her agreement. "I think you say that every time we leave the Faction."

"That's because it's true, but this time, we have an ace in our pocket." Jesse eyed Darcy meaningfully, and her insides squirmed. She liked being under his gaze when his eyes were this particular shade of blue. Roses bloomed on her cheeks, but she worked to keep her gaze steady.

"I wouldn't be so self-assured," Darcy warned. "I might have some pull with the Elite, but that only goes so far. I'm surprised we've made it this far."

Jericho snorted from his seat, though his eyes were still scanning the invisible screen above their heads. "You got that right."

Tick admonished, "Don't be such Debbie Downers! We have thirteen more days to get to the finish line. We can't lose hope now." Her wild blonde locks were drying in soft waves around her face, and Darcy was once again struck by how beautiful she was. There was something about Tick that didn't quite fit with the other Mods, even with the robotic eye shifting back and forth in its socket.

Jesse took a swig from his beer and looked out over them all. Tick was busy clicking away, and Jericho was scanning through the air. Jesse smiled at Darcy as she sat observing the systems in motion around her, and her

CHAPTER 3

insides turned to liquid fire. There seemed to be something almost secret about the smile, as though he was openly admiring her unbeknownst to the Mods surrounding them. He wasn't doing it to make fun of her or make her feel embarrassed; he was doing it as a show of admiration—something no other man in her recent memory had done.

The scar that marred the left side of his face, now pulled taut, didn't detract from his tempting demeanor, but seemed to add to it. She was completely helpless to him. She felt her face break into a wide grin, tucking her drying curls behind her ear. She wanted to say something to him, tell him to stop, but she didn't want him to stop. That was the real problem.

She cleared her throat and shook her head quickly. "I'm going to bed," Darcy announced to no one in particular.

Jesse continued watching her as she began moving toward the bedroom door. She suddenly felt self-conscious of her movements as she became acutely aware of his eyes roaming her pajamas. "I'm going to sleep in here. The three of you are more than welcome to sleep out here or you can share the other room."

She caught Jesse's smile slant into the boyish grin that liked to reside in his eyes when he was feeling particularly playful. "Sleep tight, Ms. Newton."

She stopped in her quest for the door and returned his smirk, feeling bold in their secret exchange. "The same to you, Mr. Riggs," she answered, and walked to her door. After the lock was securely in place, she allowed herself to fall into bed and finally end the day that had seemed to last forever.

CHAPTER 4

She awoke with a start as panic forced her into consciousness. The room was all wrong: the ceiling slanted where it should be flat, the bed too wide, and blankets too heavy. She reached her arm across the bed to make contact with a familiar form, but nothing was there. Darcy sat up quickly and searched the blankets for her fiancé, hoping to find purchase in her frantic state. He was nowhere to be found.

The events of the previous night wafted over her. She placed a hand to her forehead to stop the onslaught of images assailing her as her sleep-fogged brain began to clear. It all had felt like a strange dream. She had wished it was all a dream. Darcy had wanted to believe that she would wake this morning and find herself in her own room with the curtains pulled and the events of the previous day nothing but a long-forgotten nightmare.

Darcy wasn't that lucky.

She felt as though she had been run over by a tank, her eyes heavy and her head pounding. She sat slowly and groaned at the soreness in the muscles in her neck. She hadn't physically exerted herself the day before, but the stress of it all had worked her muscles like a triathlon. Her only saving grace in all of this was that the door had remained locked and it looked as though her Mod travelers had thought it best to leave her be. In all honesty, once her head had hit the pillow, she hadn't stirred for the rest of the night. She had been blissfully unaware of all of her surroundings and allowed unconsciousness to consume her.

She pulled her body slowly from the luxurious bed and shuffled her way to the bathroom. The light in the bathroom had a dimmer switch, and Darcy was happy to lower the setting almost completely. The bags under her eyes were enormous, and her hair tangled wildly at odd angles. She tried to brush it down with her fingers but abandoned the effort after a few failed strokes. She decided she might as well get herself ready for the day, for whatever was lying in wait outside her door, she knew she needed to be completely prepared.

The thought made her cringe. Last night, she had learned so much about the people she was currently entangled with, and it only seemed to confuse her position in this situation even more. Just because she knew more about them did not mean she trusted them any more than she had, but there was something inside her that had softened to the group. She was willing to admit that hearing about their lives in the city had caused her some distress. Maybe when they returned home, she could convince her father to send some aid to their area. It might not do much, but the current state of their lives was nothing short of ghastly.

As sympathetic as Darcy was feeling, it didn't change the grassroots facts of what she had been taught about Mods. They were street-smart and cunning, clearly used to lying in order to get whatever their hearts desired. Darcy was sure that they would attempt to use those tactics on her to get their way . . . if they hadn't already.

The thoughts swirled in her mind as she completed her morning routine: pulling her curls into a tight bun at the nape of her neck, using Herculean force to get them to bend to her will; applying her makeup to seem poised and pristine; and throwing on a tan pantsuit over a white camisole. She pulled an outfit from her pile of belongings—for Tick to wear—and kept her makeup bag handy. She knew today wouldn't be as challenging as the day before had been, but she was under no illusions that this day would run smoothly. She was preparing herself for the worst, and hoping for maybe just slightly above the worst. When she was ready, she collected her things in her bags and wheeled them out into the foyer.

Darcy hadn't really known what to expect when she finally exited her rooms, but what awaited her was not even in the realm of her imaginings.

CHAPTER 4

If anything, she had prepared herself for the complete opposite. She thought she would have been the first one awake, rousing the sleeping figures around the room and getting them on their feet. Instead, she was met with an almost empty space.

Tick and Jericho's voices could be heard behind the closed bedroom door on the opposite side of the wide sitting room, along with the sound of running water. Tick squealed and giggled and she could hear Jericho's low baritone echo through the space, clearly enjoying the amenities one more time before their departure. Darcy only rolled her eyes at their continued antics and headed toward the kitchen. When the space came into her view, she was caught completely off guard by what awaited her there.

Jesse was standing at the stove, flipping something in a sizzling pan. His shirt was nowhere in sight, but he was still wearing the dress pants from the night before. His feet were bare, and his left foot reached back to scratch his opposite calf. His entire back was a bare canvas that contrasted with the bright purples, greens, and blues that covered his arms. Amongst the expanse of toned skin, Darcy could see scars that had puckered and healed over; perfectly round circles the size of a quarter dotted his back and shoulders.

He turned slightly, and Darcy could see the peak of toned abs leading up to a lean figure that made her mouth water. Her pulse ratcheted up in her throat, and her breath came in quick puffs. She could feel her thighs squeeze as she took in his sleep-rumpled hair and half-smirk he was sending her way. His blue eyes danced as he grumbled, "See something you like, Princess?"

It was only then it struck her that she had just been standing there, gawking at the immaculate figure before her. Embarrassment lit her from the inside and she grumbled, "You're blocking the coffee."

He chuckled as he bowed out of her way and allowed her to pass. Her fingers shook as she grabbed a mug and turned toward the full pot. Jesse continued to smirk at her as he flipped the egg he must have uncovered in the fridge only feet from where they were standing. Apparently, he had no issue with making himself at home. "If you needed something warm to wake you up, sweetheart, all you had to do was ask."

Darcy's face flushed a deeper shade of red, and her jaw practically hit the floor. She turned to him once again and sternly replied, "It would be wise to remember who you're talking to, Mod."

He only smiled wider and slid the egg onto a plate, as though her threat was cute, and not the cutting jab it was meant to be. "I wasn't the one looking, Princess."

"I was not looking, and I don't appreciate your insinuation."

"Oh yeah?" he asked, and turned to her more fully. He crossed his arms over his bare chest—his collarbone down to his ribcage covered in symbols and swaths of color—muscles flexing with the effort. Her eyes strayed back to the bright splashes of color over his strong arms, and she felt the heat settle low in her belly. Her stomach clenched, and she cleared her throat as her eyes met his once again. He bit his lower lip, the edge of his scar disappearing behind white canines. "What were you saying?"

She gave a disgruntled huff and poured the coffee before jabbing a finger against the coy fish on his right peck. The heat sparked in her arm and she resisted the urge to pull back. "Listen, Jesse," she started, voice wobbling. "You might be used to women swooning at your words, but I am not so easily swayed. It would benefit you to remember that you might be pretending to be a part of the Elite, but I am not. If you don't watch your step, you'll find yourself in a world of trouble."

Jesse opened his mouth to retaliate, the spark in his eyes lit to a full-blown fire, when the pair heard the distinct sound of someone clearing their throat. They both jerked back only to see Tick and Jericho standing in the space just outside of the kitchen area. Tick was doing a horrendous job at attempting to hide her grin behind her fingers, and Jericho was looking between the pair like they had suddenly started speaking gibberish.

Tick giggled. "Are we interrupting something? Because we can come back."

"No," the pair answered in unison. Darcy glared at the Mod in front of her, only to see Jesse's gaze return to its playful dance.

"Tick," Darcy began, returning to business, something she was much more comfortable with discussing. Jesse grabbed his plate and walked into the living space to sit and begin eating. "I laid out an outfit for you for today on my bed along with my makeup. I'll make sure to call our next layover when we leave here to make sure the staff fully stock the closets

CHAPTER 4

and supply makeup more to your shade for you. I'll also make sure they provide some suits to fit Jericho too."

Jericho's head popped up as he poured himself a tall glass of milk. "I don't need any fucking suits."

Darcy huffed, tired of his resistance already. "If we're going to pull this off—"

"We'll be fine with me borrowing Jesse's monkey suits. No need to put on the full song and dance."

She retaliated, "If someone was to ask you to get out of the car and saw the suit was, in fact, made for a much taller person, suspicions would be raised."

Jericho made to argue again when Jesse answered, mouth full of food, "She's right, Jer."

The smaller Mod simply rolled his eyes and slammed the milk back into the fridge. "You would take her side," he sneered, and stomped away, disappearing back into the room he had just emerged from. Darcy wanted to say something snarky about forgetting the milk he just poured, but she thought better of it. No need to poke an angry bear.

Darcy felt her pulse ticking against the insides of her wrists and her face flush from the confrontation. She wasn't sure what Jericho meant by his last comment, but fighting against him for the next two weeks was going to prove to be a bigger challenge than she had anticipated. She wasn't sure what she had done to the man—considering she had said very little to him—but whatever it was, he wasn't likely to let it go anytime soon.

"Thank you," Tick whispered softly to the flustered woman, surprising Darcy by placing a gentle hand against her arm. Without thinking, Darcy pulled back away from the touch and saw the hurt flash briefly in Tick's eyes. "I appreciate all you're doing to help us. This wouldn't work without all of your cooperation."

Darcy nodded, replying, "We need to be ready to go in an hour."

"I'll make sure Surly Sam gets his shit together," Tick responded, the smile returning to her eyes as though the unintended slight were a distant memory. She bounced back to Darcy's room, entering in briefly to grab the items from her bed, and scuttling back to the room she shared with Jericho.

Darcy let out a sigh and pressed her hand against the slick hair by her forehead. She wasn't sure what to do. She liked Tick a lot—if she was being honest with herself, she thought this might be the only person she had ever considered a friend—but just because she liked her didn't mean she wasn't dangerous. It, unfortunately, could mean just the opposite. Tick had a way of lowering your guard, making you feel at home in her presence. This could be the very trick she used to disarm her enemies.

"Way to go, Slick," Jesse teased as he made his way back into the kitchen, depositing his now empty plate. "Just stick a knife in her heart while you're at it."

Darcy grimaced and replied, "I wasn't trying to upset her. I am an Elite, and you all are companions—that line cannot be blurred."

"Why?" Jesse suddenly sounded angry. "Because you're better than us? Because you're a human and we're not?"

The words surprised Darcy. Not because they weren't true, but because she was unaware that the Mods knew about the rhetoric around them. Darcy had always thought that the Mods were so far removed from society that those labels would be lost on them. "N-no," she stuttered but froze. "I—"

"Save it, Darcy. We don't need your pity."

Jesse began making his way toward the couch, picking up his discarded shirt en route, when Darcy said, "Jesse, wait." To her surprise, he stopped and turned to look at her. The hurt in his eyes was unmistakable and she began to wonder why he cared so much about what she thought of them. She was no one to them. She didn't matter in their lives beyond this mission they were on together, so why would her opinion make any difference? "I'm trying, okay?" she finally settled on.

He gave a sarcastic smirk and lifted his chin to stare up at the ceiling briefly. "But I was right, wasn't I? That's what you think? That just because we have some metal implanted in us, that it somehow makes us less than human? We still bleed just the same as you do, Princess. It might just take a little bit more to see the red."

Her throat closed, and she shook her head to clear the tears that had begun to prick at the corners of her eyes. This was more than she had bargained for. She wasn't ready to leave behind everything she had been taught and accept what he was saying, but hearing his words cut her deep. She had heard so many stories of men torturing Mods for fun, making a

CHAPTER 4

game of how long they could keep them alive. It had never bothered her before—they had never been human before—but she was beginning to think her idea of human might be wrong. She defended, "That's what I know—or thought I knew."

"I'm here to tell you, Darcy, just because someone tried to take our humanity away doesn't mean they succeeded."

He sounded morose, as morose as Darcy felt. Their gazes met for a fraction of a second, and she swore she felt a connection forming. Her bones felt electric, and her heart stammered in its rhythm. Even in her distressed state, she felt something warm bloom inside of her just looking at him. She had never felt something so pure and sweet. She felt the edge of her bottom lip curl up as a tear slipped from her cheek—her sorrow not disappearing but easier to take when she looked at him. She bit her bottom lip gently as she watched his sullen eyes spark back to life, reflecting the erratic beating of her heart.

Maybe they all weren't so bad. Maybe she could use a lesson or two in what it really meant to be a Mod. No, she wasn't quite ready to give up all she had been taught, but maybe she was ready to be open to new ideas. She didn't think she could trust her traveling companions, but maybe respecting them would be enough—recognizing that metal might not be enough to stop them from feeling the things she felt.

Jesse quickly looked away and cleared his throat, rubbing the back of his neck nervously. Darcy began wringing her hands in front of her and danced back and forth on her feet awkwardly. The connection she had felt starting to grow hung eagerly in the air between them, the shift in atmosphere enough to make her head foggy and light.

"Uh," she began as she shook her head quickly and walked toward the back window. "Be ready in an hour. I have all of my belongings by the door so you can use the shower in my room if you need it. I'll be out enjoying the morning until we're ready to leave."

Jesse nodded. She could feel his eyes on her as she walked out onto the open porch, where he had gone to smoke the night before.

Darcy took a deep inhale of the soggy air and watched the dew dance on the blades of grass as the sun began to rise over the trees. She would need to remind herself to write a thank-you letter to the owner of the land for letting them stay over. It really was a beautiful space, and she thought she wouldn't mind living somewhere similar. She and Adam could live in the mansion on her father's land for as long as they'd like, but a dangerous thought had started to brew that maybe she liked being away from home. She was still under surveillance, but being out from her father's watchful eye had made her heart a little lighter.

Her phone suddenly began to ring in the pocket of her slacks, and as though he could read her thoughts, she saw her father's name flash across the screen. She gulped and took a deep breath before answering. "Hello?"

"Good morning, Darcy," her father replied. "I trust you made it through the Border safely."

The reminder of the fiasco at the Border had her nervously pacing. "We did."

"Excellent," he responded. "Elaine Sweeney informed your mother that you stayed over on their land last night."

"Yes," she answered cautiously. If word had already spread that they were staying here, word must have gotten around that there were more than two of them.

She could hear his pen tapping on the other end of the line and held her breath as she waited for him to continue. "And I trust you'll be adhering to my timeline from this point forward. No more detours, as it were."

She was becoming more and more suspicious of his knowledge of their uninvited guests and her palms began to sweat. "Y-yes, sir." Her voice was meek once again, and she hated herself for it.

"I'm counting on you, Darcy, to make this work. Disappoint me, and you will be facing immeasurable consequences. Is that clear?" The threat in his voice had her nodding her head rapidly.

"Y-yes, sir," she agreed again.

"I'll be awaiting your call when you reach your next destination."

And with that, he hung up. She pulled the phone away from her ear gingerly and looked down as though the device might explode at any moment. Had he known? Or was this simply a precautionary call to make sure she stayed in line?

There was no need to check in to make sure she stayed in line. Darcy

CHAPTER 4

had never once considered stepping near the line, let alone crossing it. Well, except for allowing Tick and Jericho to join them in their quest for Element Five . . . and lying to the guards at the Border about who they were . . . and continuing to keep the secrets hidden from her father when she could have very easily told him just now without anyone being the wiser.

So, it seemed Darcy was becoming very familiar with crossing that line after all.

She breathed deeply into her lungs and put the phone back into her pocket, turning to meet her traveling band of Mods inside. They were all standing near the door, Tick adjusting a tie around Jericho's neck, Jericho fussing about the tie around his neck, and Jesse looking on with a smirk. The suit Jericho was wearing was just about a size too long, but tight across his shoulders, giving him a very uncomfortable look. Darcy's instincts were renewed when she thought about providing the amenities for her companions.

"Tick and I will walk behind the two of you as we exit," she said to the trio awaiting her. "You'll open our doors for us—I'll ride behind the driver since this is our vehicle and Tick will ride on the side behind the passenger—then you'll come back and load the bags. Jesse will drive the car, and Jericho will ride as a passenger."

"I have a question," Jericho interjected, shooing away Tick's fussing hands. "Does the stick ever come out of your ass, or is it, like, a permanent thing?"

Darcy opened her mouth to retort when Jesse replied, "Before you start talking about anyone else's issues, you might wanna have a doctor take a look at that mouth of yours."

"What's the matter with my mouth?"

"It never stops moving."

Jesse's face split into a grin, and Darcy found herself sporting a triumphant smile as well. Tick's eyes were sparkling with barely contained laughter as Jericho looked about two seconds from blowing his top. "Fuck off, Jesse," he grumbled, adjusting the suit jacket harshly. "Been your friend for fucking ever and you side with a hot piece of ass just because you want some of that."

THE KEY

Darcy startled at the unexpected comment and looked between the two men. Jesse's smile only grew wider as he responded, "Seems like a good enough reason to me." Tick and Darcy both balked at his boldness. Jesse grabbed Jericho in a playful razzing, which left both men chuckling and punching one another.

"Knock it off, boys," Tick admonished, though she was grinning. "We have a job to do."

The men straightened with the reminder, and Jesse opened the front door to the hot morning sun. The cherry trees blew in the slight breeze, and the two men took off down the stone staircase. Tick carefully placed the glasses over her eyes and allowed Darcy to take her arm as they exited the house.

Darcy felt a small jolt of exhilaration light her nerves all the way through their careful charade until the SUV pulled through the gates and back onto the open road. There were a few minor hiccups, but nothing so drastic that it would cause for alarm. Or so she hoped.

Once they were safely out of the watchful eye of her keepers, Darcy felt she could finally take a full breath again. The tracker that still throbbed at the back of her skull was the only thing left for her to worry about, and so long as Jesse continued to play by the rules, it would be smooth sailing until they reached Faction 8.

"I have confirmation of the lab Element Five is being stored in," Jericho announced, seemingly out of the blue.

"Faction 8?" Tick asked, lifting her head from its resting position against the window. Darcy put her phone down on her lap and watched as Jericho's eyes scanned the open air before him. They had been driving for about an hour with nothing in sight. It had been a pretty ghostly hour, not even cars passed down this stretch of road. Not unless you were traveling to the other side of the Faction, which was not done very often.

"Sure is," he confirmed. "Some lab called DymoCorp. Know anything about it?"

No one answered his question right away. Their silence filled the car, and Darcy wondered what they were waiting for. "Earth to Princess,"

CHAPTER 4

Jericho snapped, and it was then she realized he had been asking her.

She sat straighter in her seat, recognizing this as her opportunity to show these Mods she was a valuable member of the team, beyond providing a distraction and a cover story. "DymoCorp?" she asked, thinking through anything she may have heard about the lab through gala conversations or fundraising whispers.

"Figured Papa Newton might have some connections," he replied hotly.

Darcy scowled at the back of his chair but continued to flip through her brain for any information she might have.

"I think . . ." she started, her hands wringing in her lap from the lack of definitiveness of her answer. She might have a small amount of information, but anything earth-shattering would be better found on Tick's computer or in Jericho's research.

"It's all right, Darcy," she heard Jesse respond from the driver's seat of the car. "Whatever you can tell us will help."

His voice was softer than it had been in their previous interactions. Her mind flew back to the secret smile he had given her the night before. She wasn't sure that Jericho was completely correct in his assessment of their relationship—a Mod wanting an Elite was unheard of—but maybe Jesse was developing a soft spot for her. She was thankful for it if it were true.

"Today would be nice, Princess." Jericho griped from the front seat, and Tick smacked the bare skin of his neck.

"I know Edwin Ellis owns the company—"

Jesse interrupted, "The bigwig distribution guy?"

"The very same," Darcy confirmed, feeling anxiety crawling along the inside of her gut. "He's got some close ties to Darien Blake, the leader of Faction 8. I think they were allies during the Second Civil War."

Tick replied, "That makes sense since Daddy Warbucks wants to keep this so hush-hush. He must know who has it and doesn't want word getting back."

"And why he chose right now to get it," Jesse added in agreement. "Ellis and Blake will be wrapped up in Blake's daughter's wedding. With all eyes away from the lab, this is perfect timing for Newton. It also makes this ten times harder than what we originally thought. There's no guarantee that Ellis hasn't already flashed the goods to Blake. What else do you know about Darien Blake, Darce?"

"He has two daughters and a son," Darcy continued, not sure if any of this information will help, but much more confident in her ability to provide social information rather than business. Plus, the nickname Jesse had just given her made her feel like one of the team and sparked a fire in her confidence. "Daphne is the oldest and has been married for quite a few years. Max is the middle child. He moved to Faction 7 about five years ago under some mysterious circumstances and developed his own prestigious trading company. The rumor in the gossip blogs is that he's going to be the new leader of Faction 7 when the current leader passes."

Jericho and Jesse shared a look, both of them seeming to come to the same conclusion at once, but Darcy was left in the cold.

She began, "What—" But an eruption like fireworks exploded behind the SUV and stopped her inquiry. Suddenly one of the tires burst into dust on the road, causing Jesse to pull the wheel to keep them on course. Another boom, and the car began swerving erratically once again.

"What the fuck?" Jericho shouted as Jesse worked to right the vehicle.

"What's going on?" Darcy shouted from the back just as another boom sounded and the glass of the rear window exploded in a flurry of shrapnel.

"Get down!" Tick shouted at her, pushing Darcy's head below the back of the seat as she was launching herself over it to reach into her bag in the trunk.

Darcy's brain finally registered—the explosions she was hearing were gunfire. Suddenly, her brain stopped working. Her palms began sweating and tears filled her eyes as she thought that this might be her final moments. This could be the end of their journey, and she had yet to really live her life. Everything she had done had been out of fear and compliance with her family—really, with her father. She had never done anything really for herself, and now she would never get the chance. Her short streak of rebellion would be the only time in her life that she had ever lived outside of the lines, only to be cut short in a flurry of gunfire. Her breathing stopped for a second as she choked on a scream. She wanted to curse and cry, but her whole body was frozen, except for the tears splashing against her face.

Among the explosions of gunfire, the three Mods seemed to have calmed enough to design a plan, though no words had been spoken among them. Only meaningful glances as they shifted into a trance that Darcy had never

CHAPTER 4

seen before. It was as though they had shut off all emotions and gone into a place where all that existed were the bullets whizzing past their heads.

"Martyrs," Jericho shouted above the booms of gunfire and roar of motorcycles. "Have to have been following us since the Border."

"How the fuck did they sneak up on us?" Jesse asked, though it seemed he didn't really want an answer. "Tick, how's it going?"

Tick righted herself just in time and tossed two handguns to the front seat. She loaded a third and sat back in her seat. "We've got three on the right, two on the left, and one trailing," she informed as calmly as if she was describing the weather.

"Let's lose these fuckers," Jericho shouted, and turned out his now open window. As Jericho began firing, Tick climbed over Darcy and began shooting out her window, the sound of the blasts deafening to the woman lying across the seats. Her ears began ringing, and her head was swimming from the harsh sound.

Jesse shouted, "I'm losing speed. We've got to wrap this up soon. No more fucking around: shoot to kill or don't shoot at all."

"Got one!" Jericho whooped, and reloaded his gun.

Tick complained, "No fair!"

"Tick!" Darcy sobbed, terror lacing her words. "What's going on?"

"Hang on, sweetheart," Jesse called from in front of her, shifting in his seat to shoot out the broken rear window. "This'll only take a minute." He paused and let two more shots ring out. "Got one!"

"Dammit! Oh, wait—" Tick let off three more shots. "Got two! Suck it!"

She reloaded her handgun and ran a soothing hand over Darcy's face. She felt the tears she had shed dampen the Mod's palm. "It's okay, Darcy," she soothed, giving her a small smile. "It's almost over."

Tick returned to her onslaught of gunfire and seemed to be enjoying every second of it. Something about the calm manner of her companions within this moment of chaos made Darcy feel protected. Even Jericho's wild whooping as he hit his target once again was a balm to her nerves. Darcy's stomach rolled, and her throat ached with the lump that had grown as her tears fell. She was desperate to stay strong, to appear unbothered by what was happening around her, but she was failing. Her heart felt as though it would explode with the hysteria that had consumed her.

"Done over here!" Tick called, and wound herself back through the window like a snake being charmed into a basket. She crawled back over the seat, narrowly missing the whiz of a bullet hitting the windshield and sending Jesse swerving erratically once again.

"Jer!" Tick called, and tossed him another cartridge loaded with bullets. "We have one coming up quick, and one—"

Jesse let a shot ring out his window and Tick whistled. "Scratch that, just one coming up quick."

Darcy wanted to raise her head and see what was going on, but terror had her frozen. She knew the Mods would want her to stay out of the way, but she felt as though she was losing control—about to burst at any moment. Her hands were sweating, pressed against the hot leather beneath her cheek, her rapid breath creating condensation on the slick surface. She squeezed her eyes shut as her brain began to fog.

Jericho let off a few more shots and cursed under his breath, "This motherfucker just won't quit."

"I got him; take the wheel," Jesse shouted, and let go of the only thing that was keeping them from careening into the vast hills beside them. The car jerked violently to the left, and Jesse quickly turned in his seat and fired four shots between Darcy and Tick, blowing out the only remaining window in the rear of the SUV. He paused and fired one last shot. "Got him!" he called, and the other two Mods cheered.

Jesse slipped back into his seat and took the wheel once again. Darcy remained pressed against the safety of the leather beneath her, hands shaking and tears streaming across her lips. "You all right back there?" Jesse called out, but Darcy couldn't answer.

"Took a shot to my ego that Jer got one before I did, but I'll live," Tick quipped with a smile. She busied herself with collecting the weapons and beginning to pack them away once again.

"Aw, I'm sorry, baby," Jericho crooned, and turned in his seat so he was facing her. "Next time, I'll let you get first shot."

Tick huffed, "It doesn't count if you give it to me."

"How about I make it up to you." He winked at her, curling his tongue behind his teeth seductively. Tick giggled and leaned forward, her lips pressing hotly against his.

CHAPTER 4

"Get a room, you two," Jesse griped.

Tick responded, "That's the plan," while staring deep into her lover's eyes.

They continued on as though nothing had happened, slipping back into their normal banter as though they all hadn't been so close to death that Darcy could still feel it pulsing in her neck.

"Sweetheart?" Jesse finally called out, but the hysteria had already gripped her tight, keeping her in its claws like a demon.

Tick pressed her hand to Darcy's cheek tenderly—trying to wake the woman from her trance—but Darcy shot back against the mangled door of the SUV as though she had been branded. Darcy began flailing and kicking, her stomach flipping violently; the scream she had been holding back finally erupted from her chest.

Tick ordered frantically, "Jesse, pull over."

"Seriously? We have to make it to a body shop—" Jericho complained but looked back to see Darcy sobbing, hands swiping at the air. "Jesse, pull over now."

Jesse pulled the car to the side of the road—the mutilated hunk of metal tipping and tilting dangerously on the rims of the back tires. Once the car was stopped, Darcy launched herself from the vehicle and vomited on the side of the road, sobs wracking her body as she wretched into the hot asphalt. Darcy stumbled to the opposite side of the car and melted into the grassy plain. She hiccupped and coughed through the pain, her hands continuing to shake and her lips trembling. She grabbed at her once tidy hair, now pulled free from its confines and sticking to the sweat on her face. Flashes of Tick loading her gun and firing out her window shot across her mind's eye and she fell forward so her forehead pressed against the hot blades of grass in the afternoon sun.

"Darcy." Jesse's voice was smooth and even. She was shocked that he was the one that came for her and not Tick, but her body couldn't register the thought. "You've got to breathe. You're going to hyperventilate." He placed a hand on her back and she turned toward him, hands raised to fight against the attack she was anticipating. Her entire body was shaking, terror causing her to lash out. "Sweetheart," he tried again gently, not pulling away from her harsh attack. "Breathe with me."

He knelt before her, his blue eyes swimming into her view. The sobs continued to assault Darcy from every angle, but his eyes seemed to ground her in some odd way. "Th-the bullets and Tick—" she desperately tried to explain. "They'll be back for us!" Panic seized her once again as she tried to stand.

"Sweetheart," Jesse soothed, placing his other hand on her shoulder and pressing lightly so she sank down in front of him once again. "You're safe with me. Breathe." He began inhaling deeply through his nose and exhaling through his lips, modeling what he wanted her to do. Darcy was too wound up to listen or even to breathe, but she could watch. She watched as his chest rose and fell slowly with each breath, a small wet stain on his right lapel and his tie askew. She watched intently as his deep-blue eyes etched with worry and searched her face, his blonde hair windblown but still looking just as beautiful. She watched as his lips pursed when he exhaled his deep breaths.

"Good girl," he rewarded—Darcy not realizing until that moment that she had calmed enough to follow his orders—and something about the way he said it made her heart finally break. Gone was the mania and hysterics, and in its place was a melting sense of sadness that flowed over her suddenly. She launched herself forward and into his arms. He didn't back away—he didn't even flinch—but instead, he pulled his arms around her and held her against his strong chest.

Darcy wasn't sure what she thought being wrapped in his arms would feel like, but this was not it. He was strong and sinewy, but his hands rubbing up and down her spine were soft and gentle. He pet her hair, hands trailing all the way to her lower back, as though he were worshipping her. His fingers tangling gently in the mess of curls and trailing a sturdy line down. He cared for her like she had always hoped someone would care for her, and she knew she would never be able to repay him for that. She sobbed into his neck; the blooming roses and deep-green vines blurred by her tears were no less beautiful but more settling to her raw nerves.

"It's okay, sweetheart," he crooned over and over into her hair. She slid farther into his lap so she was sitting on his folded knees and her legs straddled his lap. She was fully aware that cars could pass them by and possibly see them; she just hoped the highway stayed as deserted as it had

CHAPTER 4

been for the last hour, because she couldn't think of a single thing that would get her to move at that moment.

There was not a force on Earth strong enough to move her from Jesse's arms.

"Let me go!" Darcy heard Tick shout, her nerves jumping at the possibility of another attack. She could hear the woman's shoes hitting the grass before she felt the pressure of her body against her back. "Darcy," Tick whispered against her skull, wrapping her arms around her from behind. "I'm so, so sorry, Darcy. I didn't realize—"

Jericho interrupted suddenly, "Come on, Tick." His voice was sympathetic rather than annoyed, and this might have been the first time she heard his voice so sweet. "She's all right. Come on, baby, give her some space."

His coaxing must have worked because Darcy felt the weight of the Mod pull away, and she was left sniffling into Jesse's jacket. She knew it would be proper and decent in this moment to back away, but she couldn't. She was safe with him. She wasn't ready to leave that yet.

"Well," Jericho began again. "We can't go anywhere looking like this."

"Do we know anyone in the area?" Jesse's voice was muffled against Darcy's hair, his hands still roaming up and down her back in soothing waves, lulling her into a trance-like state. She had passed hysteria, the sadness had flowed through her, and now she was sinking into a pool of nothingness. She was completely numb.

Tick responded, her voice thick with emotion, "I can call Spin and see if she can make it out here."

Jesse sighed. "If we wait any longer, Newton'll be knocking on our door. She's not ready to go anywhere, but I can't keep her here. Someone will see."

There was a pregnant pause.

Darcy was fully expecting Jericho to gripe about her holding them up or not pulling her own weight. Or maybe even suggesting that they leave her behind. To her surprise, he didn't say anything. It was Tick that finally suggested, "Let me take her, Jess. We can take the car to a station up the road, and I'll get her cleaned up."

"Too many cameras," Jericho protested. "Ask Spin if there's somewhere off the grid we can take her. Get her cleaned up, but keep moving toward the Border. If we go backward, he'll be calling."

Darcy heard retreating footsteps and assumed it was Tick going to call her friend. She breathed into the silence and waited for Jesse to ask her to move or just move her off of him, but instead he continued to rub slow circles into the wrinkled shirt on her back. His fingers gingerly gliding along her spine was the only thing keeping her from floating into space. She stirred slightly, rubbing her cheek against his shoulder. "Darcy," he whispered, close enough to her ear that she could feel the tickle of his breath ignite a completely different feeling within her. A fire started low in her belly and spread out as the intimacy of their position became more apparent to her. "I'm going to take you to the car now. Hold on to my neck."

She couldn't deny the command. There was no room to deny it. She reached her heavy arms up and wrapped them around his neck gently. He backed out from under her and scooped her knees into his arm, his other arm wrapping around her back. He stood quickly, his movements fluid and not at all strained as she expected them to be. She kept her face tucked in tight to the roses and vines, allowing them to shield her from the bright reality of the day. Now that the hysteria and sadness had worn off, she wanted nothing more than to be out of this place and to never see that car again.

CHAPTER 5

The woman Tick had described arrived on the scene—her left hand completely gone and replaced with a sort of drill bit piece that she exchanged out every few seconds as she worked to remove the remnants of the old tires on the SUV and replace them with new ones.

Her black hair was pulled into a tight ponytail at the top of her head, and she wore a one-piece jumper and clear goggles that protected her almond-shaped eyes. "These tires will get you all to the next stop, but that's all I can do out here. You'll need to bring her to my shop to scrap it."

"Scrap it?" Tick practically screamed. "We can't scrap this. The big man will kill us on sight if we don't come back with this car."

Spin responded, "Tick, I appreciate your healthy dose of fear in whatever it is you guys have gotten yourselves into, but I'm telling you, I can't get this car back to running."

"What are our options?" Jesse asked, standing next to the open doorway where Darcy sat in her cationic state.

The mechanic sighed heavily and brushed her greasy hand over her hair. "Exactly what I told you. This car isn't going to make it out of the Faction. Even if you made it to the Border, you think the Border guards are gonna let three Mods—and whoever the fuck this girl is—pass through?"

Jericho snapped, "Well, that's the best we've fucking got for now."

"You said we can scrap it?" Darcy finally asked, her voice groggy from her cries. Every Mod looked in her direction carefully, as though she might break out into sobs again if they moved too quickly.

"Yeah," Spin replied. "We can scrap it for parts, but there's not gonna be much else we can do."

"Can you get the GPS tracker out?" Darcy asked the woman, gazing up at her through squinted eyes.

Spin looked around at the other Mods before answering, "Most likely, depends on how much damage it took. If it's superficial, I can have it back up and running in no time flat."

Darcy nodded. Jesse seemed to read her mind, his eyes flicking back and forth as he worked to catch up with her. "We'll need an SUV that looks just like this one, Spin," he ordered, leaving no room for argument. "Pull the plate off of this piece of shit and pull the GPS out. Put it on the other car and no one will be the wiser, so long as the GPS fucking works."

Jericho huffed, "Where the fuck are we going to get a black SUV exactly like this one?"

"I know a guy," Tick answered, a smile breaking out across her face. "He owes me a favor anyway."

"I don't like that look," Jericho warned her.

"Don't get all worked up, baby," Tick chirped, kissing him lightly on the lips. "We can trust him."

"We better," he grumbled, but his eyes had turned all gooey as Tick began prancing away, her thumbs already tapping at the screen of her phone.

A few more minutes passed, and the plan was set. They drove in silence toward the Border, and luckily, Spin was able to have some of her workers bring her the parts she needed. Darcy sat in the front seat next to Jesse, his eyes flicking to her every few minutes to gauge her emotions. She was all cried out, the terror she had experienced beginning to fade, and all that was left in its wake was exhaustion. She just wanted to be past the Border and away from this place.

They pulled off the main road and bumped precariously down a dirt pathway to a crumbling wooden shack. The team of Mods exited the vehicle, and Spin began barking orders as soon as her feet hit the dirt. Tick pulled Darcy to a small covered outpost on the far side of the shack and began cleaning her face with wet towels and applying makeup to her like

CHAPTER 5

she had done it a thousand times. Darcy wanted to ask if Tick needed help applying her own, but it appeared that the woman had it completely under control. She swiped through the motions easily, and Darcy was amazed at how well she had picked up on the process. Tick fixed Darcy's hair back in its tight bun and did what she could to right her clothing. Once they were back to looking semi-presentable, they joined the others at the car.

Spin replaced the GPS tracker and license plate in no time. Darcy noticed that Jesse paid the woman in food ration cards instead of money, and the woman's eyes glassed over.

"I can't take these from you, Jesse," Spin resisted, attempting to hand back the cards. "You'll need them when you get to where you're going."

"Didn't you notice?" he asked, giving her one of his award-winning half-grins that Darcy liked so much. Jealousy suddenly sat hot in the pit of her stomach. "I've got myself a free meal ticket for about a month or so." He gestured toward Darcy and Spin laughed. Darcy crossed her arms over her chest and felt anger drip like hot acid into her heart.

"Can we wrap this up?" she asked, her snarky tone reflecting her sour mood. Spin and Jesse exchanged a glance and Spin finally took the papers from Jesse. He shook her hand, holding her palm in his own for longer than Darcy would have liked.

"If you're ever back this way again," Spin began, smiling brightly at the man across from her, "feel free to drop by. It looks like I owe you a meal anyway."

The innuendo was clear in her words, and Darcy felt her stomach jerk. Rage filled her veins as she worked to keep her temper in check. It had been such a long day, and she just wanted to be out of here. She didn't have time for any of this ridiculous flirting.

She stomped her way to the new vehicle and slammed the door behind her for emphasis. She saw Tick duck her head at the sudden noise, but she quickly followed her companion to the car. Jericho wasn't long behind Tick, and Jesse finally let go of the woman's hand long enough to pull himself into the car. Darcy crossed her arms over her chest and glared out the window for the remainder of the ride.

The Mods surrounding her seemed to catch her somber mood and rode in silence through the Border. Whatever tricks Tick pulled must have worked because they received no arguments and very little questioning at the Border. Thankfully, they made it through to Faction 4 on time and were able to make it to their destination before dusk.

If she was honest, Darcy would admit that the second they passed through the gates, she had been checking over their shoulder to make sure they weren't being followed. She waited for the sounds of gunfire or the roar of motorcycles the entire way to the small apartment they were staying in. She knew they would face retaliation for what happened on the road so many miles ago, but she hoped she would have the protection of the Elite when that moment came to call.

The apartment they were staying in was on the land owned by another one of her father's connections. These apartments were reserved for the more upper-middle Elite of society as they passed through. It wasn't the red carpet treatment Darcy was used to, but at this point, all it needed was a shower and a bed for her to be elated.

Darcy entered the apartment and barely registered her surroundings. She knew there was a small sitting room and a kitchen beyond that, but the only amenities that caught her eye were the two adjacent bedrooms at the back of the space. She hauled her bags from the door down a luxurious hallway to one of the rooms, not uttering a word to any of her companions. A shower was all she desired at that moment.

She dropped her bags unceremoniously at the bedroom's door and moved toward the ensuite bathroom as though she were answering a siren's call. She cranked the water all the way to hot and stripped herself down carefully. When she slipped into the scalding stream, she hissed slightly but pushed until her entire body was covered by it. If the water was hot enough, she could boil away the events of the day and come out the other side the same as when she had left Faction 2.

At least, that's what she told herself.

She appeared from the steam of the shower and gazed around the large room. Her ears were still ringing from the blasts of gunfire, and her eyes burned from her tears. The previous night, she had felt so exhausted that all she wanted was to fall into bed and never move, but tonight, the feeling

CHAPTER 5

was tenfold. She hoped that sleep would pull her under and keep her there until her body returned to normal, but she wasn't sure that would ever happen again.

Something inside of her had changed that afternoon—as much as she had hoped for the opposite—as though she had shed a skin she had been wearing for too long. She had wept and screamed and batted her fists at the horror she felt, but that same horror had changed her. She was still the same woman she had been the day before, but maybe a little wiser. Maybe a little less naive than she had been twenty-four hours before. The girl who had never so much as heard anyone speak about violence—unless they were speaking about the Mods, of course—had now been involved in a fight for her life, and she hadn't even seen the enemy.

Darcy quickly turned the lights off and slowly curled under the blankets. Her eyes closed, but images of the day's events assailed her. She could still feel the shards of glass raining down on her head, feel the hot press of leather mixed with her own tears slipping against her cheek. Her eyes snapped open, her heart racing and her pulse thumping in her wrists. She reached across to the nightstand and lit the small fireplace at the end of the bed with the remote she found there. The light from the fire allowed for a small amount of security against the shadows of the day, but a lingering fear was hollowing out her stomach.

Fluffing her pillow between her hands, Darcy tried to remind herself that everything had turned out decently enough. She hadn't been hurt, no one on the team had been hurt, and the car situation had been resolved. Her father had been none the wiser, and somehow, they had made it to the next checkpoint without a hiccup. Tick and Jericho would need to borrow clothes for another day—she had been too emotional to make the call to get them supplies—but in the grand scheme of everything, she should be sleeping easier because they had made it to the other side.

So, why was she finding it impossible to lull herself into the peaceful darkness that she desperately desired?

A sharp knock against the bedroom door had her jumping up with a shriek. She imagined bullets splintering through the thick wood at any moment; her fear at reliving the past drove her to leap out of the bed in search of shelter. The problem with leaping was that her feet were tangled in her silk sheets, sending the top half of her body toppling to the floor while her feet remained at the top of the mattress.

"Fuck!" Darcy cursed as she twisted to face the intruder, the door gliding open smoothly.

"Jesus, Darce." Jesse laughed, tipping his head to the side to get a better view of her disheveled state, a half-smirk smeared across his face. "You kiss your mother with that mouth?"

Darcy glared up at him as he crossed his arms in front of his chest and continued to laugh at her expense. He was wearing a plain white T-shirt and gray sweatpants. The art crisscrossing his hands and arms, vining its way up to his throat, seemed more vibrant against the stark white of his shirt. She blew some errant curls out of her face with a frustrated huff and shook her head so she could properly pin the Mod with a withering sneer.

"You're just chalk full of wit, aren't you?"

"I've been told I'm chalk full of something else, but wit seems like an upgrade, so I'll take it."

She twisted and turned in the sheets to no avail; then flopping onto her back, she began thrashing her feet in an attempt to remove them from the snare above her. Finally, Darcy pulled her knee back so it was tucked in the hollow between her shoulder and collarbone, shaking her ankle roughly until it popped free from the tangle of sheets. She reached a hand out to Jesse for assistance in standing upright and noticed his cheeks had grown pink as though someone had slapped him, his eyes blazing a hungry sapphire and his tongue dancing across his lower lip.

Darcy gulped at the sight, her arm lowering slowly and her eyes tracing every subtle move of his body. He seemed to not notice her change in demeanor, nor did he try to hide the change in his own, but she felt it as acutely as a physical touch, her body heating and electricity sparking in her stomach. Her throat had gone dry, and her teeth grazed into her bottom lip, nervous of what he would find in his appraisal. His eyes were scanning over the long expanse of exposed leg and tousled chocolate curls.

She had only thrown on a large shirt and sleep shorts for tonight, not anticipating seeing anyone until the early hours of the morning, but now felt vulnerable in her state of undress. She didn't imagine she would be under someone's scrutinizing gaze. Embarrassment mingled quickly with

CHAPTER 5

her arousal, and she tucked her hair behind her ear, shielding her face and breaking the connection between them.

"Need help?" Jesse hastily asked, seeming to pull himself out of his trance.

Darcy shook her head and flailed her leg wildly until she finally disentangled herself from the sheet, falling haphazardly to the floor.

"I can manage," she grunted as her foot finally freed itself. She pushed herself to an upright position and stood abruptly, crossing her arms over her chest for protection. "Did you need something?"

Jesse rubbed the back of his neck self-consciously, and Darcy felt the movement in her gut. She swallowed thickly and made her way quickly to the bed, wishing for this interaction to be over. He finally answered, "I just came to make sure you were all right."

"I'm fine."

"Clearly," he said, deadpanned and gave her a smirk. "Stubborn as a bull in mud," he added under his breath.

Darcy balked at his boldness; even being with him for this long, she was surprised by his antics. She got the feeling that her status in society made no difference to the man. "Not stubborn," she disagreed, pulling the blankets over her. "I'm being honest. I'm fine."

"Yeah, and Jericho's a housemaid in his spare time."

She huffed at his sarcasm and watched as he padded his way across the floor toward her. His bare feet slapping lightly against the wooden floor, his long, loping strides making her lips tingle and her palms sweat in the best possible way. He stopped beside her, his hips hitting against the mattress next to her arm. Darcy pulled the blankets up to her chin and eyed him suspiciously.

Her nerves were already raw, and her heart fluttered like a caged animal, but having him this close sent a strange desire pulsing through her veins. It was as though something had shifted between them on the side of the highway. She had thought he was attractive before they left, but something in the way he looked at her made her want him more than she had wanted anyone in her life. Guilt tucked in tight to her stomach as the image of Adam flashed across her memory. She had all but forgotten he existed.

"Look me in the eye and tell me you're fine," he demanded, pinning her with a fiery stare.

She jutted her chin defiantly, set on reiterating her point and sending him on his way. She opened her mouth when she felt her lower lip quiver, tears suddenly springing into her eyes at the flash of memories assailing her.

Because, if she was being honest, she wasn't fine. She was the opposite of fine.

All of her comrades were acting as though what had occurred only hours before was nothing more than a minor inconvenience—something they could sweep back under the rugs of their lives and continue on—but Darcy couldn't. This seemingly small encounter had left her broken in her beliefs and unsure of where she stood. The ground beneath her feet looked the same, but felt entirely different.

"Scoot over," Jesse requested.

His words could have sounded like a demand, but she understood the question in them. She knew she could tell him no and he'd walk away, no harm done. She wasn't really sure when she started to have these instincts about a Mod she knew so little about, but something inside of her was calling something inside of him, and whatever it was, responded in kind. They were kindred spirits, it seemed.

She did as he requested, dropping the blankets along with her pretenses of modesty, and crawled to the opposite side of the bed. He kept the veil of friendship closely tied together by remaining on top of the blankets as he sat, and Darcy was forever thankful for that. She wasn't sure when a line between decent and indecent had needed to exist between them, but suddenly it was at the forefront of her mind.

"I remember the first time I saw active fire," he said as he settled his back against her pillows, his head leaning against the bare wall behind them. Darcy mirrored his posture, settling herself back against the wall, though she would prefer to snuggle back against her pillows. "Didn't sleep a wink for about a week."

"Why not?" she asked quietly, afraid to raise her voice above a whisper. The fire cast shadows along the planes of his face, igniting his scar to a florescent red and sending his beard and hair into a strawberry hue.

He chuckled without humor. "I was scared shitless." He rubbed a tired hand over his face and cast his solemn gaze over to where the flames

CHAPTER 5

danced. "I was barely old enough to hold a gun, much less be enlisted in an army."

"How old were you?"

His eyes went far away, and she knew he was no longer in the room with her but in some distant past that she wasn't sure she was ready to endure with him.

"I was only seventeen. I got drafted into the People's Army and so did Harper, but she was only fifteen then. She didn't want any part of anyone's war, but we were past having a fucking choice in any of it. They told us we were lucky we had been drafted at the very end of the shit show, instead of when it started. I didn't understand why they told me I was fucking lucky, like I had won a prize or something. The end was worse than anything I could have ever imagined.

"I had been happy that we both got called to join the People's Army at the same time. We had been in foster care for as long as either of us could remember, and we were the only family the other had. If one of us went and the other stayed behind, it would have been unbearable. We had spent our whole lives in a broken system that the government had designed, and I couldn't wait to dismantle those motherfuckers. Harper didn't feel as bloodthirsty as I did. She just wanted to grow up—go to school and have a boyfriend—without watching buildings being bombed around us. We lost more friends to bombings than I could count. I wanted to burn them to the ground for all the torture Harps and I had been through. I was young and angry, blinded by my hate for whatever had made my life such shit. I didn't realize that the big name corporations I was about to go fight for would put me through something even fucking worse.

"I spent the first six months of my enlistment in an army triage hospital getting ripped apart and put back together again. They rewired my brain—cut off my nervous system and made me numb to any physical pain. They implanted metal into my hands and arms to make them stronger; put steel pipes lodged with springs in my legs to make me jump higher and run faster. They wanted to create a super soldier to win some game none of us knew the rules to. The only thing they couldn't take away from me was my heart. I asked about Harper every day. They promised me we would be reunited after my modifications were over. Those bastards knew how to lie, and I fell for every fucking word—letting them do whatever they wanted to me just so I could see her again.

"They sent me to the front lines in what used to be New York, but at that point, the whole country had crumbled. This was before the Factions had been set up and before anyone really had claim to anywhere. They were dark fucking times for us on the battlefield.

"I remember the first kid I killed like it was fucking yesterday. The whole fucking city was a burning pile of rubble. The smoke was so thick, you couldn't see in front of your face. The fucking kid came out of nowhere, popped right out of a crumbled building, and started firing. I didn't even know if he was on our team or not. I almost pissed my pants, I was so scared. I had never shot a gun in my life until that day. I'm not sure if it was the shit they put in my brain or just dumb fucking luck, but somehow I managed to get him right between the eyes. One minute, he was screaming, veins popping out of his neck, and the next, he's staring up at the smoke-filled sky with nothing but blood gushing over his face.

"I remember I turned and puked, and some of the older guys made fun of me for it. Told me I would get used to it over time. I hoped to God I would never get used to something so fucking savage. But, they turned out to be right. After a while, I learned that shooting and fighting were just a part of my life. They became as routine as brushing my teeth. All of the faces of the Mods I killed in the name of the People's Army started to blur together as I became the killing machine they had designed me to be.

"The gunfire wasn't even close to being the worst part. The bioweapons were way worse. You would hear a *pop! pop!* and suddenly, guys would be dropping like flies—foaming at the mouth or skin melting off of their faces. You couldn't see where it was coming from, or if you had been hit with it already, you just covered as much of your body as possible and got the fuck out of Dodge. Run as fast as you fucking could; leave all your goddamn friends behind. That's another thing you learned in war: There are no friends when shit hits the fan. You gotta look out for yourself because nobody is gonna look out for you.

"At least, that's what I thought until I met Jericho. He was wild as a fucking banshee in the thick of it. He would send out war cries and go running straight for danger, guns fucking blazing and eyes wild. He didn't

CHAPTER 5

give a shit about his life and wasn't afraid of death the way the rest of us were. The thing was, we all had people we wanted to see again. We wanted to get out of this hell so we could find them, but Jer didn't have anybody. He had been beaten and abused in every way imaginable by the streets. He was an orphan, had been abandoned in the streets as a kid, and no one ever came to get him. He looked out for himself and did whatever he had to do to survive. He didn't even get drafted; he showed up hoping this shit would kill him.

"It took me a long time to get him to trust me. We butted heads and fought in the streets more times than I can count, but eventually, he realized I wasn't going to leave him like everyone else did. We were in that shit together, and we were going to get out of that shit together, no questions asked. He started to calm a little, but there wasn't any taming Jericho. Well, Javier—he was called Javier back then."

"Javier?" Darcy finally asked, feeling brave enough to break Jesse from his story. He shook his head and looked down at her as though he finally remembered that he wasn't still on that battlefield.

"Yeah." He sighed and sunk lower into the pillows so his head was resting on top of them, his eyes trained on the ceiling. "Tick, Jericho, Spin—they adopted these names after we left the army. Most Mods did it as a sign of their release from the human world. We weren't who we were before we went in, and most Mods ditched their human names as a sign of that."

"But you didn't?" Darcy asked, sliding down so her head hit the pillows too, and she turned to watch him. He crossed his arms behind his head; the pops of color that slicked across his muscles appeared to dance as the flames swelled over them.

"I wanted to make sure Harper could find me," he admitted, his voice sounding tight. "Jericho and I finally were released from the army five years after we went in. We decided to stay in Faction 2 because I wanted to find Harper, and Jericho stayed because he had nothing better to do." He smiled ruefully, and Darcy squashed the sudden reflex to lean over and run her hand along the strong line of his jaw. "So, I spent the next five years looking for Harper. Jericho and I traded smuggling jobs for information from people that might know anything about where she was . . . if she was even still alive. I did it as a way to gain information but realized I was really fucking good at it and started charging people for it. Of course, it didn't hurt that Jericho was a literal genius, and eventually, Tick came along."

"What was Tick's name before the war?" Darcy asked.

He hesitated and then responded, "I'll let you ask her that. That's a whole different story in itself."

Darcy felt her cheeks warm at the knowledge that she had mis-stepped in this minefield of new knowledge, but urged, "Was Jericho as surly to Tick as he is to me?"

Jesse laughed. "Abso-fucking-lutely not. It was love at first sight for him. He was fucking smitten with her from the minute he met her. He used to follow her around like a little puppy, doing anything and everything she asked of him."

"Seriously?"

"No lie," he confirmed, and they shared a smile. He was looking at her now, his gaze traveling over the planes of her face, and this time, she didn't feel the creep of embarrassment. Only the warmth of desire flushed through her veins, and she fought against the urge to slide her thighs against one another under the blankets. "Once she joined our crew, we were pretty much unstoppable. We ran into a few kinks, but we pulled through and were better smugglers for it. Even with the smuggling—and the rewards we were able to share with our people—I still felt lost. I still wanted to know where Harper was, or if she had even made it out on the other side. Leads were scarce and mostly false identifications that led to dead ends."

"Until you met my father," Darcy whispered, all of the dots suddenly connecting for her.

"Until Charles Newton confirmed what I had been after for ten fucking years. She's alive, and she's somewhere within his reach, which means she's not safe. I have to get this Element Five shit back to him as fast as fucking possible and go get her. Even if he doesn't willingly hand me the information, I'll get it from him."

Darcy responded, sitting up on her elbow so she could better read his face, "He'll give it to you. He's a man of his word."

"I wouldn't be so sure, Darce," Jesse said, rolling so his eyes were now in

CHAPTER 5

line with hers. "I know he's your dad and all, but that doesn't make him an honest man—"

"But he is—"

"He was one of the men that drafted kids like me and Harper and Jericho to the front lines. His company funded the modifications that were happening—shit, he even provided the parts for it. I know you want to believe that he'll keep his word, but I'm not so sure he's as trustworthy as you say."

A thought struck Darcy then, and she almost didn't ask, but felt if there was ever a time for her candor, it was now. "Is that why Jericho hates me? Because of my father?"

Jesse sighed heavily and rubbed a tattooed hand over his face. "That's a complicated question, sweetheart. He doesn't necessarily hate you; he hates what you represent. You represent the people that literally took out his brain and replaced it with a machine. You represent the people that forced us to kill one another for five years just so they could take control. Your people were the ones that threw us on the street like trash after all we had done to secure that power. We did everything while the Elite sat on their asses and reaped all of the rewards, pawning us off into the slums like we didn't even matter. Shit, I think the real reason they put us there was that they were hoping we'd just off one another and they wouldn't have to deal with the mistakes they made.

"Those Borders aren't lines to remind each other where their power ends—they're there to remind the Mods that the Elite are the ones that have the power. Mods aren't allowed to even cross a Border unless they're on official business and have proof by a Faction Elite that they are supposed to be out. We're treated like criminals after we sacrificed our lives for freedom. If you need more reason than that for Jericho to resent you, I don't know what else to tell you." His voice had gone hard and ended with a snap. It seemed that his own prejudice had started to sneak into his words and bared its gnarling teeth.

The seconds ticked by as his words hung heavy in the air. "Do you?" she asked quietly, afraid that his answer might burn her hotter than the flames reflected in his eyes. "Resent me, I mean."

He chuckled, shaking his head against his hand and falling back on the pillows. His eyes crinkled and cracked at the corners, and Darcy finally saw how weary he was. He had seemed so carefree and jovial in their previous interactions, but now he seemed jaded and bone-tired. She wondered if he had always been like this and she had been too self-centered to notice—focused on her own feelings and motives rather than those around her. Or maybe he hadn't trusted her enough to show this side of himself. But why did he choose tonight to expose all of his secrets? Why tell her about Harper or Jericho? She had to admit, the knowledge she had gained about the Mod across the hall had shed new light on his ill-tempered demeanor toward her.

"I wish I could resent you," Jesse finally admitted, not looking at her but staring instead at the shadows dancing on the ceiling. "Hell, I tried to hate you. I did everything I could possibly think of to get you to hate me right back, but it didn't seemed to work."

She bit her lower lip and pressed herself back against the pillows again. She whispered, "The truth is, I was afraid of you."

"Afraid of me?" he asked incredulously as though the idea were completely out of the realm of possibility.

"I had been taught that all Mods were killers and thieves. I was never allowed to be around any Mod alone, and my father made sure that I was suspicious of every Mod I came into contact with. When he told me I was going across the Factions alone with a Mod, I thought he had lost his mind. I had myself convinced I wasn't going to make it out of this alive."

There was a pause; the only sound was the gentle wave of their breaths in and out as they both processed her words. "Are you still afraid?"

She smiled against her will and shook her head quickly. "After what happened—back on the side of the road—I don't think I've ever felt safer."

He turned quickly so their eyes met again and her heart seized. She had the distinct feeling that he might lean down and kiss her right there in the bed. She wanted to feel repulsed by the idea—not because he was a Mod, but because she was engaged—but she found herself wetting her lips in anticipation.

"I told you I tried to hate you," he finally whispered, only a breath away from her mouth. "The truth is, I thought you were just like the rest of them. I saw the way Newton talked to you in his office, the way you

CHAPTER 5

cowered at him, and thought you were just like everybody else in those fucking high-rises. Ever since we pulled away from your mansion, I could feel it. Something inside of you is different."

She shook her head against her pillow. "No," she argued. "I'm no different than any of the other Elites. I have been raised to think and act exactly like they do. But . . . I think being with you—all of you—has changed me. I think I'm starting to unlearn those things."

He smiled at her, big and wide, his scar pulling at the corner of his mouth as though it wanted to stretch it farther. She watched as his eyes trailed across her face, then down to her mouth, his tongue darting out to wet his supple lips. She wanted nothing but the touch of his mouth against hers. She wanted to feel the wet heat of his tongue in her mouth. Her heart raced with it and lust pooled low in her belly at the thought. It wasn't right and it wasn't decent, but her body had other ideas of what was right and decent.

He reached a hand out and pushed a curl back behind her ear. Neither had said a word in what felt like a lifetime, but their eyes were having a full conversation. Darcy could see the desire reflecting back to her from his sapphire gaze, fire blazing from within him. She could feel the tantalizing press of his hips against her stomach even through the layers of blankets between them. What she wouldn't give to feel them pressed fully against her. What she wouldn't give to feel the naked pull of his skin rubbing against her own.

Her cheeks flamed at her thoughts, but she was powerless to them. Darcy knew she had no right to think them, but her mind and body were not playing by the same rules. She knew she had to stay faithful to Adam, had to be the good wife he had always wanted, but a deeper part of her wanted this more. She wanted to feel what it was like to enjoy your partner, and maybe even have them enjoy it too. No more passionless rutting and pain. She wasn't sure how she knew, but somehow, she knew that sex with Jesse would be an experience unlike any she had ever had.

"And what about your fiancé?" Jesse asked, seeming to pull her thoughts straight from her brain. She opened her mouth to tell him that Adam could go to hell when he continued, "Do you think he'll understand when you come home and he finds you've unlearned all of these things?"

His words were like a bucket of water against Darcy's skin. She pulled away slightly and felt her face pull together in a scowl. "No," she started hesitantly, thinking through her answer. "No, I don't think he will. I think that I'll have to relearn my place in this world when I get back if I want to be a good wife to him."

"Are you that anxious to be who he wants you to be just so you can claim that you're a good wife? Because you're so much more than just that."

"Being a good wife is the best way to show your husband your obedience and loyalty."

"And that's all you care about."

"No," she sighed out in frustration. It was so hard for her to get him to understand when she didn't entirely understand herself.

"Then why does it matter if you go back to him as a good wife? Wouldn't you rather be good to yourself?"

"That's not the way my world works," she rebuked. "My father worked hard to establish this engagement, and if I were to come home completely savage, it would undermine everything he has worked for."

Jesse pulled a face and subsequently pulled back from her. "Your father put you up to this engagement?"

"It's the way things work," she repeated, more slowly hoping he would understand. "In the Elite, we don't choose who we end up with; it's chosen for us based on the best moves for the Faction. Adam will rule Faction 2 someday, and it's my father's job to pick the best candidate for that position."

He looked stunned, well and truly stunned, by this information. "So, you just let him arrange a marriage for you and didn't think there was anything fucked up about that?"

"It's the way things work."

"Heard you the first time, sweetheart."

Her temper flared and she bolted up onto her elbow so she was looking right at him. "I know it's difficult for your brain to comprehend, but we're not all free to do whatever we please. You Mods might be allowed to run wild, but in the Elite, we're governed by a set of rules in order to keep things working without violence."

"Oh, here we go," Jesse groaned, sitting up so he was facing her again.

CHAPTER 5

"Us Mods are all just a bunch of lawless heathens, while the Elite are so fucking sophisticated."

"That's not what I said," she defended, feeling a lot like she wanted him out of her bed and out of this room.

"No, but it's what you meant."

She huffed and pushed onto her knees so she was practically towering over him. "Are you saying that the Elite are just as barbaric as Mods?"

He smiled sarcastically and turned the full force of his gaze on her. "Arranging a marriage for your daughter to someone she doesn't even like sounds pretty fucking barbaric to me, sweetheart."

"It's not barbaric! It's a tradition there to keep the Factions from falling into the wrong hands. The current leaders are able to pick their successors, which keeps the Factions running. A fact, I'm sure, you are very pleased about."

"Never been happier."

"And I do like Adam. We are in love. I don't know what would give you the impression otherwise."

"If you love him so much, why do you look like you just sucked on a lemon every time you say his name? Why haven't you called him a thousand times just to hear his voice? Why hasn't he called you?" His tone had a superior edge to it that Darcy wasn't keen on.

She pressed the palms of her hands against the tops of her thighs, pushing herself so she was practically nose to nose with Jesse. "Just because we don't call one another every second of every day doesn't mean we don't care for one another."

He snorted and rolled his eyes. Darcy wanted to slap the snark right out of him, but kept her body still. "That's where you've got it wrong, sweetheart." His tone had gone deep and quiet, the lids of his eyes lowering as he scanned her face in a sultry, smooth trail across her skin. "You see, if a man has something he wants—something he can't live without—it's all he's going to be able to think about. His days and nights would be filled with nothing but you: where you are, what you're doing, who you're with . . . The thought of not having that body of yours pressed against his would be so fucking unbearable that he'd be calling you just to hear that sweet little voice of yours, imagine kissing those lips, and grabbing that fine ass. He'd want to know exactly what you're wearing and how you made up your hair. He'd want pictures of you and messages telling him how badly you want him. These are the things that a man in love desires most from the woman he can't live without."

Darcy gulped. And then gulped again. Her breath was stuttering out between shaking lips. The images floating through her mind were causing her to pant like a wild animal. His vivid descriptions had her practically melting with the heat of it. A sudden pulsing had begun to accompany the wetness that had spread between her legs. She wanted to squeeze her thighs together to dull the ache but knew that would be a clear indication of the effect his words had on her. Darcy had a suspicion that Jesse knew just exactly what he had done to her—the sexy half-smirk appearing at the corner of his lips as he watched her face flush and her chest rise rapidly with each breath—but she wouldn't give in so easily. She was an engaged woman, and he was a Mod. There was nothing that should attract one to another.

But what Darcy felt wasn't attraction—it was an inferno of lust and heat that had exploded inside of her, and she knew there would be only one way to quell the fire inside.

Her voice was low and shaky as she responded, "It sounds like you know from experience."

He leaned forward, his nose grazing lightly against her own. She sucked in a quick breath, intending to move away, but was frozen to the spot. Anticipation vibrated beneath her skin, causing her hands to shake against her bare thighs. What would it be like to feel those lips against her? She was afraid to find out, but more afraid he would deny her the chance.

"All I know is," Jesse began on a whisper, his lips only a breath away from hers. All she would need to do is tip her head a fraction of an inch and they would be fused together. "If I had what he—"

A knock at the door sent Darcy shooting back away from Jesse as though she had been burned. She felt like she had been burned. Every inch of her skin was on fire, her legs and arms shaking, and her heart speeding like a freight train.

"Jesse!" Jericho shouted from the other side of the door. "You in there?"

Jesse lowered his head into his hands and let out a frustrated sigh

CHAPTER 5

before pushing himself from the bed and starting toward the pounding at the door. Darcy leapt back against the pillows and covered herself once again. She watched with wide eyes as Jesse pulled the door open to reveal their interruption.

"Why the fuck are you in here?" she heard Jericho ask. She saw his dark eyes scan the room behind the man before him as Jesse began to say, "I just came in to—"

"Fucking Christ, Jesse," Jericho admonished as his eyes landed on Darcy. She wasn't sure what he saw, but she knew that whatever it was did not look innocent. She could feel her cheeks still burning even with the distance between herself and the Mod. She had been biting her lower lip raw, the skin there sensitive.

"Jer—"

"Fuck, Jesse, fuck no. Are you trying to get yourself killed?" Jericho looked desperate as he pleaded with his friend. Jesse began shoving the Mod out the door as he tried to explain the situation. "This isn't what it looks like, Jer. Nothing happened." He shut the door behind them, blocking Darcy from the rest of their conversation.

She laid in her bed in silence, waiting to see if Jesse would return to her tonight or if he would think better of it and sleep out on the couch. She hoped he would stay out there. Darcy didn't trust herself to make good decisions around him, and she resolved to never be alone with him again. She just hoped she could stick to it.

CHAPTER 6

Rain pattered lightly against the window beside the bed. Darcy could hear the light trickle of it, a soothing tune waking her lightly from her deep slumber. She had thought that she would have been too terrified to sleep, or at least that nightmares would have hounded her through fitful bouts of rest, but neither was the case. She had waited for what seemed like a lifetime for Jesse to return to the room, but he never did. She was secretly disappointed by his abrupt departure but would never admit her true feelings. The things she was feeling for Jesse were wrong—as confusing as they were—and she knew she needed to put a stop to them. She had only known the man for three days and already he was taking up more space in her mind than he should. She should be focusing only on their goal ahead and what that would mean for her when she returned to Faction 2. She vowed to only allow Jesse the barest of thoughts, and even then, only where their shared mission was concerned.

She stretched wide as a crack of thunder roared through the early morning sky. As Darcy's arms reached above her head, they came into contact with something warm and scratchy. She pulled her hands back swiftly and tucked them against her chest. It was then that she registered the weight of a body next to her, an arm slung over her hip from behind, and realized that the warm and scratchy object was, in fact, a beard.

Holy shit. Jesse was in bed with her.

Darcy could hardly breathe, and she didn't dare move. Her resolution from just seconds earlier seemed laughable now as he was the only thing filling her mind already. She was practically sweating with the knowledge that he was so close to her in such an indecent position. When had he come back to her room? She didn't remember his return, nor did she recall asking him to stay with her, so what gave him the idea that any part of this was okay?

And what gave her body the idea that it should be enjoying this?

The familiar throb and ache from the night before were reignited with vigor, her knees practically quaking with the heaviness in her lower belly. His light snores at the back of her neck tickled the curls tucked there, sending shivers down her arms and over her legs. She could imagine his lips pressed against her nape and gave a small moan at the thought. How delicious it would feel to have him pressed fully against her from behind, his whole body wrapped around hers like a python.

Her small moan must have disturbed Jesse, his body shifting and his snoring interrupted for just a breath. He squeezed her hip with his enormous hand, the grip of it nearing toward the side of pain but stopping just at ecstasy. He shifted again, his snores continuing as though he had never stopped, and Darcy felt the familiar press of something long and hard against her tailbone. But this was much longer and harder than the one she was used to. She felt a tickle of rebellion at her heart, the press of him against her fanning the flames. She knew it was wrong to think this way, and even more wrong to act on such impulses, but something inside her lit every time she was with the Mod, and she couldn't help herself. Darcy bit her lower lip between her teeth and gave a small press back into him.

"Shit, baby," Jesse groaned, grabbing her hip harder, pressing her more solidly back against the hard cock pressed against her. "You keep moving like that and we won't make it out of this bed today, let alone across the Faction."

Embarrassment shot through her like a bullet, and she turned quickly to face him. He took her breath away, looking gorgeously disheveled and handing her a shit-eating grin that showed off his silver caps. His eyes were raking over her body playfully, but he didn't try to hide the hunger lingering in their depths. He was openly gawking at her, inviting her to

CHAPTER 6

play. Darcy longed to run her fingers through his sleep-tousled locks, or scratch her fingers down the vibrant red roses along his throat.

Instead, she demanded, "What the hell are you doing in my bed?"

"Oh, sweetheart, I love it when you talk dirty."

She tried to jerk upright, but Jesse pushed her back to the mattress with the flick of his wrist against her shoulder. Darcy blew the curls out of her face even as she lay there glaring up at him. "I asked you a question."

"You didn't seem to mind it so much just a few seconds ago."

Her face matched the roses on his neck, and she averted her eyes. "I thought you were someone else," she lied, sounding just as ashamed as she felt.

"Still missing Mr. Perfect?" he asked, his voice taking a harsh tone. She knew he was talking about Adam, and their conversation from the previous night flashed back into her mind. Darcy turned her head slightly and watched his face. He had gone from playful to hateful in a matter of seconds, and Darcy felt the swift shift of it in her gut. He couldn't be jealous, could he? She quickly remembered her uncharacteristic response to his interactions with Spin and reconsidered her incredulity.

"Jesse," she warned, placing a hand to his chest and shoving him back away from her so she could sit upright. "Why are you in my bed?"

He sighed. "Is that a yes?"

"I want to know how I ended up going to sleep alone and waking up with a person sleeping next to me. Whomever I thought you were or didn't think you were is not in question currently."

"I came back in to tell you the news from Jericho, but when I got in here, you were sleeping. I figured I'd just go crash on the couch like I did before, but then you started making these little cry noises and I thought I would stay in case you woke up. I remember those first nights during the war. I would wake up in a total panic, ready to start shooting at the next thing that moved. The only thing that ever calmed me down was having my bunk mates there with me. They could talk some sense into me and I was able to calm enough to not kill someone."

Her heart melted. Well and truly melted from her chest cavity into her abdomen. He looked bashful as he admitted his truth to her and she went from angry to smitten in a matter of seconds. Darcy wasn't sure if it was appropriate—given their previous state—but she didn't think she cared. She launched herself across the bed and wrapped her arms around Jesse's neck in a hug she hoped expressed all of her gratitude. Her legs pressed against his, thick layers of blankets keeping them from fully pressing into one another.

It wasn't just the fact that he had stayed with her; it was the fact that not one being on the planet had ever cared for her the way he did. The way he had held her on the side of the road, the way he had rubbed her back and petted her hair through her sobs—everything he had done was because he must care for her well-being. He wasn't here with her because it would look good to the press or because he was trying to impress her father. Jesse was here with her because he cared about her, and maybe that was all she had ever been looking for.

The tears fell quietly from her eyes, and she wiped them away before pulling back to look at him. He still had his arms raised at his sides as though he wasn't sure what to think about what she had done. His brow furrowed, and his eyes watched her curiously.

"Thank you," she whispered. "For everything. For taking care of me and making sure I was safe."

"It's what anyone would do."

She shook her head and pushed her curls behind her ears. "You're the only one who has ever done something like that for me."

"Not even Mr. Perfect?"

Darcy couldn't stop the smile that crossed her face, even if she did feel bad. "Not even."

She stood from the bed to make her way to the bathroom to get ready for the day when Jesse called out, "Hey, Darce,"

"Yes."

"This morning, when you said you thought I was someone else . . ."

"Yes?"

He stared at her knowingly, letting his eyes rake up her legs and across her face like he already knew the answer. "Who were you thinking about?"

Her face flamed again, and she bit her bottom lip. "That is not something a lady shares with company."

His smile widened, taking his scar with it as he traced his lower lip with

CHAPTER 6

his tongue. "Then it's a good thing I'm asking you and not a lady."

Darcy scoffed and continued her trek toward the bathroom. Only forty-eight hours before, that would have been enough to throw her into a fit of offense, but today, she seemed to tolerate his playful banter a little easier. "You'd be wise to leave this room before someone finds you in here and gets the wrong idea."

"As you wish, Princess" was his snarky reply as she closed the door behind her. Her heart thumped at his gravelly tone, and she pressed her body back against the closed door. The smile that was pressed to her face reached all the way to her eyes, and she couldn't have stopped it if she tried.

She knew Jesse was a flirt. He carried a swagger on his shoulders that was irresistible to almost everyone he came into contact with, and Darcy tried to remind herself that she was no different than anyone else, but she couldn't quite make herself believe it. She wanted to believe that she was different to him, that she was somehow special in his eyes. She had never been special to someone before—except for the benefits her father could lend to those around her. She felt a flutter in her stomach at merely the thought of Jesse; thinking she might be more to him than just another woman made the feeling erupt out to her fingertips.

Getting ready for the day had been quick work. Dressed in a floor-length white sundress, dotted on the bottom with cerulean-colored flowers and yellow swirls at the top, across the chest, and over the cap sleeves, she finished the look with a denim jacket and strapped sandals. She left a pale-pink pantsuit out for Tick that she felt would washout the woman's tawny skin, but it would be appropriately comfortable for their journey. They wouldn't make it across the Border to Faction 5 on this leg of their journey, so there would be no need to keep up pretenses.

When Darcy exited her rooms, she was met with the dreary sight of rain pelting the windows that lined the hall leading to the bedrooms. She had lacked the mindfulness to take any of this in the night before. She wished the clouds would have rolled on by now, only so she could see the sunlight streaming into the space, but knew that rain would plague them throughout their journey. Darcy stepped through the small sitting room and back into the kitchen, where she heard the hushed tones of voices.

"Shh," she heard Tick soothe. "Drink this, baby. It'll make you feel better."

She watched from the corner of the kitchen as Tick handed Jericho a mug of something warm and pungent.

"Come on, Tick," he griped, and grimaced as he took a small sip. "This shit is fucking painful."

She rubbed at his temples, his bare head falling back against the thin fabric of her tank top. "You know it'll make you feel better. Just kick it back real quick, and it'll all be over." She kissed the top of his head and continued to rub against his temples. He was seated in one of the lower kitchen chairs, and she stood behind him, rubbing the bare skin of his head and soothing him with her words.

"Is he all right?" Darcy asked, expecting one of the pair to jump at her sudden words. Neither moved, seeming to be lost in their own world.

"Headache," Tick finally whispered, moving so her hands massaged against the base of his skull and back of his neck. "The rain always brings them."

Darcy cringed slightly. Now that she knew the extent of Jericho's modifications, she knew that the headaches must be a result of them. The government had altered his life more than she had ever thought. Jericho winced again and swallowed the offending liquid in one smooth gulp. Tick kissed the top of his head, his forehead, his nose, and finally pushed herself onto her tiptoes to plant a kiss against his lips. He smiled against her lips and reached up to hold her face between his palms.

Darcy suddenly felt embarrassed. She knew she shouldn't be watching this—though she knew her presence made no difference to the couple. They were so completely wrapped up in the other that the world outside of themselves seemed nonexistent. Darcy moved so she was out of sight of the kitchen and sat herself on the warm leather couch in the small sitting room. She could pour herself some coffee when the couple was finished.

Jesse appeared from the hallway, scratching his wet hair with a towel and looking out the windows at the rain falling in sheets from the sky. Darcy's heart felt like the rain against the glass, pattering against her ribcage at the sight of the man that now resided in almost all of her waking thoughts. He

CHAPTER 6

was wearing his black button-down shirt, the buttons undone, exposing a white undershirt. His black pants were slung low on his hips, and his shoes were missing as he padded across the floor in his bare feet.

"Morning," he called to her casually, though his eyes scanned her from head to toe in a spine-tingling appraisal.

"Good morning," she returned, watching his eyes and feeling the blood rush up her neck to her cheeks. She bit the corner of her lip, trying to keep the smile from her face.

To anyone listening, their conversation was completely harmless: two people greeting each other for the first time that day. But all Darcy could think of was his hand wrapped around her hip, his breath light against the nape of her neck, and his hips thrust against hers. She was burning on the inside, needing the feel of skin against skin to cool the fire that had started within her.

"No coffee?" he asked, continuing past her toward the kitchen. She opened her mouth to tell him about the couple in the next room but didn't get the chance. Three shrieks of surprise rang through the small apartment, followed by Jesse's quick exit into the sitting room.

"Jesus!" he shouted, shaking his head and walking past Darcy. "You know, there are bedrooms in this fucking place."

Tick was the next body out of the kitchen, buttoning her pants as she followed her friend, giggling. "Come on, Jess, like you've never done something like that before."

"Not when there's other people three fucking feet from me! Fucking Christ, people eat there!"

"They should probably sanitize before eating, then." Jericho chuckled, throwing his white T-shirt back over his head. He gave Tick's bottom a firm swat to which she yelped and turned a beautiful shade of burgundy. He gave her a toothy grin and grabbed around her waist, fusing their mouths together once again. Darcy turned her head quickly, shielding herself from the couple currently mauling one another.

"Enough already! We get it!" Jesse griped, walking past them and into the kitchen once again.

Tick removed her tongue from Jericho's mouth long enough to sigh. "Don't be jealous, Jess."

"I'm not jealous!" he grumbled from the kitchen.

Darcy longed for a change in subject and finally turned her head to say, "Tick, I left a pantsuit on the bed for you for today."

Tick turned her head to the side curiously. "I thought I wasn't going to need clothes from you today. I actually got an outfit ready for you."

"An outfit for me?"

"Sure," she continued, looking to Jericho for reassurance. "I thought you could use one since we're going into the city tonight. Obviously, you won't have to wear it until we're settled at wherever—"

"We aren't going into the city," Darcy insisted, pulling herself off the couch and into a standing position. "What gave you the idea that we would be going into the city? If we continue on our path, we should make it to the Border at dusk. The city would take us ten miles out of the way."

Tick and Jericho exchanged a wary glance, and Tick fidgeted as Jericho sighed heavily. "What did Jesse tell you?" he asked sharply, his tone suspicious.

"Tell me?"

"About the plan for today," Tick supplied as Jericho opened his mouth to make a scathing remark, she was sure.

"He hasn't told me anything." Darcy was confused and a little annoyed that she seemed to be an afterthought in all of this when she should be the one making plans. After all, two of them were not even supposed to be on this trip in the first place.

"Of fucking course," Jericho muttered, and ran a rough hand over his face. "Well, here's the deal, Princess. Tick found a guy that she's been chatting with in the deep Mod systems about Element Five. Guy claims that he knows everything about it and is willing to meet up with us to give us some information. For a price, of course. He's supposed to be running supplies for his employer in Faction 4 today. He wants to meet in the city and have a talk."

"No," Darcy challenged, no trace of hesitation in her voice. Jericho's eyes grew to the size of saucers and he advanced on her slightly.

"What do you mean no?"

"I mean," she continued, her voice stronger than she felt. "If my father were to find out that we were talking to anyone about Element Five, we

CHAPTER 6

would be jailed for insubordination or worse. We cannot risk going to the city when he could be tracking us. If he gets so much as an inkling that we may not be following his orders to the letter, we could all be dead."

"And we could be picking up a dangerous chemical that could blow us all to little bits. And then we'll all be fucking dead anyway."

"I said no," she insisted, her voice raising.

"I don't give a shit what you said. This isn't Faction 2, Princess. This isn't some fantasy land where you snap your fingers and we do your fucking bidding. This is real life out here, and in this part of the world, we rule."

"Jesse!" Tick called toward the kitchen as the pair stared menacingly at one another.

"I'm not asking that you follow my orders. I'm telling you that this is a risk I'm not willing to take. My father could choose any moment to check in on us. It's too—"

"Bullshit!" Jericho yelled, throwing his hands in the air. "It took us three fucking days to find anyone who had any kind of information, and you're hell bent on fucking it all up."

"I am not!"

At that moment, Jesse appeared from the kitchen, looking wide-eyed between the battling duo. "What the fuck—"

Jericho interrupted, "Seems you were so busy between her legs last night that you forgot to explain the fine details of our plan. Now Little Miss Prissy thinks she can tell us all what to fucking do."

Darcy refuted, her ears burning like they were on fire, "I never said that! And for your information, he was not between—"

"Guys, this really isn't the time." Tick tried to mediate, but the voices surrounding her piled on top of her gravelly tone.

"Woah, woah!" Jesse yelled, stepping between them with his arms out. "Time the fuck out!"

The pair finally listened and both stopped yelling for a moment. Darcy wasn't sure why she listened to Jesse. She wasn't sure if it was the lust burning between them, the bond she felt they somehow shared, or his natural ability to make people listen to him. Whatever the reason, he had command of the room.

"What the fuck happened?"

"She thinks she's Queen fucking—"

"Apparently, there's a plan in place to go to the—"

"They both came out here out for blood—"

"Stop!" Jesse yelled once again. "One at a fucking time." He took a deep sigh in and finally looked to Jericho. "Jer, what the fuck happened?"

"Why are you asking me what happened? You were the one that told me you were gonna tell the Princess the plan we came up with last night. I guess you got a little distracted and decided not to tell her. Now I look like a jackass trying to explain to her what we already decided."

Jesse ran an inked hand over his face and shook his head. "She was asleep when I got in there. I didn't have a chance to tell her."

Things started to click for Darcy as she remembered their conversation in bed this morning. Jesse had said something about Jericho's plan, but she had been too caught up in their conversation to register that one important detail. Her face flushed again at Jericho's insinuation of their relationship, and how close he was to being correct. If it weren't for the ring on her finger, Darcy had a feeling that things would have played out the way Jericho had described.

"Bullshit," Jericho muttered, not believing what the other Mod was telling him. "I didn't come on this suicide mission for some Elite bitch to boss me around like she owns the fucking universe." His gaze turned to Darcy, who was currently fuming at his words. "We are going to the city tonight to meet with this informant. You can either put your big girl panties on and join us or scamper on back to Daddy. Your choice."

With that, the Mod stomped back toward the bedrooms, and the distinct sound of a door clicking shut echoed through the space left in his absence. Darcy harrumphed and stormed back to the kitchen. Her judgement on Jericho may have changed slightly, but she wasn't willing to surrender herself to the verbal abuse he subjected her to daily. It ran her nerves raw and made her feel as though she constantly needed to be on the defensive. She fired up the espresso machine and began gathering her supplies to make herself a cup of coffee. It didn't matter what he said, they were going to the next stop, no detours.

"Darcy," she heard Tick's raspy voice call from the corner of the room. "Look, I understand why—"

CHAPTER 6

"You really don't."

"I think you'd be surprised."

"Am I the only one that understands the precarious situation we are currently in?" Darcy slammed the delicate demitasse cup on the counter. She was surprised the frail porcelain didn't shatter with the force of it. "You all think that this is a game—that this is another one of your smuggling operations, but it isn't. My father is one of the most powerful men in the world. He has a way of finding things out, and we must be the luckiest people alive that he hasn't found out what we've been up to so far."

"Darcy, I know what the risk is. I have been in your shoes many times before."

"Oh really?" Darcy responded, feeling the acid creeping into her words. "When, may I ask, have you been the daughter of a powerful Elite hiding two Mods on a cross-country trip to find a mysterious and powerful element?"

The Mod gave a sad half-smile and stepped fully into the kitchen. She sat at the table, where Jericho had sat not twenty minutes earlier, and patted the seat beside her, saying, "Sit, Darcy."

Darcy wanted to argue. She wanted to tell the Mod that she had already made up her mind and there was no changing it, but she couldn't bring herself to be so cruel to the woman. Her heart seemed to have a soft spot carved deep within it, with Tick's name planted firmly on it. Darcy slumped into the kitchen chair, though her dark eyes were still sharp, refusing to give up her stance on the matter.

"How much has Jesse told you about us?" Tick asked, her eyes going somber.

"Very little," Darcy admitted.

The Mod sighed again as though it pained her to continue, and Darcy began to feel a queasiness set into her stomach. "Have you ever been to Faction 13?" Tick asked.

The question caught Darcy off guard, and she stared momentarily. She felt herself begin to wring her hands beneath the table as sweat broke out along her spine. "Only once," she squeaked out.

"Did you come for Homa's funeral?"

This struck Darcy like a slap. She had, in fact, been there for Homa's funeral. Homa had been the daughter of Kareem Abdari, the leader of Faction 13. She had gone missing months prior, the media swarming the story like vultures, each wanting their exclusive look into the tragedy of her family. The family pleaded for months for their daughter to be returned, but there was never a trace of her. Eventually, they gave her up for dead and held a funeral in her honor. There was never a body to be buried, but the sentiment was there. The family needed closure, and this was the way to move on.

Charles Newton and Kareem Abdari had never been particularly close—the distance between their Factions making it difficult to form any sort of business deal during the war—but Charles never missed a chance to be in the spotlight. Darcy remembered her father instructing her to quietly weep when the cameras pointed in their direction. Her mother even went as far as wearing a black veil to hide behind as she delicately swiped at her own tears. It was a complete farce that had gained them their own media coverage for well over a month. Her father had been elated.

But that had been almost ten years ago now, the memory tucked away behind mountains of other tragedies and trips to the Factions. Darcy was struck by how distant that memory seemed now—fuzzy and faded around the edges but just clear enough for her to recall vague details when asked.

"Did you know her?" Darcy asked quietly.

Tick laughed quietly once, humor gone from her normally cheerful voice and replaced with the thick press of unshed tears. "Know her? I am her."

Darcy gasped and sat bolt upright in her chair as though an electric shock had passed straight through her arm. Tick's robotic eye searched erratically around the room as her human eye seemed to do the same. "You?"

"Me," she sadly responded, a tear slipping gracefully from her eye. "I was sixteen years old. I was practically a child—no, not practically, I was a child." She sniffed and roughly swiped her palm against the tear on her cheek. "The war was coming to an end—the Factions in full swing by now. My father had just come into power, and we were in a very insecure position. There were rumors of a full mutiny from one of my father's most trusted advisors. We were watching our backs like our asses were on fire. No one moved—no one so much as breathed—unless my father okayed it first.

CHAPTER 6

"This wasn't the first time that someone had tried to take power from my father. We weren't established enough yet to have the ability to silence the threats politically, and people saw my father as weak. My father had me specially trained by the top hackers in the Faction to track down his enemies and watch for anything suspicious that they might be planning. He was so paranoid that he only trusted the family to work for him, and only a few close advisors and security men. I had gotten good—I mean, I was the best in the business—and I liked hacking and working with computers. It was probably the only valuable thing my father had ever done for me.

"Times were dark for our family, but even darker times for the Faction. They needed a leader. Someone strong and fearless to conquer the traitorous villains out for his throne, and someone brave enough to keep the Faction from being overrun by the other Factions. People began to panic, uprisings began in several of the smaller communities outside of the Elite. My father was desperate to keep his power, but he needed to show them he could rule with an iron fist.

"So, he devised a plan. It seemed simple enough. He hired some men that he trusted to whisk me away for a few weeks. They made it seem like I had been kidnapped—ransacked my room, took me under the cover of night, the whole nine. The next day, my father went to the media claiming that one of his rivals had taken his daughter and he wouldn't stop until he found me. That's when the beheading started."

"No," Darcy whispered out, hardly believing her own ears. She had only been about thirteen at the time, too young to really remember the details of what had happened, but surely, she would have remembered something so barbaric.

"Oh yes," Tick continued, a sad smile crossing her face once again. "Weeks turned into months that I was in hiding. He was using the ploy of my disappearance to get rid of every rival he could get his hands on. Soon, there were no rivals left, but his thirst for blood was so strong that he started beheading innocents as well. People across the Faction feared him. Leaders in other Factions began to fear for their own safety. He had finally gained the power he had always desired.

"While he was climbing the ladder, I spent all of those months being tortured in a rundown hovel in the woods. No one but my father knew where I was or who I was with. It was the perfect opportunity for my captors to unleash their rage upon a defenseless girl. They took it easy at first—only binding me so I couldn't move and refusing to give me food or water for days at a time. When they realized that no one was going to come looking for me, they really amped up the abuse. I was beaten, tortured, starved for days on end. These men that my father had trusted knew that there was no value in me, and they used that to their full advantage.

"There wasn't a part of me that they left unscathed. I had wished for death more times than I can count. I had begged and pleaded for death, anything to make it all end. They had only laughed and spit in my face. I had tried to escape so many times, I lost count, and each time they brought me back, the beatings became more brutal. Eventually, I became numb. I hoped they would kill me, but they seemed content to keep me alive—if that's even what you could have called me. I was nothing more than skin and bone. My hair was clumped with blood and torn out in chunks. They had cut out my eye, and the other was so swollen that I couldn't see out of it half of the time. They had broken my legs so many times that walking was nearly impossible. I was dead, but somehow my heart kept beating.

"The men had gone out for supplies one day. I had been tied up and dragged into a closet so no one would see me—not that it mattered. I had long since given up hope that I would escape or that anyone would find me. But it was at this lowest point that I heard the sounds of tires crunching on gravel outside of our tiny hovel. I heard two voices—two male voices—arguing about being lost and it almost being sundown. I knew it wasn't my captors, but I was too afraid to hope that it was anyone that could help me.

"The sound of their footsteps up to the door still rings in my ears from time to time. The second I heard them knock, I started screaming for help. At that point, I had thought I was beyond wanting help. I thought I had been reduced to nothing more than a pile of bone waiting to turn to dust. It was only when the option of freedom had been presented that I understood that the instinct to survive might lay dormant, but it never truly goes away.

"I wasn't sure if they could help me, but I knew it couldn't be worse than what I had already gone through. I screamed and screamed until it was

CHAPTER 6

all I could hear. I was sobbing by the time they finally opened the closet door and found me. I couldn't walk, and I could barely form words, but Jer leaned down and picked me up without so much as a 'who the fuck are you?' He put me in the car and held me while I screamed and sobbed. Pulling away from that place was like removing a knife that had been lodged in my throat. I was so relieved to be away from that place that it never struck me that where Jericho was taking me could be worse.

"Thankfully, the boys took me to a Mod sublet in the city and called in every favor they could just to get me back up and running. Imagine that. They had never met me, had no idea who I was or what had happened, but they cashed in all their chips to save me. I think I fell in love with them right then and there. I had just about every Mod in the city come to give me some sort of care for my wounds, all soothing and sweet against my raw and anxious nerves. Jer never left my side, no matter what. He just gripped my hand or sat so I could lean my cheek against his chest. There was no ill intention behind any of it—he just cared.

"One Mod even implanted my eye and fixed my legs so I could walk again. No anesthesia in the slums, so Jer got me rip-roaring drunk and held me while she worked. I screamed and fought as hard as I could against him, but he held strong—just whispering words of love and encouragement in my ear while pain seared me from the inside out. Eventually, I passed out and the healing process had to begin. It was a long journey, but well worth it. They're fitted with some titanium steal and work better than ever."

"The Mods did all that?"

"They were there for me when no one else was," she continued to explain. "I had been tortured for months, barely alive, all because of some close confidants of my father's. I was supposed to trust them. I had been lied to and double-crossed by the very people set out to protect me. I was saved by the very people I was taught to fear. These things we were supposed to see as less than human had quite literally saved my life using the little supplies they had. They had no ties to me, no bond to keep them coming to my aide, but there they were. Sure, Jericho and Jesse had called in favors at first, but there was no reason for any of them to continue to care for us—least of all me. I owe my life—more than my life—to them and I will do everything I possibly can to repay them all."

Darcy was quiet for a moment. Tick's words sinking into her brain, igniting thoughts she wasn't sure she was ready to explore. Tick was an Elite. "Did they ever find the men that had tortured you?"

The Mod gave a rueful smile, then sat slightly back in her chair. "When I had healed, Jericho and I spent more time alone together. We told one another all our secrets, our desires, our dreams . . . He told me about his life before the war, and I told him about mine. I knew right from the start that he was my soulmate. He was everything to me, and I would be damned if I hid anything from him. I told him the story—the whole story—one night when we were alone. I thought he might be irate or at least try to defend my honor, but he simply held me while I cried and told me everything was going to be all right.

"That was the last we spoke of it for months. I had all but forgotten that he knew about any of it, except for the pitying glances he threw my way when he thought I wasn't looking. He waited until right before we left to go back to Faction 2 to make a move. I had heard that my family had held a funeral for me while I had been healing in the Mod slums. I figured things would never be the same and decided I was ready to leave it all behind.

"I wasn't sure why the funeral felt like the final push for me to move on, but I knew it was the right thing to do. I could have gone back to my family, but there was no guarantee they would accept me back into their lives. I had been gone for months, modified almost beyond recognition, and living with a pretty serious case of vengeance for the blood of my captors. I would have been surprised if they didn't shoot me on sight. My father must have known what had happened to me, or he really thought I was dead, but either way, I didn't want to face it. There was nothing left for me there, and according to Jericho, he and Jesse had a full life waiting for them back in Faction 2. Why not join them and become part of their traveling band of misfits?

"The night before we left, Jericho told me he was going out for a while. Jesse was with me, so I didn't mind so much that he was going. As the hours passed without his return, I started to panic. I wasn't used to him being gone for more than an hour at the most, and he had been gone most of the evening. Jesse was normally the one that would make runs to get supplies or trade with other Mods, so Jericho being gone for so long really struck a

CHAPTER 6

nerve. Jesse and I even discussed going after him, but Jess convinced me he was fine. He had made it through the Second Civil without help, he could make it through Faction 13.

"When Jericho finally came back, he was covered in blood from head to toe. There was a crazed look in his eyes as he rushed through the door—something feral and wild glinted just below the surface. Jesse and I both thought he had been in a fight—or worse. I responded the only way I knew how: I panicked. I rushed him and fussed over him, my hands shaking and brain buzzing, but he was grinning from ear to ear like he had won the lottery. He came sauntering over to the oversized box we used as a table and dropped two eyes directly in front of me."

Darcy gasped as Tick chuckled and shook her head at the memory. "He looked at me with the biggest grin on his face and said, 'An eye for an eye, baby.' I swear I have never loved the man more than I did in that moment. I could have wept. The story was out the next day that some crazed murderer was running the streets and had killed two close companions to the Faction leader—taking an eye from each. My father knew I was somehow involved but could never prove it without revealing that he knew I was alive. His men have been searching for me ever since, looking for revenge and to silence the only loose end my father has."

Darcy sat quietly once again and pondered all that she had heard. She had known that something was different about Tick from the moment she met her, but she never imagined that she was part of the Elite. Even worse, Darcy had a sick feeling in the pit of her stomach that Tick's double-cross was not so uncommon, and if she wasn't careful, she could be next.

"Why tell me all of this?" Darcy finally asked. "You must know that this only proves my point."

Tick sighed heavily and ran a hand through her wild locks. Darcy flinched at the movement, picturing the long locks ripped out by the root and bleeding from her scalp. "Because I want you to know that you're not alone in this. I have been terrified of my father before—of his power and reach—but it still led me to the same fate. I did everything he asked of me, was the perfect daughter and soldier when he needed me to be, and he still tossed me aside like I was worth less than the shit on his shoe. It was only after I broke out from under his thumb that I recognized that being free and running from his wrath is a whole hell of a lot better than living under his command and cowering to his will."

Darcy protested, "But I'm not like you, Tick. I can't just leave my family behind. I am an Elite and I always will be."

"That may be true," the other woman conceded. "But, you can find small freedoms in rebelling just a little bit. You'll still bring home Element Five and prove your usefulness to your father, but you'll do it on your own terms. You have the rest of your life to be loyal to Faction 2 and his rule. Why not use this opportunity—this trip—to rebel just a little before going back to being perfect?"

Tick's eye shone with emotion, and Darcy felt it pressing against her like a weight. She wanted to tell the woman that it was no use. She knew her father well enough to know that rebellions—no matter how small—were not tolerated and would be punished. But she would be lying if she said the idea of breaking free from his hold for just a fraction of time made her blood pulse with fire.

She had her entire life to be good. Was it so wrong to be a little bad?

CHAPTER 7

The phone felt heavy in her palm later that evening. There were two calls she needed to make, and if she was being honest, she didn't want to make either one. Well, technically, she only had to make one call, and the other, she felt compelled to make. Her conversation in the late hours of the night with Jesse fussed in her brain all day. Why hadn't Adam called her yet? She had been gone for three days, and she hadn't heard so much as a peep from him—which, before she had talked to Jesse, she would not have found odd in the least. They weren't like that. They gave each other space . . . maybe too much space. She wasn't sure. In any regard, she needed to call him to check in and make sure that things were running smoothly in her absence.

The second call needed to be to her father. He had not been in contact with her in over twenty-four hours and that worried her. He had warned early on that he would be keeping close tabs on them. So, either he had been bluffing in the hopes that she would follow his word to the letter, or he had been tracking them using the SUV's GPS and their trackers.

She hoped for the former but expected the latter.

She sighed begrudgingly, pulling her hand through her dark locks, before finally entering Adam's name into her phone and placing it to her ear. It rang a few times before he answered with a gruff, "Hello."

"Hi," she answered back. "How have you been?"

"Darcy?" he asked.

"Yes, it's me."

"I hadn't expected to hear from you until your return."

"I wanted to talk to you—maybe just to feel closer to you. I wanted to make sure you've been well since I left."

"Why wouldn't I be?"

She stared at the phone for a minute before finally replying, "I just thought you might miss me or want to hear my voice . . ."

He gave a short laugh. "Miss you? You've barely been gone. What has it been, now? Two days?"

"Three," she corrected, feeling her cheeks warm and a knot forming at the back of her throat. The ring on her left hand suddenly felt heavy and uncomfortable on her finger. She wanted to rip it off and fling it across the room. "It's been three days."

"Well, there you have it! You've barely been gone for the blink of an eye. Krista has been doing an excellent job. It's as though you've never left. Honestly, there are some things you could learn from her upon your return. She is an excellent wife and housekeeper. Truly stunning to have around."

A sinking feeling hit her straight in the gut. She was going to spend the rest of her life with this man. She had been gone from his life completely for three whole days, and he acted as though it made no difference to him at all—as though her absence was a welcome reprieve from her day to day. She wanted to weep and maybe even scream—she might have done both of those things—but being the perfect wife meant being nothing less than appreciative. He wasn't allowed to see her break, so she had to continue.

"I'm so glad." Her voice was shaking with the effort to keep her composure. "I'm fully confident in her abilities."

"I completely agree. She's been everything a man hopes to find in a wife."

Another gut punch. Was he falling in love with her sister? She had never heard him speak of her in that way. "Oh?"

"She's sweet and demure—barely makes a sound as she wafts through the house. She deals with the staff through electronic communications only and keeps me abreast of all of my social obligations well in advance. She is remarkable."

Her voice trembled, teetering on the edge of heartbreak, as she

CHAPTER 7

whispered, "I'm so glad you're pleased."

"Yes, but I am very busy, Darcy. If there was nothing you needed . . ."

The expectation was clear, and Darcy would be lying if she said she wasn't ready for this entire conversation to end. "I'll let you get back to it, then."

"Yes, thank you. I'll see you upon your return."

"See you then."

There was a pregnant pause as Darcy waited for him to end the call. She wasn't sure if she expected him to profess his love to her or maybe to even give one last indication that she might matter to him at all, but nothing ever came. There was a click on the other end and the line went dead.

And with that, she knew. He didn't love her. She was merely a business arrangement that he continued to indulge.

This time when the urge overcame her, she didn't resist. She took the ring from her finger and let it fly across the bedroom. It hit the metal of the large window frame with a ting and rolled delicately to the floor. She approached the offending object and stared down at it as it lay on the plush cream carpeting.

The ring was nice. She had liked wearing it and even got a thrill from showing it off at parties and fundraising events, but it had never truly been her. Cushioned by about ten smaller diamonds cascading down the band, the central diamond was large enough that she might have been able to see her own reflection. It had been too flashy and showy for her, but she had been so wrapped up in the drama of finding a life partner that she hadn't said a word on the matter.

She had mistakenly thought that with the ring would come a love and passion she had been craving for most of her life. She couldn't have been more wrong.

Darcy bent slowly and placed the ring in her palm. It weighed heavily there, like the remaining thread tying her to Adam. She held it delicately between her thumb and forefinger and squinted at it as it danced in the light of the room. She knew she needed to put it back on—it was worth more than her life, she was sure—but a deep resistance to the idea took hold of her. For the first time ever, she didn't want to put it back on. Her hand felt lighter without the press of it—as though a chain had been broken from her wrist and she was finally free.

Her heart raced as she shoved the ring deep into the pocket of her denim jacket. She pulled her arm back and stared down at her hand for a long second. The ring wasn't gone forever, but a lightness had taken its place that Darcy wasn't sure she would want to concede when she returned home. There were a lot of things that had come into her life these past three days that she wasn't sure she wanted to give back when the time presented itself.

She palmed the phone once again and quickly dialed her father. The phone rang twice before she heard his low voice greet, "Darcy, how are you progressing?"

She swallowed hard before answering, "Fine, Father. We have stopped near the Border of Faction 4 and 5 for the night. We should be able to make it over the Border in the morning. We might even make it to Faction 7 a day early if we move quickly."

"Excellent," he praised. "I trust Mr. Riggs has been playing the dutiful companion without complaint?"

Darcy couldn't help the smile that crossed her lips or the eye roll that accompanied it. Complaining seemed to be his only ability when he donned the role, but she wouldn't let her father know that. "Yes, Father," she lied. There wasn't even a slight hesitation in her voice as she professed the falsity. She would have been shocked at herself, but it seemed something within her had drastically changed in a short period of time and she was beyond the surprise of it.

"I expect that your trip has been rather uneventful as well. I would assume you would have informed me if anything less than standard had occurred."

"Everything has gone to plan," she lied again, but this time, a familiar pulsing at the back of her skull told her he knew more than he was letting on. She stood her ground, though, waiting out the silence that followed her blatant lie. A fine sheen of sweat had broken out over her upper lip, and she felt her leg begin to bounce as she waited for his response.

"Then I will be awaiting your call tomorrow."

"Yes, Father."

And just like with her conversation with Adam, there was a pause and

CHAPTER 7

then the line went dead once again. She was glad that he hadn't tried to engage more in the conversation, and that she was free from his hostile appraisal for another night. She just hoped her anxieties were lingering from her knowledge that lying to her father—and siding with the Mods—was wrong. She knew being home again, and back to reality, was going to be a rude awakening from the life she had adopted since leaving. Things had changed within her, and she needed to find a way back to the old her.

"Is he suspicious?" she heard Jesse ask from the doorway. She jumped slightly and turned quickly to see him pressed against the doorframe, arms crossed over his chest and a booted foot crossed over the other. Casual in his stance, but his words were tense.

He was dressed almost exactly as he had been the day they had met. A blue and gray flannel was unbuttoned and layered over a white T-shirt that had seen better days. His jeans were obsidian—ripped and worn from years of use, she was sure—to match his scuffed black boots adorned with chains. The only thing missing from his ensemble was his signature leather jacket. His blonde hair was pushed back away from his face, exposing a freshly buzzed layer at the sides and back of his head. His eyes were electric, the brown splash of his left iris coming alive. Darcy's heart stuttered a tattoo against her breastbone, and her cheeks suddenly flamed. His scar pulled as a shit-eating half-smirk crossed his face as he watched her. She knew she should be ashamed of her reaction but couldn't find the decency to care. He looked mouthwatering in every sense of the word, and she'd be lying if she said she didn't want a bite.

"You were listening?"

"Only to part," he admitted, pinning her with his gaze, searching for a hint of a lie or suspicion. "I came to see if you were ready and heard the end."

She nodded and thought about lying to him. It would be easy enough given her newfound talent for it, but there was a gnawing nag at her gut that made her reconsider. "He hasn't come out and said it, but some of the questions he asks makes me think he might be."

"Do you think he's suspicious enough to track us tonight?" He stepped further into the room, his footsteps muffled by the plush carpeting around them. He prowled more than walked, and her heart dropped into her stomach at the sight. He was lethal, and powerful, and whatever raw and aching thing that lived inside of her pushed toward him. It was like he had a magnetic pull over her that she couldn't stop. She didn't want it to stop.

She shook herself from her thoughts briefly and looked up at him. He had stopped before her and sat on the edge of her bed, his dark jeans in complete contrast to the mauve comforter below him. "I don't know," she answered honestly. "I don't see why he would feel the need to track us tonight. It wasn't as though he gave any real indication that he thought something was amiss. It was more of a general idea that we haven't been telling him the whole truth."

Jesse pulled a cigarette from the pocket of his flannel and flipped it across his fingers a few times, the letters scrawled across his knuckles flashed back and forth. "That's still not great news, sweetheart. If he thinks we're up to something, he could decide to get trigger happy. I'm not liking our odds."

Darcy didn't like their odds either, which is why she had fought so hard earlier that morning to not make this mistake. "If we're going to do this," she began, advancing on him slightly and pressing her hip into the mattress next to his leg. The energy hanging heavy in the air zigzagged and sparked in the short distance between them. She swallowed hard and looked up to catch his eyes. "We have to do it tonight. I won't be brave enough to try it again."

Her voice had gone small at the end, meek like she was used to using around her father. Jesse smiled sadly and shook his head. He pocketed the cigarette once more and used his knuckles to graze beneath her chin lightly. Sparks flew from his fingers to her sensitive skin. She resisted the urge to moan at the contact. "Sweets, when are you gonna realize you're so much braver than they let you think?"

She was startled by his words. She knew she was a coward, and after all he had seen of her, how could he not think the same? She had never been brave enough to stand up to her father or even her siblings, never strong enough to be seen as a valued member of their family or the business. She was merely a mistake and a burden to be passed around.

"You think too highly of me," she admitted, and turned her cheek, not quite far enough for his fingers to break their contact.

CHAPTER 7

"I've never been accused of thinking before," he joked, and she gave a small chuckle. He used his thumb and finger to grip the tip of her chin and turn her face back to him. This time, the pull in his eyes was so demanding that she nearly floated until her nose was only centimeters from him. "And I don't think you give yourself enough credit."

With that, Darcy thought for sure he would close the space between them and finally quell the fire that had been aching in her gut since the moment she saw him in her father's office. Had she been aware enough to realize it then, she would have recognized the electric pulse between them for what it was. Like a moth being drawn to a fire, she knew he would be the death of her, but she didn't care. She was going to enjoy the burn while she could.

"Let's go, lovebirds!" Tick called from the doorway.

The two flew apart like shrapnel, and Darcy worked to calm her stuttering heart. She could have stomped her feet and pouted like a child. She had been so close to finally getting what she wanted. With the ring gone from her finger, she felt powerful.

"Perfect timing as always, Tick," Jesse grumbled as he moved past her and out the doorway.

Tick patted his shoulder gently a few times, saying, "You'll thank me in a few weeks when your head is still attached to your body."

Darcy's cheeks flamed, and she immediately felt embarrassed. Tick was fully aware of what they were going to do and was doing everything in her power to stop it. Darcy and Jesse both knew the punishment for having any sort of relationship with an Elite was death, but having a sexual relationship with one—now that was grounds for a fate worse than death.

"You're not even dressed!" the Mod admonished as she sauntered into the room. She was dressed in her usual cargo pants and beater shirt over combat boots, but Darcy was still wearing the white sundress she had put on that morning. "Come on, we better hurry before Jericho blows a gasket."

Darcy smiled, relieved that the Mod wasn't going to lecture her on the dangers of her previous state, and allowed her to take control. After a few minutes of Tick's silent pampering, she finally stepped back and looked at Darcy, seemingly satisfied with her own work. Darcy was currently sporting Tick's clothes, which were easily two sizes too small for the woman.

Darcy had always been on the thinner side, but Tick was another level of thin. She hadn't had a decent meal in about a decade, and what little meals she had were enough to keep her muscles toned, not to add meat to the woman's bones.

The white beater rode up Darcy's stomach to her midriff, skin bumping at the exposed air. The shorts she was wearing barely buttoned and came indecently close to exposing her to the entire room. One wrong move, and everyone would have a view of Darcy that only Adam had ever had before. Her curls were tossed up in a high ponytail, much like Tick wore her own hair, and her makeup was much darker than she would ever dare to wear. She looked every bit like a Mod would, and it was shocking how freeing it felt.

"You look the part," Tick congratulated herself, giving a few small claps in celebration.

"You really think I'll fool anyone?"

Tick's face fell slightly, and she sighed. "Just"—she pushed a hand through her wild blonde locks—"try not to talk to anyone."

Darcy's cheeks flamed, and she began wringing her hands in front of her exposed stomach. "Remind me again why it's necessary that I go with you. Wouldn't it be easier if I stayed behind? No risk in that."

"We killed about half a dozen Martyrs close to two days ago. A slight like that doesn't go unnoticed, and you won't want to be alone when their buddies catch up to us."

Darcy gulped and began following the woman out the door. "Who are the Martyrs? I've never heard of them."

"They're some crazy sons of bitches, that's who," Jericho supplied as he finished tying the laces of his boots and stood. He looked at the women entering the room and did a double-take when his eyes hit Darcy's. "Damn, baby, you worked some magic on that one."

"You think she'll pass?" Tick asked self-consciously.

"If I didn't know her already, I'd think she was one bad motherfucker," he praised, taking Tick around the waist and pulling her to him. She grinned wide, and her eyes sparkled at his compliment. Darcy used to find their public displays of affection vomit worthy, but since she learned about Jericho—the real Jericho, and all he did for her friend—she didn't mind as

CHAPTER 7

much. "Just don't let her talk to anyone. The second she opens her mouth, the stick climbs right back up her ass."

"Hey!" Darcy squeaked, and began advancing on the couple.

"Whose ass are we talking about?" Jesse asked as he emerged from the opposite bedroom and around the corner. He was grinning at the group, clearly enjoying the quip, when he stopped dead in his tracks.

His eyes slowly roved over every square inch of Darcy. She had felt exposed before, but now she felt completely bare. It was as though his gaze were stripping the few items of clothes she had left on her body. Her eyes sought Tick as she waited for Jesse's word of approval. Her friend gave her a small thumbs up, but Tick's smile wavered as she watched Jesse. His jaw clenched tight, and his eyes flamed bright in a need so deep it almost took Darcy's breath away. The throbbing ache that seemed to only fade was back with a vengeance, and she bit her lip in an attempt to hide her own need.

"No way, Tick," Jesse ground out, stomping down the steps to where they were standing. "No fucking way."

Jericho sighed. "Here we go."

"It's the only way, Jess," Tick reminded Jesse, placing her hands in front of her in a placating gesture. "No one is going to believe she's a Mod if she wears one of her outfits, and if anyone thinks she's Elite, we're toast. We'll stick out like sore fucking thumbs if she walks in there with one of her pantsuits."

"And if she walks in there like that she's going to have Mods crawling all over her."

"Better that than Martyr bate," Jericho grumbled, and Jesse lit him with a furious gaze.

"Who are the Martyrs again?" Darcy piped up, hoping to end the argument before it got too heated.

"They're Mods," Jericho started, sounding annoyed. "The ones that got too fucked up over the war. They all banded together across the Factions, and their sole purpose is to kill as many Elites as possible."

"But why? What do they gain?"

"Revenge," Jesse supplied before Jericho could answer. "They kill the Elite and take their teeth. Keep one molar to themselves and send the rest to their family."

Darcy gasped and put a hand over her lips. She had never heard of this group of savages before now, but she hoped that fact meant that they had stayed far away from her family and would continue to do so. "Why were they firing at you then? They must have known you were Mods."

Jericho gave a short bark of laughter. "They don't give a fuck who they take out in the process. They just want to take them all out. I can't say I blame them."

The last words felt like a shot to her gut, but Darcy remained silent. She could only guess at the hatred Jericho harbored for her kind, and she couldn't say she entirely blamed him. His life had been hard, but what they had done to him was unforgivable.

"So," Tick continued as though the previous conversation hadn't occurred. "Everyone ready?"

Jesse gave one last look over Darcy's exposed legs and sighed heavily. "Stay next to me all night. Do not move," he ordered.

Darcy nodded quickly and cleared her throat. "I guess it's now or never."

"That's the spirit, Princess," Jericho joked, and opened the door for them to file out. Jesse and Jericho led the way, attempting to hide the women from the prying eyes of the cameras until they were safely in the SUV. Darcy hoped that no one would be paying too close attention to the cameras at this hour, but she felt anxious even at the thought. If they were caught at this point, there would be a lot of explaining to do.

It had been agreed—through a series of phone conversations and messaging on Mod platforms—that their SUV would be housed in a garage just outside of the Elite area in which the foursome was staying. They dropped the SUV and picked up an old car that looked as though it should have been sent to the junkyard years ago. It was a rusted orange, and whether that was from the actual rust or an unfortunate choice in paint could not be determined. There were only two doors, one on either side of the vehicle, which caused Jesse and Darcy to have to climb behind the two front seats to make their way to the back. Jericho insisted on driving, and Tick was more than happy to be his passenger.

Because their current vehicle was about a third of the size of their SUV,

CHAPTER 7

Jesse and Darcy were pushed so their knees pressed together between the two front seats. Jesse looped his arm behind Darcy's head and across the tops of the back seats. Somehow sitting with Jesse in this position felt almost more intimate than when they were in the bed together. They were forced to look at one another or out the front window. Darcy caught Jesse's eyes trained on the straining top against her chest or at the obscene amount of thigh exposed below the shorts that had ridden all the way up to the crease where her legs met her hips.

And Darcy's full attention was on Jesse's. The flannel shirt had been rolled to the elbows, showing off pops of color across his skin. The vines and flowers across his neck intertwined down into the star at the dip of his throat. Darcy was sure she was melting into a puddle of lust. She burned with the urge to reach out and run her fingers across the intricate lines of his throat. Run her tongue along the petals of each rose. Scrape her teeth against the rough hair on his jaw.

"Sweetheart," Jesse warned low in his throat. Darcy bit her lip and tried to pull her eyes away, fully aware that their companions in the front seat could hear and see everything that was transpiring between them. She longed for the privacy of a room, where they might be able to explore her fantasies in private.

But she knew it would never happen. What she was thinking—no matter if they both wanted it or not—was wrong. She had left her ring far behind in the pocket of her suitcase, but that didn't make her engagement any less real. Even without the ring on her finger, she would still have to marry Adam in three months' time. No matter if she craved the wild touch of the man currently pressed against her, it couldn't be. The retaliation they would face would be fierce, and her father's reach was unmatched.

They could never run from the consequences of their actions.

They quickly bumped along the road as Jericho pushed the limits of the old rust-bucket they were currently enclosed in. Tick seemed to be enjoying the freedom as much as her partner, her wild hair free from its confines and blowing in the summer breeze coming from her open window.

The sun had long since set, but the heat was unrivaled. Darcy was glad Tick had opened the window because she was sure this vehicle did not have the capacity for air conditioning and the night was stifling. She only hoped that wherever they were heading was much cooler than where they had come from. It had only seemed to grow hotter as the days progressed, and Darcy was afraid soon they would hit a boiling point.

Once they hit the city limits, Darcy became acutely aware of just how desolate things were for Mods all over. This city seemed to have crumbled decades ago, but somehow beings were still trying to inhabit the space. Buildings were left without roofs, but tarps and thick blankets had been tented over the space to create a vulgar imitation of one. The road was nothing more than dirt and crumbled cement. Holes as big as buildings broke apart the illusion of having a road at all.

Mods still milled about in the spaces even given the late hour. Men and women stood around barrels lit with roaring fires, cooking food and having conversation. Others sat on enormous piles of rubble and drank. Some even rutted in the shadows like wild animals, and Darcy had to look away. The whole scene made her stomach turn, and she felt her face fall ashy. How did anyone live like this? How did they survive in such conditions?

She felt the tight pull of the pants she wore across her hips and remembered how hard it had been for her to get them buttoned. Tick was one of these people. She had stood around those fires and built homes out of nothing but ash and tarp. She had starved. She had begged. Jericho. Jesse. They were all exactly like these people. And Darcy had done nothing at all to put a stop to it. In fact, she had hated them because of their misfortune. Blamed them for the wrongdoings of her own people.

A deep-rooted shame overtook Darcy suddenly, and she felt bile lift to her throat. They had become beasts because the Elite had forced them to. They had thrown them away and expected them to die, but the Mods survived—no, thrived—in the face of unimaginable circumstances. They refused to give in to the impending darkness, and instead, became one with it.

"Okay, folks," Jericho chimed, rousing Darcy from her dark thoughts. "It's showtime."

The car came to a stop in front of a hole at the center of a building. Darcy could see Mods traveling in and out, some stopping and leaning against the precarious structure with bottles in hand, and she guessed this was what passed for a Mod bar. She wasn't so much judging the appearance

CHAPTER 7

of it, but more concerned about her ability to look as though she belonged.

The Mods clambered back out of the vehicle, but Darcy stayed tucked into her seat. The moment she left the safety of their rust bucket, she would be putting herself in the deepest of trenches with her traveling band of misfits. She knew that once she left, she had to leave the Elite piece of herself behind, and Darcy wasn't sure she could do it.

"Darce," she heard Jesse call from the open door. Her eyes reached up and found his. "You're so much braver than they let you believe. Remember that."

His words sunk deep into her bones and she internalized them. He was right. She was brave, even if she didn't feel like it. She knew she could do this because she had to do this. They had to find Harper, and this was the way. With renewed resolve, Darcy pulled herself from the car and let Jesse press his hand to the exposed small of her back, leading her into the bar and further away from who she used to be.

CHAPTER 8

The bar was about what Darcy had expected, but that didn't make her feel any better. She knew it would be nothing close to what she was used to, but the state of it really made her head spin. Most of the tables were falling apart, missing the pieces that would keep them standing. None of the chairs seemed to match, and it was a gamble to find one that would hold your body weight. Everything had a sticky shine to it, and the smell of smoke was heavy in the air. The bodies around them were all pressed closely together, sharing what little air the space had to provide.

All three Mods beamed at one another.

Jericho took a deep breath in through his nose and puffed out his chest, saying, "Home sweet home."

"Or close enough to it," Tick agreed, and looped her arm in his.

None of the Mods surrounding them seemed to give them much notice, but Darcy was aware of a few lingering stares she received from a group of Mods in the corner nearest to them. They looked rough—like they would start a brawl at any moment—but Darcy worked to squash the prejudice voice in her head. If she had learned anything on her trip, it was that there was more to these Mods than what she could see. But something about the predatory gleam to their eye sent shivers down her spine. She wouldn't want to meet with any of them in a back alley anytime soon.

"Martyrs at three o'clock," Jericho muttered to Jesse as they snaked their way through the crowd. Darcy's stomach flipped, and she felt herself stiffen as she looked around.

"Take it easy, sweetheart," Jesse soothed against her ear as he pushed her along. "There's no reason for them to come sniffing around you unless you give them a reason to. Just stick by me and we won't have any issues."

His words helped relieve some of the pressure that was building in her chest, but it didn't stop her from looking around. It didn't take her long to find them. They were standing at a back corner, watching the crowd like vultures waiting for their next meal. They spoke lowly to one another, none of them so much as cracking a smile, each with a leather jacket and black paint smeared across their eyes in a tribal warrior facade. Jericho had warned her that they were crazy, but bile reached Darcy's throat when she saw the glint of pearly white teeth strewn in layers across each one of their necks. That could be her. She could be next. Tick reached back and squeezed her hand twice before continuing their trek into the bar.

"How much time do we have?" Jesse asked Tick when they found themselves perched at a table, drinks in all their hands thanks to Jericho.

Tick shrugged one shoulder and took a long sip of the greenish liquid in the murky glass in her palm. "About twenty minutes give or take. He wasn't real specific on the platform, sounded pretty nervous to me. I wouldn't be surprised if he decided to bolt."

Jericho scoffed, "He's smart enough to know who we're bringing with us." The insult didn't go unnoticed by Darcy, but she kept a tight leash on her anger. It wouldn't do to bring more attention to the small group or someone might be suspicious. "Haven't touched your drink there, Princess. What? It's not good enough for you?" He sneered at her as she stared at the grayish liquid, gulping nervously.

"Enough, Jer," Jesse commanded. "We don't need any of your shit tonight. We've got to at least pretend to be in this together for tonight. You can get back to being your charming self when we get back to La-La-Land."

Jericho tossed back his drink and grumbled into the empty glass, "I'm going to get another."

He pushed through the crowd surrounding them, earning him a few glares and even some heckling, but Jericho didn't seem to notice or care. The crowd pressed against them more closely in his absence and Darcy

CHAPTER 8

began to feel claustrophobic. She weaved her body closer to Jesse as a slender man began pressing into her from behind.

The whole scene made Darcy feel queasy, but Jericho was right in the end. She hadn't even touched her drink because she was convinced she'd contract some sort of communicable disease from the offending liquid. She had just spent most of the ride contemplating how much she had separated herself from the Mods in an effort to shield herself from their pain, and here she was, continuing to turn her nose up at them. Sure, the drink looked vile, but it was the best they had to offer. Darcy could put her prejudices aside for one night and, at least, enjoy her farce as a Mod.

Feeling Tick's and Jesse's eyes on her, she tipped her glass back and downed the drink as quickly as she could. She heard Tick give a whooping cry and Jesse a wolf whistle as she tried not to gag. The drink was strong—stronger than any drink she had ever had in her life—and she couldn't quite detect what kind of liquor it was. It burned like whiskey but had a sharp finish like a vodka. She shook her head to clear the fog that had begun to burn into her brain.

"Well I'll be mother-fucked," Jesse murmured, pressing his hand to her back once again and igniting the fire beneath her skin. If he wasn't careful, she was going to take him to that back alley and finally quench the thirst she had for him.

"We'll make a Mod of you yet!" Tick cheered just as Jericho returned with drinks for everyone . . . except Darcy.

He asked, "What'd I miss?"

"Just Darcy shoving your words right back up your ass," Tick informed, taking her drink and a superior gulp.

Jericho looked around the table like Tick had grown two heads before his eyes landed on Darcy's empty glass. He made a big show of rolling his big brown eyes and scoffing, "Big deal. So she drank a little fucking moonshine, who cares?"

"I think it was pretty fucking impressive," Jesse disagreed, and pulled Darcy tighter to his side. "Let me go get you a drink," he offered, and began walking to the bar.

"That's all right," Darcy quickly interrupted. "Let me go get it."

Three pairs of eyes balked at her. She felt a blush creeping up her spine and resisted the urge to wring her hands. "No way," Tick finally responded. "I mean, why don't you just go with Jesse?"

"Yeah," Jesse agreed. "We could use a little one-on-one time."

Darcy's body pulsed at the idea of having any sort of one-on-one time with him, but her mind was resistant to the idea. She had been catered to this entire trip, and now she wanted to feel as though she was able to do the hard things. The drink may have been pushing her courage, but she was sure it had always been there.

"It's okay," she insisted. "I'll just be right up there. It's not as though you can't see me. I'll order my drink and be back before you know it. I'll be fine." She hopped off of her precarious perch and began marching to the bar before anyone could change her mind.

Darcy was already part way to her destination when she realized she had no idea what to order. She didn't know what the drink was called or if there was a special way in which she needed to ask for it to be made.

The thought of turning tail and running back to the safety of her group crossed her mind, but she banished the thought just as quickly. She had convinced herself to be brave enough to make this first step, and she needed to see it through. No more falling back into the habit of letting someone else take control of her life. She was going to have to fake it on her own.

The crowd seemed to have only thickened as Darcy wound her way through it. She finally pushed through the edge and found herself pressed into the bar by the suffocating crowd around her. A woman, with half her face gleaming in the low lighting, was behind the bar, mixing drinks in glasses that looked as though they hadn't seen a good wash in about a century. Darcy watched as the woman spun around more quickly than her eyes could catch to fill the glasses with different colored liquids from bottles without labels. She wasn't sure how the woman kept everything straight, but there was apparently a method to it all.

Darcy listened as people ordered drinks, but none of the names sounded familiar to her or even looked similar to anything she might indulge in during gala events or charity fundraisers. She usually let Adam order for

CHAPTER 8

her, and he always got her a white wine. Something dainty and sophisticated. Darcy did not feel dainty or sophisticated when she had kicked back the drink in her glass just a few moments before. She had felt real and raw, almost like she had climbed into a new skin and enjoyed the feel of it for the first time.

"What's your poison?" a Mod beside her asked. She turned abruptly to look at him, expecting to see a Mod, but was surprised at what she found. He looked deadly. Sharp in every aspect. His eyes were sharp like daggers, pointed ears and nose, his teeth razor sharp and metal from one side of his mouth to the other. He looked as though he could bite through iron. Darcy swallowed hard but tried to slide her mask in place to keep from seeming out of place. His hair was long and stringy, black and pulled back into a ponytail at the base of his neck. His skin was sickly white with a hue of green that made her wonder if he was ill. He was wearing a grin that looked as though he could see right through her and the disguise she was trying to wear. It worried her more than his closeness and she thought about ditching her effort for a drink all together.

"I'm not sure yet," she answered, trying to make the words sound light, not as though she was fighting for every breath.

"Not sure?" His voice was curious, but there was an edge of suspicion to it. "Why don't you let me help you figure it out?"

"No, but thank you," she declined, hoping he would take the hint and move on.

"I said, let me help you." His hand curled around the arm that was closest to him. She startled and began to jerk her arm away. "You good, baby?" he asked, still sporting his cat-that-caught-the-canary grin, his grip only becoming tighter. "Not afraid of little old me, are ya?"

She cleared her throat. "F-fine," she stuttered. "Just waiting for my friends to join me."

He let out a bark of laughter. "'*Waiting for my friends to join me.*' The way you talk"—he shook his head and took a large gulp of his drink—"I don't think I ever heard someone talk like that." He leered at her, and Darcy looked over her shoulder to make sure her shield of support was still fully blanketed around her. The crowd had gathered tightly behind where Darcy was perched, and she couldn't find the familiar faces she was searching for.

125

"It sounds real nice. I think I'd like to hear you talk more like that. Why don't you come with me? We can spend more time together."

Panic crushed against her ribcage, and she fought to keep her face still. "No, I don't—"

"Aw, come on now." He pressed his cold fingers into her forearm. "Don't be like that. I won't bite." He snapped his jaws twice, the threat clear in the look he gave her as he did so. She tried to swallow the knot of fear that had begun to form inside her. She glanced back again, hoping to find Tick or even Jericho, but came up empty. She knew they would be leaving for the back alley to talk with the informant soon, but she was hoping someone would stay behind to keep an eye on her. But why would they? She had claimed that she would be fine, that they didn't need to worry about her, so why would they be looking out for her? Darcy wondered if she would ever learn her lesson and stop being so stubborn.

"I have some friends—"

"They won't mind. They let you come up here all by your lonesome. What's the matter? Afraid the Martyrs will sniff you out?"

That truly shocked her. Darcy whipped her head to look at him fully. He was really smiling at her now, that knowing glint to his eyes sparkling. Terror gripped her once again, but she fought to keep her exterior appear calm. The only way she would be able to get out of this was by staying calm. "I don't know what—"

"Oh, darlin'," he drawled, taking another long sip of his swill, the grip of his clawed hand on her arm digging painfully against the bone. "I think we both know what I'm talkin' about, so let's drop the fucking act. Here's how this is gonna play out. You're gonna slide that fine ass off that there stool and follow me out to my place. I'll show you a real good time. Might even share you with my friends." She started to struggle against his hold and looked frantically around for someone she recognized. "Now, let's not do all that. You keep that up and one of those Martyrs is likely to come over and pull one of those bright-and-shinies right from your skull. I've seen them eyein' you."

At that, her scalp began to tingle. Her legs felt jittery, and her calm demeanor slipped all the way out. She began wildly tugging at her arm, looking for a weak point in his robotic grip, but there was none. "Let me

CHAPTER 8

go!" she shouted, hoping to draw someone's attention. Several pairs of eyes slid toward them, including the black painted glare of one of the Martyrs. Darcy knew now that she had been discovered but couldn't find it in her to care. She wanted to go home. She wanted the security of her hired protection and her high stone walls with gates that locked. Darcy was desperate for safety. "Let go of me this minute!"

"You got some fire in you, girl!" he whooped, and the grip on her arm tightened as he laughed jovially. "This is gonna be a good time!"

Darcy opened her mouth to scream for help when she felt a hand grip the nape of her neck. Pure fright surged up her throat, and she began fighting against the wall of a human behind her. "If you wanna keep that arm where it should be," she heard Jesse drawl, "I suggest you fuck off." Her body responded immediately to the sound of his voice and stopped its thrashing. She pushed herself more into his atmosphere and hoped the man next to her would take the hint.

"Beat it, pretty boy. I saw her first," the Mod threatened, his grip becoming tighter. Darcy whimpered in pain and began jerking her arm once again. Jesse looked completely calm, except for a ticking in a muscle in his jaw, which appeared to be going haywire like it had been lit with an electric current. He reached a strong hand forward to grip her at the elbow, stabilizing her arm and effectively halting her wild yanking.

"Now, you see, that's just it." Jesse rubbed his other hand along the stubble on his jaw and eyed the predator dangerously. "This Elite belongs to me, and I don't like to share."

"Woah, now, partner," the Mod placated, his grip not yet releasing from her forearm. She would have a bruise blossoming before the night was out. "This fine young thing and I were just starting to get to know each other, weren't we darlin'? I don't think it's within your rights to take her away just yet."

"We definitely—" Darcy began to rebuke.

Jesse interrupted, nodding in a sort of amicable way. "Friendly kind of guy, huh? Why don't you go get friendly with someone else?" Jesse pulled a switchblade from his pocket and stabbed it into the bar for emphasis. The Mod didn't move right away, but the glint in his eye had died and something darker took its place.

"She really worth starting a brawl over? A little bit of pussy worth losing your life?" the Mod questioned, eyes narrowing at Jesse. He pulled his own switchblade from his pocket and waved it slowly in the air before stabbing it beside Jesse's. Not a single Mod looked in their direction, but Darcy felt a crawling under her skin like eyes pressing against her. She felt the possessive hand against her arm release her and move to her hip, pulling her back against him so her ass pressed against the rough fabric of his dark jeans.

"Last chance to back out." Jesse's voice was light, but there was a pulsing beneath it that made Darcy snap her eyes back to his. The tone struck the atmosphere around them like the snap of a whip. Darcy had seen Jesse angry before, but never like this. She pressed harder into him and felt the grip of the Mod loosening.

"I'm not the kind to back away from a fight."

"And I'm not the kind to run with Elite, but here we are." Both men stared at one another for a solid breath, daring the other to be the first to draw.

"What's the holdup?" Darcy heard Tick chime as she sidled up to the bar. "We have a deadline to meet." Her eyes scanned the scene before her briefly before a scowl pressed between her eyes. "What the fuck do you think you're doing?" she addressed the Mod, looking just as fierce as Jesse.

"Jesus, not you too!" he grumbled, and rolled his eyes.

"Yeah, me fucking too. If you think for a second I won't gut you for this woman, you're dead wrong."

Suddenly Tick was sticking her own knife in the top of the bar and scowling at the man still attached to her. The trio stared hard at one another again before the Mod let out a heavy sigh of defeat.

He let go of Darcy for good. She quickly pulled her arm back and retreated fully into Jesse's arms. She rubbed the pulsing flesh and cradled her hand against her chest. "What? Her pussy made of gold or something? Is there anyone in this fucking place that isn't trying to claim her?"

"I'm not," a familiar voice answered as Jericho made his way through the crowd. "You can have her as far as I'm concerned. A real big pain in the ass."

"Jericho!" Tick chastised, and gave a small slap to his chest. "You don't mean that!"

CHAPTER 8

"You know he fucking does. And in this current situation, I fucking agree," Jesse grumbled as the Mod pulled his knife from the bar top. "A big fucking pain in the ass." He gave her denim-covered cheeks a solid swat, and Darcy yelped in surprise, her face turning scarlet in embarrassment.

The disgruntled Mod mumbled, "Fucking weird Poly-Mods." Then turning on his heel, he disappeared into the mass once again.

"Great," Jericho groaned. "Now people are gonna think I'm fucking around with her."

"Don't worry, Jer," Jesse answered, clapping him on the shoulder playfully. "No one in their right mind would think she'd settle for your ugly ass."

"She'd be lucky to tap this fine ass," Jericho returned, and grinned at Tick. She bit her lower lip and leaned her hip into his as he wrapped his hands around her waist.

Darcy finally whispered out, "Thank you."

"Learned your lesson on going on your own?" Tick admonished, like a mother scolding a young child. Darcy nodded her head quickly and vowed to never leave their sides again. She would even stoop to sticking herself to Jericho like glue if she needed to. She shivered at the memory of what the Mod had said, and how close she had come to being a plaything for some degenerate Mod.

Jesse pressed, "Let's get out of here before we become Martyr jewelry."

"The guy should be out there," Tick agreed, and led Jericho by the hand toward the back door. Jesse took both of Darcy's hips in his hands and pushed her forward through the crowd. Her brain short-circuited. All she could focus on was the heat pressing between his bare skin and hers. An electric shock flicked from his fingers to her over-stimulated skin.

Tick and Jericho ducked out into the alley using a crude wooden imitation of a door hung precariously on two rusted hinges. Graffiti covered every available surface, making it seem more in place than it would have if it were bare. Instead of following the couple out the door, Jesse gripped Darcy's bicep and pulled her into a dark corner that was somehow free from bodies.

He pushed her back against a damp wall and pressed his body over hers, covering her almost completely from head to toe. "Never again," Jesse demanded, his eyes penetrating her skin and digging deep into her bones.

She wasn't quite sure what he was saying, but she was afraid to ask. She had never heard his tone so sharp, like a slap cracking against the skin of her cheek. "You won't leave my side ever again. Do you understand?"

Darcy wanted to argue. To tell him he would only be with her for a week more, at the most. Tell him that he wasn't allowed to bark orders at her. She wanted to tell him she didn't actually belong to him, but she wasn't sure that was entirely true. The more she was with him, the more it felt like she might just belong to him in every way that mattered. And that terrified her more than any Mod could.

The demand had lit a fire low in her belly and molten lava was seeping between her legs. His possessive grip on her arm combined with the fire in his eyes and the tone of his words set her body on fire. Something about his command sent lust careening through her veins.

"Yes," she breathed out unevenly.

"I will tie your ass to my hip if I have to."

She gulped. "I-I understand."

"Good," he breathed, inching his face ever closer to hers. She gulped again and worked to keep her heart from beating into her mouth. Every inch of her body was on fire. She hated the idea that their clandestine kiss would be shared in the back of a filthy bar, but she felt she might actually explode if he didn't press his lips to hers this minute. The throbbing pulse in her body had to be building to something, and the only logical explanation was an explosion so terrific that it would level them both.

Jesse's hand lowered from her bicep and smoothed down her sides so both of his hands were gripping the rough denim that barely covered her. He pressed her fully against him, the hard plane of his chest pressing into hers. She could feel the tips of his fingers digging into the bare skin of her ass and she moaned at the contact. "Goddamn," he growled in his chest. He opened his mouth to continue, his nose pressed to hers before the slam of the door next to them broke them apart slightly.

"Jesus Christ!" Jericho shouted, and grabbed Jesse by the collar. "I leave you alone for five fucking seconds and you're trying to get your dick wet. The informant is here! Get your ass out there now!"

Jesse allowed Jericho to pull him through the door, but Darcy stayed for a beat to catch her breath. Her chest was heaving like she had just sprinted,

CHAPTER 8

and her arms were humming with an energy so intense she had to shake her hands to get them working properly again. She ran a hand through her tousled hair and let herself take a deep cleansing breath. She should be ashamed of herself, but all she felt was the desire to stomp out to the alley and slam her lips right against Jesse's.

But tonight, they had bigger concerns than her untamed desire.

Darcy marched out the door and looked both ways down the dark corridor. There were no lights in the small space, which made finding her friends harder than she thought. She could hear the sound of low voices coming from the deepest part of the alley but hesitated before going down. She had only just vowed to stay right by Jesse's side, and she was already on her own again. What if the voices belonged to someone more fearsome than the Mod from the bar? What if they were Martyrs?

"Darce," Tick called from the direction she was looking. The voice set her nerves at ease, and she jogged to their position. They were talking with a man that was the size of a small house. Tick was standing directly next to him, while Jesse stood face-to-face with the man and Jericho slightly behind Jesse's right shoulder. Darcy wiggled her way between Tick and Jesse, where she felt safest.

The man was enormously tall and had a large belly sticking out over the tops of his jeans. There was no outward sign that he was a Mod, but Darcy knew he must be. He had strawberry-colored curls that fell down over his ears and forehead. His once white shirt was now a putrid shade of off-yellow. His jeans were faded and rough around the edges, holes dotting his knees and the bottoms of his pockets.

The immense being before them stopped mid-sentence and looked to the newest member of their group. "She—" he began, staring directly at Darcy. "She's here." His voice was breathless, almost stunned as his green eyes scanned her from head to toe. Her eyes were still adjusting to the dim lighting.

"Who?" Jericho asked, looking around to see who the man could possibly be talking about. "Her? She's nobody. Don't worry about her," Jericho soothed, looking at Darcy and waving her off as though she was nothing more than a nuisance, and she had the sneaking suspicion he wasn't wrong.

"No," the man disagreed. "She's everything."

Jesse rolled his eyes and groaned deeply. "Someone remind me not to bring her anywhere ever again," he grumbled, and advanced on the mountain of a man. "Hey, Jolly Green, she's already claimed. Back the fuck off."

"No, no . . ." he worked to remedy. "I have no interest in claiming her. She's her. She's the key."

"The key?" Darcy squeaked out, finding herself moving out from between her companions. She stood before the large man but stayed close enough to Tick that if he made a move toward her, she would be safe from his wrath.

"The key to everything," he breathed again, wonder coating every syllable.

Jericho huffed, "Hey, Paul Bunyan, more information about Element Five, less about her."

"It's all entwined; the element, her, the Revolution . . ." He stopped and sighed, looking around the small group suspiciously. "I've seen it." He tapped his head a few times with a pudgy forefinger and looked meaningfully at Tick. "Element Five, it-it's the most powerful weapon on the planet."

"Weapon?" Jesse interrupted. "What kind of a weapon?"

"Powerful enough to wipe us all off the face of the Earth. Think *Dawn of the Dead* meets *The Day After Tomorrow*, but for Mods."

Darcy chimed in, "What about humans?"

"Of course, she's worried about herself," Jericho groaned under his breath. Darcy sent him a nasty glare.

"This is exclusive to the Mods. Something about the way it interacts with the metal in our skin. One drop is enough to melt us into a pile of goo," the informant continued. "Put it into a bomb . . ."

"And that's lights out," Jesse finished for him.

"So, how do we stop it?" Tick asked, anxiously bouncing from foot to foot, her blonde hair swinging behind her head.

"Destroy it."

"How do you suggest we do that?" Jericho asked, frustration lacing his words. "Three Mods stop something that could melt all of our faces off?"

CHAPTER 8

The informant looked meaningfully at Darcy, and her companions swung their eyes in her direction. "The key."

"Of fucking course," Jericho cursed, and shook his head.

"How?" Darcy asked, her voice barely above a whisper. She began wringing her hands, biting the corner of her lower lip with her nerves. Jesse reached out and placed a steadying hand against her bare hip. She jumped slightly at the contact, but otherwise did not sway from her position.

"She needs to—" His voice was cut short as he suddenly fell forward onto his knees. The force of it was so powerful that he pushed into Tick and knocked her off her feet. Darcy back-pedaled into Jesse's embrace and felt herself gasping for breath. The man began screaming, shrieking out in pain as he writhed on the crumbling floor beneath them. Darcy attempted to shield herself as she watched the man roll in her direction.

Suddenly, he lifted his head, and Darcy watched as the skin melted from his face, his eyes exposed and bleeding. She could see the raw white bone of his jaw as his screams turned to gurgling moans. His hair began falling to the ground in tufts of bright-red scalp. Darcy tried to climb into Jesse's arms as the man dragged himself toward her. The sockets of his eyes were exposed as his eyes melted down into sludge that poured over the skeletal remains of his cheeks.

Jesse screamed, "Bio!" and tore his shirt from his shoulders. He covered Darcy's face with the flannel as he covered his own with his T-shirt. From behind the shirt, Darcy saw Jericho cover his face and then turned to Tick. She was sitting, frozen on the ground, watching as the skin began to disintegrate from her arm. Blood poured from an expanding wound, her eyes trained to the spot, her mouth open in a silent scream.

"Tick!" Darcy shouted, and shoved Jesse to the side. His hands reached for her as she evaded his grasp and fell to the ground before the Mod. She heard the muffled cries of her name from behind cloth, but she didn't care. She couldn't stand by and watch as her friend was melted into nothing more than sludge on the filthy street. She grabbed the woman's hand as reality sunk into Tick's system. She began wailing—the sound emanating from her throat terrifying and otherworldly.

Darcy knew close to nothing of bio-weapons or how to stop them, but she knew she would move heaven and earth to stop whatever was

THE KEY

happening before her. Without thinking, Darcy pulled the small woman into her arms and lifted them both to standing. She wasn't sure how she did it, but she began walking while carrying Tick, her legs shaking with fear and the weight of the woman in her arms.

"Open the door!" she screamed at the men watching her. Her voice seemed to break them of their stupor and they both rushed into action. Jericho pulled Tick from Darcy's arms while Jesse flung the door open. Darcy stormed through the crowd that once intimidated her and pushed Mods left and right. She wasn't sure what she was doing or where she was going, but she found herself pressed once again against the filthy bar.

She shouted, "I need alcohol! I need alcohol, now!"

"Don't we all, sweetheart" was the sarcastic reply. No one else seemed to give her any mind. They all continued on their way as though the haunting cries of their fellow Mod were nothing more than a slight disturbance to their atmosphere. The rage boiled beneath Darcy's skin, and she felt herself let out a fierce cry. She grabbed the nearest glass, climbed onto the gummy surface, and launched it against the wall right beside the bartender's head. "I said!" she shouted, all eyes on her. "Give me some fucking alcohol, now! She's dying!"

Right at that moment, Jericho slid Tick's shaking form on the top of the bar, his shirt pressed to her skin. "It's melting! It's melting!" she was screaming. The bar was completely still, no one moved. A Mod to the left of her jumped from his chair and pushed through the crowd. He had a knife sticking from his stump of a wrist and came upon Tick as a surgeon does his patient.

"I need moonshine in the cleanest glass you can find," he instructed to the crowd. The bartender stood, glass in hand, staring as he pulled the T-shirt—and a good amount of skin—from Tick's arm. Darcy jumped from the bar top and grabbed the woman by her shirt front.

"Moonshine," Darcy ordered, her voice sounding very much like someone else completely. The Mod looked genuinely frightened of her as she moved quickly to grab the bottle with clear liquid. Darcy tossed it over the bar to Jesse—doing her best to ignore the feral cries coming from her writhing friend on the bar—and began searching for a clean glass.

"I need something to cauterize the wound!" the faux surgeon shouted

CHAPTER 8

again. There was shuffling and the whooshing sound of a blowtorch before a Mod brought his prosthetic leg forward. "When I say, press it hot against her arm," he instructed Jericho. "She's going to fight like a bull and then pass out, but she'll live."

Darcy shouted, "Glass!" as she tossed the glass to Jesse. The medic Mod finished his digging on Darcy's arm and took the moonshine by the neck of the bottle.

"Get ready," he instructed Jericho. He poured the liquid over Tick's arm and then moved back quickly. "Now!"

Jericho rushed forward and pressed the hot appendage against her arm. The Mod had been right. Tick kicked and screamed like she was fighting for her life. She managed to knock Jesse in the nose with the back of her head, blood spurting down his white shirt, but he didn't move away from her. Jericho was whispering words of love against her cheek as sweat and tears poured down his own. She finally fell into a heap against her lover, her cries disappearing almost as quickly as they came.

The room was silent, every eye in the place watching while the small group at the bar heaved air back into their lungs as they gazed at one another. Darcy's felt her breath shaking between her teeth, her hands gripping each other so tightly that the knuckles had gone completely white. Gone were her thoughts of the Martyrs; gone were her fears of her own safety among these beings. All she could think of was her friend. The woman she loved lying lifeless on the bar.

"Jer...," she stuttered finally. "Is she...?" She couldn't finish her thought. Her throat closed and her voice choked.

"She'll live," the surgeon finished for her, pulling the clean glass over to where he was sitting on a bar stool and pouring himself a tall glass of moonshine. "She'll need to rest for a few days, but she'll live."

Darcy let out a sigh of relief and stumbled back against the wall of liquor bottles. The rattle of glass mirrored the rattling of her bones. She wanted to fall to the floor. A wave of exhaustion suddenly came over her, and she wanted to close her eyes. Tick was safe. She needed to get her home. She couldn't think about the body now lying half disintegrated in the alley where they sat. She would unpack that—along with all of the information it had imparted—when she was safely behind the walls of her palace.

THE KEY

"Sweetheart," she heard Jesse mumble as the crowd began to disperse and return to their own festivities. He approached her softly, as though he was afraid she would fall into a million pieces. "Let's go home."

He reached his hand over the bar toward her. She stumbled haphazardly toward him and let her fingers twine into his. The comfort of his touch was almost enough to break her, but she wouldn't allow herself that luxury yet. This was not the time for her tears. Tick needed her strength.

She pulled her foot up on a box of used bottles and pushed herself to a seated position on the wooden top. Jesse wrapped his arms around her waist and pulled her down into his chest. Her cheek was met with the cool whip of his blood-drenched shirt. She didn't mind the feel of it, cooling her overheated skin slightly. She should be disgusted, pull herself away, and wipe her cheek until it came out clean. Instead, she pressed herself more fully against him and allowed him to press his inked hand to the back of her head, holding her against his heart.

Darcy watched as Jericho slid Tick from the bar clumsily, teetering on his feet as he worked through the crowd. Darcy detached herself from Jesse's side and pushed to catch up with Jericho's uneven steps. She rushed outside to where they had parked their poor excuse for a getaway car and opened the passenger door, pushing the front seat all the way forward. Jesse and Jericho juggled her carefully as they laid her in the back, her head ending up on Jericho's lap. He continued to whisper words of admiration to her as he stroked her hair lovingly. Jesse pushed himself quickly into the driver's seat just as Darcy closed her own door.

They drove to the SUV in relative silence. There were no words sufficient enough to describe the horrors they had all just witnessed.

CHAPTER 9

Darcy stared at her reflection in the bathroom mirror. Blood slicked across her right cheek—Jesse's blood, not her own—and her curls had been pulled and tossed from the tight confines of her high-ponytail. Her eyes were red ringed with unshed tears, her lower lip bruised and puffy from biting it ferociously. Bright blue-and-purple spots cascaded across her arm from her brief run-in with the Mod at the bar. She had all but forgotten the event, her mind whirling through the never-ending cycle of melting flesh and blood-curdling screams.

She had helped Jericho bring Tick to the bedroom, watched as he curled his body around her prone form across the mattress and wept. Darcy had averted her eyes and followed Jesse from the room, shutting the door quietly behind her. She had hoped that Jesse would pull her into his arms again, hold her through her tears as he did when they were back at the bar, but he had seemed to pull completely away from her. He hadn't so much as looked in her direction since the second they entered the car. He had rushed out the front door and ran down the steps before she could utter a single word. She wasn't sure where he was going—or if he even knew—but she wouldn't follow. She knew if he had wanted her with him, he would have taken her.

So, that left her alone. As steam filled the small bathroom, she watched her reflection in the mirror, trying to reconcile what she saw now with what she had seen just four short days ago. How could she have changed so much with so little time? How was it possible that she could have the same hair and eyes and cheekbones, but the woman staring back at her was someone completely new. She had looked into the face of death. She had snarled and bared her teeth at a room full of Mods—wild and feral like she had been raised by the wolves—not thinking twice of the repercussions.

Who would she be when she returned? She would have to return, but in what state? She had seen firsthand what would happen to the Mods—to the people she loved—if this element fell into the wrong hands. She would do whatever she had to do to keep Element Five from the dangers that were undoubtedly waiting to strike, but in the end, it would be handed over to her father. She needed to return home, and Jesse needed to find his sister. There was no other option but to return.

She finally pulled her eyes from their trancelike gaze and pushed herself into the shower. Normally, showers were her refuge. She would allow herself to wallow in her misery under the hot oppression of the beating water, but today, she could find no solace. Her tears streamed down her face, but she found no comfort in the spray. She longed for strong arms to wrap around her, inked fingers trailing over her back and hair. Then she would allow herself the peace she longed for, but for now, the empty space of the shower was all she had.

She stepped out of the stall to an enormous banging coming from her bedroom door. Her heart leapt suddenly in her chest as she worked to quickly throw on a shirt and sleep shorts. She would recognize that fierce knock anywhere, and the fact that Jesse had come to her sent her soul reeling. She had needed him since they left the bar, and her need was finally going to be fulfilled. She swung the door open wildly and looked into his icy blue gaze.

"Jesse," she breathed, not even attempting to hide the relief in her voice. He pushed past her roughly, not pushing her out of the way exactly, but shouldering his way past her. This caught her off guard. He had been perfectly controlled since they had encountered the man in the alley, and he seemed to be losing his composure. His shoulders were tense under his white shirt, and his painted fists clenched at his sides. He turned to look at her, his gaze fire and fury, his scar pulling taut with the scowl he was currently sporting. "Jesse, what's wrong?"

CHAPTER 9

"How did they know where to find us?" he growled dangerously.

Darcy almost gasped. His words burned her like acid, the accusation clear in his voice. How could he even think that she would have done this? Didn't he know her by now? She expected this from Jericho because he had always expected the worst from her, but now she was faced with her worst nightmare. "Jesse, I would never—"

"How the fuck did they find us, Princess?" he shouted, his finger pointing right at her chest. The nickname crushed her ribcage against her sternum, and she felt the breath whoosh out of her. "The list of people that knew what the fuck we were doing begins and ends in this fucking apartment. How the fuck did they find us?"

"I don't know, Jesse!" she shouted back, tears pressing hard at the corners of her eyes and in the hollow of her throat. "Why would I risk it? Risk us?"

"You told me earlier that he was suspicious. Why would he be suspicious if you didn't give him a reason to be?"

"You know why he's suspicious," she groaned, already tired of this game. "We haven't done a single thing according to plan since we left the mansion. Of course, he's suspicious! He isn't stupid."

Jesse rocked his head back against his shoulders and gave an incredulous laugh. "I should have seen it before now. I should have listened to Jericho from the start: You've never been with us. You've been working against us the entire fucking time."

"Why would I do that, Jesse? What purpose would it serve me to ruin any of this for us? I have a stake in this game too."

"But do you?" he questioned, inching closer to her and lowering his eyes so they were in line with hers. "There is a reason for all of us to be here, but why are you here? Old Chucky boy elected you with nothing more than some bullshit about needing a companion."

"What are you saying?" Darcy fired back, stepping closer to him still. "That I tipped my father off, and he sent someone to melt this guy? That I'm so diabolical that I wouldn't care if any of you were caught in the crossfire?"

Jesse scoffed, "You've got that innocent, goody-two-shoes act down pat, Princess. You should teach an acting class."

"You've got to be fucking kidding me!"

"Oh, you're a big girl now, huh? Take a walk with some Mods, and now you think you're tough?"

Darcy spat back, "I know I'm tough. Tough enough to save Tick from whatever the fuck melted that guy into goo. Tough enough to not have to take this from you."

"Oh yeah? You gonna run to Daddy and tell him I was mean to you? Maybe he'll blow my brains out before morning."

Her jaw unhinged, and she felt the tears tip over onto her cheeks. She hated herself for crying in front of him at this moment, but her body needed to release some of her repressed emotions. "I cannot believe you," she whispered, her voice shaking. "If I had tipped him off, why would I . . .?" She stopped mid-thought, caught suddenly by the form that had appeared in the doorway.

Jericho was standing against the doorframe, nose rosy and eyes puffed with the constant stream of tears. She bit her lip and moved further into the room. She wasn't prepared to defend herself from both of them, especially with her protection currently unconscious in the other room. She would be obliterated by them both.

"Jer—" she started again when suddenly he was moving toward her. She tried to backpedal into the room, but he was faster. He caught her biceps between his hands and stared at her briefly before pulling her hard against his chest and wrapping his arms around her.

Darcy was stunned. She didn't know if she should wrap her arms around him or if she should keep her guard up and be ready to defend herself. Just as she started to wrap her arms around his broad back, he sobbed, "Thank you."

She fully embraced him, his shoulders shaking as her fingers gripped the hard muscle beneath them. "Jericho," she whispered, relief settling hard in her stomach and her tears matching his.

He sniffed hard and pulled back slightly, still holding her waist in his arms. "You saved her. I fucking froze like a fucking statue, and you-you pulled her away and saved her. I won't ever be able to thank you enough."

"I-I couldn't stand the thought of her being hurt," Darcy admitted, her true feelings making themselves known just as she was speaking them.

CHAPTER 9

"You've got my loyalty, Princess," Jericho declared, his voice shaking slightly. "I swear to God, I'll do whatever you want me to."

"Just take care of her, Jer," Darcy instructed, finally feeling as though she could take a full breath. She wiped the stream of tears from her chin and gave him a watery smile. "I just want her to be okay."

"This has got to be a joke," Jesse groaned, sounding every bit like the old Jericho that Darcy knew so well.

"I'm not laughing," Jericho responded, pulling fully away from Darcy and glaring at his friend.

Jesse accused, "How are you not suspicious of her right now? She breathes in the wrong direction and you accuse her of working against us, but now, suddenly, you trust her?"

Darcy would be lying if she said his words didn't sting. She couldn't believe that Jesse thought so little of her. She had always thought that he was in her corner, but now it seemed she had been mistaken. "She saved her, Jess," Jericho stressed. "She could have just stood there and watched that poison take her from all of us, but she didn't. If she had set all of this up, why would she risk it all to save Tick?"

The reality of his words settled around them, and Jesse shook his head between the Mod and the Elite, bewildered. "How did they find us?" he whispered, trying to grasp any straw he could.

"The trackers? Random fucking bad luck? Who the fuck cares! All that matters is we all made it out of that alley."

Jesse looked chagrined and shuffled from foot to foot, fuming. "Fuck this." He stormed from the room, and Jericho and Darcy both jumped with the slam of the front door. Darcy felt another tear fall from her lashes but swiped at it quickly. These weren't tears of sorrow, they were tears of anger. She was furious with him. If she was honest, she didn't want to see his face again anytime soon.

"I need a favor," Jericho interrupted her musings. "And you don't know how bad this chaps my ass to ask."

"Anything," Darcy answered, figuring she would do whatever she could to mend this current relationship despite the crumbling embers of her previous.

"I need you to give us more time here. I'm going to get some meds for her, but she won't be well enough to travel for a few days."

"A few days? I don't know if I can convince him to give me that much time."

"Get whatever you can out of him. Stall us. I need her to get back on her feet, and moving her now won't help her any."

Darcy nodded and rubbed the back of her aching neck. "I'll call him in the morning. If I call him now, it'll raise suspicion." Darcy looked over at the clock on the wall and realized it was already the early hours of the morning. The sun would be rising in just a few short hours, and she hadn't been to bed. She knew she should feel exhausted, but the adrenaline of the night seemed to be keeping her standing.

"I'll do whatever it takes," she vowed, knowing in her heart she would do whatever she needed to do for her friend.

"I'm meeting with a connection of Tick's to get some antibodies in her. I'll be back."

And with that, he was gone. It was so abrupt that Darcy hardly had time to squeak out a goodbye. And once again, she was alone with her thoughts.

Never in her wildest dreams did she ever imagine she would be held in the arms of her biggest critic while simultaneously defending her honor to her biggest champion. Life had taken a turn, and Darcy wasn't sure what she would do if it didn't right itself.

She needed her friend. She knew if Tick had been there, none of this would have ever happened. She had a way of calming everyone around her and getting them all to see reason, and without her, they were falling apart. Tick just had to be okay.

Darcy looked at the luxurious bed awaiting her and considered slipping beneath the sheets, but she knew she wouldn't be able to sleep with the way things were left. She trudged out to the front room, dragging her feet along the plush carpeting and running her fingers against the wall. Everything looked impossibly clean, every surface perfectly pristine—the whites and creams surrounding her seemed in such contrast to the dark she had been shrouded in. She stepped to the large bedroom door and knocked quietly, the sound echoing off of the quiet walls around her.

No sound came from the other side, not a whisper of movement from within the room behind the door, but Darcy didn't honestly think that

CHAPTER 9

Tick would answer. She was stalling for time. Seeing Tick crumbled on the bed, cradling her arm that had been disfigured and wrapped crudely in Jesse's old flannel, had crushed her. She wasn't sure she was ready to see the aftermath again so soon, but she also knew this wasn't about her. Darcy didn't want Tick to wake up alone, scared, and maybe even traumatized in a strange place. She wasn't sure if Tick would feel the same about her—considering Jesse's extreme reaction—but being angry would be better than being terrified.

Darcy opened the door slowly and pushed herself over the threshold. Her feet dragged across the carpet as she moved toward the sad lump in the center of the mattress. Tick was lying on her right side; her face and the majority of her body were covered by her knees pulled to her chest and her chin tucked down into her knees. Her wild locks were free falling over her face, further shielding her from Darcy's gaze. She could see the blood-stained fabric of Jesse's shirt tossed over her hip and around her back. Darcy tried not to look too closely at the exposed flesh before her; instead, she slid into the bed next to her friend.

The mattress dipped below her weight and disturbed the sleeping figure beside her. The woman turned suddenly, gasping out, "Baby?"

"It's me," Darcy soothed. "It's Darcy."

She wasn't sure what reaction to expect from the woman, but she should have known it would be nothing less than an expression of love. The woman calmed instantly and melted back into the bed, rotating to face Darcy and smiling with her robotic eye squinting. Darcy caught a sharp glimpse of the raw red flesh of Tick's arm and took a sharp inhale through her nose. "Oh, Darce," Tick whispered, petting her face. "I'm all right, love. I'm all right."

Darcy wrapped her arm over the woman and held her tight. "I was so scared. I was so worried that you were going to . . ."

"But I didn't."

"And then when we were at the bar and you were screaming . . ."

"No more screaming. Just thankful."

"And Jericho—oh, Tick—he was completely wrecked with guilt."

"He'll get over it."

Darcy smiled wide at her friend and pulled back to look into her robotic stare. "How can you be so calm? I thought you would be terrified."

Tick nodded somberly. "It's nothing I haven't survived before. This was nothing compared to what I've been through."

Darcy gasped. "Tick, I-I didn't think—"

"Darcy, it's okay. I am fine. Honestly, you're worse off than I am." She was chuckling now, seemingly forgetting all about her mutated limb. "How are you? How's Jesse? My poor, sweet Jer was a mess. I think he finally calmed down enough to get his shit together. He wasn't too hard on you, was he?"

"He was a complete gentleman," Darcy admitted, thinking back to his strong arms around her. "He thanked me and hugged me. He was so sweet."

Tick sat upright on her elbow suddenly, her jaw unhinging with shock. "Jericho? Like, hates-all-Elite-no-matter-what Jericho?"

"One and the same."

"He hugged you?"

Darcy giggled and nodded quickly. "He even stood up for me when Jesse started in—"

"Jesse?"

Darcy hesitated, she wasn't sure if she should divulge the drama that had unfolded in her room just before. She knew that Tick and Jericho had an inkling of her feelings toward Jesse, but if she told Tick about their fight, she knew she would have to admit to their untidy affair. "I'll tell you about it later. You need to rest."

Tick scoffed, "Spill. Now."

Darcy couldn't help the half-grin that spread over her face, though it was a little wobbly with emotion, and began her tale. She spared no detail as Tick commented along the way, nodding and confirming all of her suspicions. It was as though Tick had just been awaiting this moment for Darcy to confirm everything she had supposed.

"Can you believe him?" Darcy finally ended, feeling bold in their tight hold of one another. Tick had kicked one of her legs over Darcy's hip, and Darcy found herself wrapping her arm over her waist. This was what she had always imagined being friends would be like: whispering secrets in the dark and holding tight to the fantasy that they were the only ones in the world. Darcy couldn't imagine a world without this woman or her friendship.

"Yeah, I actually can," Tick disagreed, giving Darcy a knowing smile.

CHAPTER 9

Darcy balked at her friend. "You're not serious."

"Of course, I am! It's so obvious."

"If it's so obvious, why don't you enlighten me?"

Tick giggled and ran one of Darcy's curls over her fingers lovingly. "He was terrified. He was pissing-his-pants terrified. Normally, you run away from the danger—cower down and wait for him to save you—and this time, you ran to the danger. You ran straight for it, and his heart couldn't take the thought of losing you. So instead of being vulnerable and telling you how he really feels, he got angry. Classic Jesse."

Darcy was stunned. She didn't think that Tick could have been more wrong, but something in her heart wanted Tick to be right. She wanted Jesse to feel so fiercely for her that he couldn't stand the thought of being without her. Something electric wiggled its way into her bloodstream, and she could feel her face go hot with it. "That would be indecent," Darcy denied, even as her feelings grew stronger.

Tick scoffed, "Indecent as it may be, I've seen the way you two look at one another. There's no denying the laws of attraction—you want most what you're not supposed to have."

Darcy's heart sank a little at that. "Do you think that's all it is? He wants me because he's not supposed to have me?"

"Maybe." Tick shrugged, wincing as her arm smarted. "He's only known you for a week. I just don't know how you could really know someone in that amount of time; know them enough to want them forever."

The sound of her final word bounced in Darcy's ear like a pinball. Forever. She hadn't thought about that. There was no such thing as forever with the two of them. Their roles in one another's lives was coming to an end very shortly, and there was no way out of it. Even if, by some miracle, Darcy and Jesse were still able to keep in touch—or, God forbid, see one another—when they returned to Faction 2, the price was too high to risk. If they were discovered having anything more between them than a simple business relationship, Darcy would be exiled and locked away for life, and Jesse would be subjected to a public execution. She couldn't indulge her wants for the consequences that were lying in wait.

"You're right," Darcy finally sighed out, feeling an unwelcome tightness in her throat. "Whatever it was we were playing at needs to end. It isn't right to string one another along."

"Woah, woah! I did not say that," Tick defended, lifting her head slightly to look the other woman more fully in the eye. "Remember what I said about small rebellions?" The Mod smiled, her robotic eye twitching with the effort.

"Of course, but I don't see—"

"Jesse isn't stupid, and neither are you. Both of you are smart, consenting adults that are far enough away from the world that you can choose to make these small rebellions while you have the chance. Have a little fun, make this trip worth every second, because lord knows you won't get a chance like this again."

Darcy smiled right back at her friend. Tick was right. She was never going to get an opportunity like this ever again, so she needed to seize the moment and take hold of it while she could. Even if the thought of leaving Jesse ripped a hole in her gut, she could enjoy every second with him while she had the chance.

"Thank you," she whispered to her confidant.

"You know I would—"

"All right, hens," Jericho interrupted suddenly from the doorway. Both women squealed with fright and rolled away from one another. "Stop your clucking. Time to get some sleep."

Both women looked to one another and began to giggle. Soon, the giggles turned into peals of laughter, and before either one knew it, the laughter turned to hysterics. Neither could catch their breath, the lack of sleep and emotion of the day seemed to finally break them. Darcy couldn't remember a time when she had laughed so hard. Her stomach muscles burned, and her eyes watered as she worked to calm herself down. Tick seemed to be incurring the same fate as she wrapped her injured arm around her midsection. Jericho looked bewilderedly between the two as though they had both sprouted second heads.

"And I thought I was the crazy one," he mumbled as he approached the bed. "All right, Princess, off you go. Your Prince Charming is sulking in your room, no doubt waiting for you to get back so you can both angst together."

Darcy's laughter had died to sporadic chuckles as she slowly moved herself from the mattress. Tick grabbed her hand and squeezed it once,

CHAPTER 9

hysteria still lingering on the outside of her smile. Darcy returned the gesture and moved around Jericho to leave the room at last.

Her friend was okay, and that was all she needed to finally fall asleep.

Her walk to the opposite bedroom was more serene than it had been earlier that night, her feet moving more quickly against the soft platform beneath her. The sky had gone a milky gray with the rising sun, and Darcy knew it was well past time for her to get to bed. She felt exhausted now, though her heart was lighter. Her mind was set at ease seeing Tick acting like her old self—if a little more subdued—which made relaxing into sleep seem like a possibility.

Jericho's words followed her to the bedroom door, and she paused slightly. She wasn't sure which version of Jesse would be waiting on the other side. Any other night—or morning, she guessed it was—she would be barreling through the door to see him, but tonight, she wasn't so sure she was ready. His words still sat sour on her stomach, and she wasn't certain she was ready to incur more of his wrath.

But she needed to be brave. If anything came out of this night, she knew for sure that she was brave.

She opened the door quietly and slid her body through, watching carefully at the form sitting on the edge of the bed. He was slumped forward slightly, fiddling with a switchblade, an unlit cigarette hanging from the edge of his lips. His eyes were focused on the knife in his hands, but Darcy knew that he had heard her. He was no longer wearing the sullied white shirt he had been wearing earlier, but a new gray one with a pair of black sweatpants. His hair looked damp, and the air felt foggy as though he had just pulled himself from her shower. The thought thrilled her slightly, but Darcy worked to keep it from her face.

Ice blue finally reached up to her face, steady as a mask, giving nothing away. She tried to harden her own expression but could feel her eyes soften as they landed on his face. Her hands itched to reach out to him, her body on edge just seeing him sitting at the corner of her mattress. But she refused to move. She would not be the first to fold in this game they were caught in.

"Go ahead and let me have it," he finally spoke, putting the knife down on the bed and pulling the cigarette from his lips. Darcy crossed her arms over her chest but said nothing. "I was a fucking prick and I deserve all of it, so go ahead and let me have it."

He sounded just shy of ashamed as he spoke, and the tone made Darcy's lips pull in a half smile. "You're right," she agreed quietly. "You were a prick."

Jesse returned, "I don't think I'll ever get used to hearing you say shit like that."

Darcy's face flamed slightly. "I think it's appropriate given our current situation."

"I don't hate it," he continued. There was a pause, and they both looked at one another. Darcy resisted the urge to begin apologizing to him. She was so used to bending to Adam and her father—really, anyone in her life—that it came almost second nature to her to apologize.

"You have to know it wasn't me," she started, not an apology, but her voice still sounded unsure. "I would never put her in danger like that."

He nodded solemnly. "I know. I never really thought—I mean, I know that if you were going to go after anyone, it would have been Jericho." The last part was said as a joke, and Darcy conceded a full smile this time.

"I would do it again if I had to—I mean, I would help Tick, no matter the consequences."

His eyes darkened slightly, and he narrowed his gaze. "You won't do it again, not while I'm around. You could have gotten yourself killed. And then what? We lose her and you?"

"At least, she wouldn't be alone!"

"You're too soft for this, Darcy. You haven't seen—"

"You're right, I haven't seen what you've seen, but I am not soft."

Jesse shook his head and sighed heavily, running his hand over his short beard. "Your heart is too soft, Darcy. Out there—out on the front lines—you have no friends. You have to look out for yourself in order to stay alive. You can't throw yourself at an invisible enemy and expect to win every time."

Darcy took a few short steps closer. She was feeling bold—maybe a little nervous—but she needed him to understand. She needed him to see her. Darcy stood between Jesse's knees, her hips just centimeters from his, and held his jaw between her shaking hands. He looked up into her face in a combination of lust and surprise. She was honestly surprised by herself.

"These aren't the front lines, Jesse," she whispered, making sure his eyes

CHAPTER 9

met hers. "We're not on the battlefield. I have friends here—people I love—and I will not hesitate to risk my life for theirs. If you see that as softness or weakness, then I'm sorry for your lack of perception."

They stared at one another, Darcy's heart thumping so quickly against her chest she was struggling to keep up with it. The look in Jesse's eye told her he welcomed the intrusion, his normally icy blue darkening to a cerulean, his lids lowering to capture every inch of her face. She knew she should back away—his tongue darting out to lick his lips entirely too enticing for her to take—and continue her path of faithfulness. She knew she would feel wrong if she gave in to her desires. After all, cheating on your fiancé, no matter how far from home, was still adultery in the worst way. She should be ashamed that she was even considering it.

But a small voice in the back of her head reminded her that she would never get this opportunity again. Once Element Five was provided to her father, she would be back in the arms of her soon-to-be in their mediocre attempt to bring passion into their relationship. Darcy wondered if the same would be true with Jesse. Would she find if she pressed her lips to his that all of this tension was for naught?

Small rebellions, Tick reminded her subconsciously.

Darcy lowered her head slightly, her lips just a breath away from Jesse's. His hands came up to her waist and held her there, not making any more moves than that simple expression of interest. She hesitated just on the outside of the kiss, waiting for the logical part of her brain to talk her out of this, to tell her to stop, but nothing ever came, just the rapid pummeling of her heart and the quick hitch of her breath against his face. She could smell the tobacco on his skin, and she wanted to feel revolted, but it only added to the warmth that was currently pooling in her lower belly.

Without anything left to stop her, Darcy leaned forward ever so slightly and pressed her lips against his. The kiss lasted only a second before she pulled back, waiting for her better sense to kick in. Nothing came. Only her body and her brain screaming at her to get her skin against his as soon as possible, but she never got the chance.

Jesse's lips chased hers instead as he leaned up slightly and captured her mouth with his. His lips pulled and sucked at hers, driving her insane. He was clearly more experienced in this avenue than she, but she was happy to let him take control. He tightened his grip on her waist as his teeth grazed the overstimulated flesh of her mouth. She felt a shaky sigh rattle out between her lips, and he chuckled in delight. He loved what he was doing to her, and she couldn't say that she hated it. She had never experienced a kiss so searing in her life.

She could feel this kiss in every molecule of her body, from the roots of her hair to the tips of her toes. Nothing had ever been so intimate or magnificent. She never wanted the moment to end. The wetness of his tongue danced along the seam of her lips as he worked to get her to comply. A sudden shyness took over her as she contemplated this next step.

She gasped as his teeth nipped at her lower lip, her whole body jolting with the pleasure of it. He took the opportunity to grant his tongue entrance and her whole body lit with a building pressure at the slide of his tongue against her own. His hands quickly lowered to her thighs and lifted so she was straddling his lap, the evidence of his pleasure rock hard against her. She moaned at the contact—surprised at her own neediness—which only seemed to encourage him more. He used his hands to slide hers from his face to his neck, where she held on for dear life.

"This okay, baby?" he panted out as he pressed his hips up into hers, the hard head of his cock driving right over her sensitive bundle of nerves. A wanton cry fell from her lips as she returned the contact, looking for more friction to send her careening toward the pressure she felt building.

"More, Jesse," she whined, not recognizing her own voice. He slanted his lips hotly across hers in a kiss that melted her all the way to her feet. Her hips began rocking against his without her permission, seeming to have a mind of their own.

Her fingers dug into the skin at the back of his neck, urging him to press deeper and harder into their searing kiss. He finally shifted his hips up against her as she came down, and a surprised whine escaped between her lips. He moved again, and she nearly melted into him. Their hips began to grind together in a race toward a finish line neither was ready for. Her small gasps of pleasure at the intimate contact filled the space around them. She swore that she had just died and gone to heaven. Nothing in her entire life had been as sensational as this moment, and they both still had all their clothes on.

CHAPTER 9

"More?" he growled between his teeth, his voice strained as though he were using all of the strength within himself to hold back. She nodded her head in a jerky assent, knowing at this point that she wouldn't be able to stop. There was not a force on Earth strong enough to keep her from racing faster toward the pleasure it seemed only Jesse could provide.

He stood, lifting Darcy up so her legs were wound around his waist, and shifted so she was beneath him on the end of the bed, pulling her thighs around his hips so he could position himself right where she wanted him to be. He thrust his hips forward slightly and she felt the dampness of her shorts press into his pants. He made a choked sound in the back of his throat that made Darcy see stars. She knew she should be embarrassed by her lack of modesty, but it all seemed to thrill her more.

It had never been like this before. Sex had always been a chore—something to endure because it was a woman's job to please her husband. Every press of Jesse's hips against hers convinced Darcy more and more that this man had been created for the purpose of pleasing her. Every moan from his lips sent her to a high she had never thought possible.

"Fuck, baby," he grunted as she lifted her hips against his, daringly. He seemed just as lost to her as she was to him. His heart was beating a tattoo against her hands, the feelings from just moments before seeming to push it faster than she thought it ever could. He trailed his lips down the column of her neck, biting and sucking the sensitive flesh over and over. She let out small sighs of pleasure and ran her hands up his back under his thin shirt, needing the feel of his skin against hers like she needed oxygen. The shock of pleasure was like lightening in a bottle.

"Jesse," she whined as he nipped the sensitive skin of her neck a little harder. He reached his hands under her shirt and began to lift, the smooth flesh of her belly exposed to his fiery gaze. He dipped his head and kissed the center of her stomach, goosebumps fanning out across the skin beneath him, Darcy's gasp of pleasure almost too loud for her own ears.

His hands continued to trace up her ribcage, taking the thin fabric with it. Darcy's head felt as though it were spinning. Her skin was a feverish red, and every inch that Jesse exposed seemed to light under his touch. His lips followed his hands as he kissed his way up her belly to the flat expanse between her breasts, each nipple now puckered and aching for attention.

He lifted her shirt over her head, his hips flush against her again.

He ravaged her mouth, taking possession of every inch of her. She gripped the hem of his shirt and pulled until his own painted skin was exposed to her perusal. He knelt between her thighs, sultry eyes taking in every inch of her exposed skin. She had never felt so powerful in her life. This was not an area of her life where she ever felt she had the upper hand, but the wrecked expression on his face told her she was dead wrong.

"See something you like, Mr. Riggs?" she joked on a shaking breath. His eyes found hers, a smile dancing at the corner of them, as he gripped her ankle and yanked her down so she was once again straddling his knees.

"Oh, sweetheart, like doesn't even begin to cover it," he answered, and bit the over-stimulated flesh of her neck once again. "That's why stopping is going to be the dumbest fucking thing I ever decided to do."

"Stopping?" she asked breathlessly. "No stopping. Why are we stopping?"

His chest heaved as he licked across her collarbone. Every square inch of her brain short-circuited at the motion, and her thighs trembled around his waist. "Because if we keep going, you're going to regret it."

"Regret it? What the hell are you talking about?"

Jesse moaned, "God, I fucking love it when you talk dirty." He took her lower lip between his teeth and pulled slightly, her eyes effectively rolling into the back of her head. "I can't stand the thought of you regretting any part of this. You went through some shit tonight, and you're trying to drown out those feelings with the good feelings, and as tough as I am, I can't fucking stand the thought of you regretting us for one fucking second."

She stopped, pushing back against his chest slightly. "So, you're punishing me for Tick?"

"When did those words ever leave my mouth? I'm not punishing you for anything, just making you take some time to really figure out if this is what you want. I'm willing to face the consequences of this, whatever the outcome is. But I don't think you are."

"Jesse," Darcy protested, trying to pull his face back to where it belonged.

"Not tonight, Darce," he ground out, and pushed back, separating them from one another. The cold air of the room was like a splash of ice water, and Darcy quickly covered herself with her arms. "You have no fucking clue how hard it is for me to say that."

CHAPTER 9

Tears welled suddenly in her eyes, and she sat quickly. She looked around for her shirt frantically. "I think . . ." She sniffled. "I think it's time for you to go."

Jesse looked at her from his position gathering the pillows. He took in her hunched form, her tears, her sudden self-doubt, and seemed to register his misstep. He crawled down to her quickly and placed both of his hands on her jaw. "Baby," he crooned, kissing her lips softly. "You've gotta know this is the stupidest thing I've ever done. Like, they should probably lock me up now for the shit I've been thinking about doing to you." She chuckled against her tears, and her face flamed. "But my ego wouldn't survive if you told me you didn't want to be around me after we sealed the deal. I'm going to seal it, trust me, but not tonight."

Darcy understood, she really did, but the disappointment that filled her was not so easily satisfied. She nodded half-heartedly, wiping her tears on the back of her hand, and began pulling her shirt on her arms.

"Hold up, now," Jesse stopped her, pulling the shirt off of her. "You didn't think you'd get off that easily, did you?" He grabbed his shirt from the end of the bed and pulled it gently over her head. "I might not be able to claim you the way I want to, but I'm sure as shit going to claim you the only way I can. You're gonna wear my shirt to bed every night from now on, got me?"

She should have been offended by his demand, told him where he could shove his shirt, but instead the embers of what they had just left started to burn again. Something about the possessive tone of his voice made her thighs shake. "Fine," she huffed, and put the shirt all the way on. "If I have to."

"You have to." He pulled her against his chest and pulled back the luscious comforter. They both piled back against the pillows, and Jesse automatically wrapped an arm around her waist.

Darcy was frustrated, and throbbing in all the right places. She wanted to be enraged at Jesse's antics, but what she felt for him in that moment was something much stronger, and a lot more dangerous.

CHAPTER 10

An orange, warm glow filled Darcy's mind as she came back to consciousness slowly. There was a delicious pressure over her as a now familiar tingle spread from her fingers and toes. Warm hands tangled in her curls and rubbed at her scalp languidly. Her back arched up into the heat hovering above her as teeth connected with the skin of her neck. Her eyes blinked open, a breathless moan escaping her lips.

"There's my girl," Jesse growled against her throat, the full pressure of his body over her sending electric shocks down to her toes, the familiar pulse and burn from the night before bringing her aching need to the forefront. Darcy stretched in his arms and pressed her hips up against his pulsing cock. "You're a fucking tease," he complained even as he placed a gentle kiss against the column of her neck.

"I'm just trying to catch up," Darcy responded, her voice sounding thick. She raised her arms to scratch along the back of his head, the short hairs there crisp against her fingers. "Seems as though you've had an unfair advantage."

"I'd be looking in a mirror when you're talking about unfair, sweetheart. You should have heard the sounds you were making—all hot and sweet—that's what's fucking unfair. I'd like to meet the guy you're dreaming about. Give him a piece of my mind." He gripped her hip roughly, and she watched as his Adam's apple bobbed beneath the bright-red blooms.

He was beautiful—his blue eyes shining, his blonde locks tousled with sleep—and Darcy wished she could snap a picture of this moment. Just the two of them together.

She smiled coyly, rubbing her cheek against the rough fur of his. Everything about this man drove her wild, right down to the words he whispered in her ear. She felt her spine shiver at the thought of his resistance crumbling so easily. Darcy was not-so-secretly wishing that it would crumble enough for him to finish what he had started the night before.

"Oh yeah?" she teased, feeling bold in their current position. "And what is it you would say to this mystery man?"

"Back the fuck off of my girl."

"Your girl?" The sound of the words coming from him took her slightly off guard, but she tried to keep the shock tucked in tight to her chest.

"I don't know if you've heard, but you're mine, sweetheart. According to ninety percent of the Mods in Faction 4, I've claimed you, so you better get used to it."

Darcy pulled slightly back away from him, continuing to pull her fingers through his hair. "What does that mean, anyway? To claim someone? That must have some sort of pull around here, considering it saved me from certain torture and death."

Jesse looked suddenly serious. His eyes glanced over her head for a moment before he kissed her lips lightly and replied, "A story for another time, sweetheart. It's time for you to call Daddy Dearest."

Darcy wanted to protest, wanted to pull him back against her, and spend the morning getting the answers—and the attention—she craved from him, but she knew he was right. They had only been sleeping for about three hours, but it was enough to cause some suspicion if her father was checking their trackers. If he noticed they hadn't moved yet, he could send someone to check on them, and that would be the last thing they needed in her current state. She could climb back into bed after she took care of the business side of their arrangement.

Jesse moved fully out of the bed, unashamed of the large tent in the front of his pants as he did so. He even went so far as to leer at Darcy and send her a wink before loping into the bathroom and closing the door behind him. Darcy reached for her phone and sat in the center of

CHAPTER 10

the opulent bed. She wasn't sure what she was going to say that would convince her father to give her more time. According to his timeline, they were ahead of schedule, but that didn't mean that he would be willing to spare the little advantage they had. They had to be to Faction 8 before the wedding in order to keep their story legitimate.

Taking a deep breath in, she put the phone to her ear and waited for her father to answer.

"Yes, Darcy," he breathed into the receiver, sounding irritated with her intrusion on his life already. "I trust everything is moving along as expected."

"Actually . . ."

"Actually? There should be no actually, Darcy."

She cleared her throat quickly before responding, "I'm sick."

"Sick?"

"I must have caught something from all of our travels. I cannot travel today. I won't be able to leave the bedroom much less the apartment."

There was a dangerous pause lingering on the other end of the line. She worried her nail between her teeth and tried to keep her breathing steady. One inclination that she was nervous, and her father would sniff it out like a hound dog. "This is unacceptable, Darcy. I expect you to be on the road within the hour."

"I can't travel, Father. I'm too sick."

"Are you defying me? I gave you an order, and you will follow it if you have to drag yourself out of the pits of hell."

This was not going to plan. She knew he would push back, but she had prayed that he would give in without much more explanation. "But, Father, we're ahead—"

"Damn the schedule!" he practically shouted into the line. "You are required to listen to me, and I am ordering you to get you and your pet Mod to Faction 5 within the hour."

And with that, the sound of the dial tone thrummed in her ear. She had failed. She had told Jericho she would do everything in her power to give them time, and if anything, she had just sped things up.

Frustrated, she tossed her phone into her lap and grunted. There had to be a way to make this right, but she wasn't sure how. What would Tick do—what would Jesse do—in a situation like this? Her usual tactics weren't working, so she needed a new plan. She pondered for what felt like ages before she picked up the phone once again and placed it to her ear.

"Darcy?" she heard the ghostly moan on the other end of the line. The voice sounded tired and frail, no doubt still sleeping from a night of stiff drinks and party drugs. She knew she would never be able to win over her father, but she knew someone who might be able to sway him if she played her cards right.

"Shane," she breathed into the line, giving her most pathetic attempt at sounding sick.

Shane huffed, "Dammit, Darcy, what do you want? It's not even eight in the morning."

"I need help."

"Yeah, what else is new? I thought you were on some secret escapade for Father. What could you possibly need from me?"

Darcy heard the distinct sound of a tired groan coming from the other end of the line, and not from her brother, and her cheeks warmed at the implication. Darcy hadn't thought that Shane would have been with someone. "I need you to talk to Father."

"Jesus Christ, Darcy," Shane groaned, sounding more awake than he had previously. "What have you gotten yourself into?"

"Nothing!" she lied, not willing to give him any reason to be suspicious. "I'm sick. Father wants me on the road today, and I just cannot manage it. Can you please try to talk some reason into him? I need a day to recover."

There was a pregnant pause as Darcy heard the distinct mumbling of her brother and his lover on the other end of the line. She wasn't sure what they were saying, but she was hoping that the man was able to sway the cause in her favor. Lord knew her brother was not fond of her and was not used to granting her favors. She would take all of the help that was offered her way.

"I swear you'll owe me for this for life. I shouldn't even be considering this." He sighed heavily, and she pictured him rubbing his hand over his clean-shaven face in frustration—a move she had seen him complete hundreds of times at gala events. "Give me ten minutes, and I'll call you back. I'm making no promises that I'll be able to convince him more than you already tried."

CHAPTER 10

"Thank you, Shane," Darcy chirped in delight. "I'm forever in your debt."

"Yes, you are." Darcy began to pull the phone away from her ear when she heard her name being called back to the line. "Oh, and Darcy?"

"Yes."

"When Father calls you again today—which I'm sure he will—at least try to practice sounding sick. You're a shit liar."

Darcy couldn't remember a time when her brother had ever been so bold or so candid with her. A smile spread across her face, even though she knew she should take his advice seriously. "Thank you, Shane. I really mean it."

"Don't thank me yet."

And with that, the line went dead. She dropped the phone in her lap once again and nervously watched for the screen to light again. She knew it would be some time before her brother returned her call, but she couldn't help nervously glancing down at the screen every few seconds.

Jesse emerged from the bathroom, rubbing the back of his head lightly with a towel, shirt discarded somewhere in the steam billowing out from behind him. Darcy's mouth watered at the splashes of color swathed over toned muscles. Her fingers twitched at the thought of running them over every line and curve from the skull on his left collarbone all the way to the watercolor blotches on his forearm.

"What'd he say?" he asked casually, as though he couldn't tell that every square inch of her was melting at the sight of him.

Darcy cleared her throat quickly and answered, "Waiting for a call back." Her eyes scanned down his hard abs to where his sweatpants hung low on his hips. She wished he were closer so she could press her lips to the large expanse of skin currently exposed to her hungry gaze. He was driving her crazy, and she wasn't sure how much longer she could hold out before she quite literally exploded.

"He said he'd call you back?" he asked, tossing his towel unceremoniously on the back of one of the lounge chairs and settling himself into the bed next to her.

She fidgeted briefly with the blanket and bit her lip. "I had to call in a favor."

"To who?"

"My brother," she answered.

Jesse squeaked out, "Your brother?"

"My father didn't believe my excuse and wanted us back on the road within the hour. I was desperate and needed someone that might have enough pull to convince him to let us stay."

Jesse gripped her fingers lightly, halting their nervous dance, and pulled her chin up so she met his soft gaze. "You did good, sweetheart."

She shrugged. "We'll see if it works in our favor. It could backfire, and we could be ordered to return home—or worse, he could decide to come check on us."

"Well," Jesse started and shrugged slightly. "I guess we better start putting a sock on the doorknob just in case."

"A sock?" Darcy giggled, turning her head to the side to watch him curiously.

"Seriously?" Jesse asked incredulously. "You've never heard of putting a sock on the door."

She shook her head, and he smiled wide at her, shaking his head in bewilderment. "You're really something, Darcy Newton."

She felt her cheeks flush even as she teased, "That's Ms. Newton to you."

He hummed deep in his throat and used their connected fingers to pull her roughly into his chest, wrapping his free arm around her back. Their eyes locked, lips only centimeters from one another. "Oh yeah? Is that so?"

A shiver ran down her spine, sending goosebumps along her arms. The bright-red petals on his neck called to her like a beacon. Unable to resist the call, she leaned forward and placed her lips lightly to the petal in question and was rewarded with a shaky exhale of breath. His hands lifted to fist in her hair as she placed another wet kiss to the petal directly across from her previous victim.

"Darcy," he groaned out just as her phone began to ring once again. She pulled back quickly and searched the blankets for the source of the ringing. "Saved by the fucking bell."

She eyed him, annoyed by his persistence to keep her at arm's length, but pressed the phone to her ear. She needed to focus on the task at hand. "Hello," she greeted.

"It wasn't easy," Shane began, mouth clearly full of food. "But I was able

CHAPTER 10

to convince him to give you twenty-four hours. Not a minute over."

A smile smacked her right in the mouth, and she tried to keep her voice steady as she gushed, "Oh, Shane, I don't know how I can ever repay you. This means more than you know."

He huffed reluctantly. "I don't know what you've gotten yourself into, sister, but I suggest you get your priorities straight before Father decides to send for you."

She nodded and then realized the man couldn't see her from the other end of the phone. "Yes, Shane, I will."

"Please, whatever you do, do not call me again. I want nothing more to do with your antics."

"Goodbye, Shane."

"Goodbye, sister."

Jesse was waiting, eyes wide, as Darcy hung up the phone. She nodded her head frantically and gave him the affirmative. "We have twenty-four hours. It was the best he could do."

Jesse nodded and jumped from the bed suddenly. "That'll have to be enough. I'll tell the love birds; you get dressed. We have a lot to talk about."

She followed his orders to the letter, donning a light sundress in favor of some of her more formal wears. She was well aware the dress showed almost as much leg as her shorts did the previous night and accentuated her small curves in a pleasing way. She was hoping her wiles would be enough to drive Jesse as wild as he had been driving her. She wasn't sure what his qualms were with finally giving in to their mutual desire, but she wasn't naive enough to believe that her possible feelings of regret were the only reason he was continuing to hold back. There was something deeper hidden within him that she was hoping to discover.

When Darcy arrived in the sitting room, all three of her comrades were sitting, quietly chatting and seemingly awaiting her arrival. Tick had a crude-looking bandage across her arm that was slung across her chest. Jericho was sitting beside her on the luxurious, cream-colored couch, threading a piece of her hair between his fingers. Jesse was sitting on the floor with his back against the opposite chair. He gave Darcy a half-grin and moved slightly to the left to allow her to sit.

She passed by him, feeling his knuckles graze up her bare calf only slightly before she dropped into the seat of the chair. If either of the Mods across from them noticed the small action, neither of them commented. It took almost everything in her power to focus on speaking rather than the burning point where his skin had met hers.

"What are we discussing?" Darcy asked, crossing her legs delicately so her knee pressed slightly against the side of Jesse's skull.

Jericho began, "What that Mod said last night"—he paused and let out a great whoosh of air—"it was pretty fucked up."

"Yeah, and not in the fun way," Jesse supplied. Darcy felt a squeeze in her stomach at the memory of the man melting into the concrete beneath her feet. She fought to keep her composure, but her stomach continued to roll.

Tick agreed, "A substance that could destroy all Mods? What the fuck are we gonna do if the Elite get ahold of that? It's only a matter of time until we all go up in smoke."

"The Elite will have their hands on it," Darcy added, "whether we fulfill our duty to my father or not. It's already in Faction 8, which stands to reason that Darien Blake will have his hands on it soon enough. The sooner we can get to the lab and get it back to my father, the better."

All three Mods looked at her as though she had just suggested they strip off all of their clothes and run through the streets naked. "You're joking," Jericho said, deadpanned.

Jesse turned in his seated position more fully to look up at her. "Why in the hell would we give this shit to Daddy Dearest when we know exactly what it can do? We'll be sawdust before you can blink."

"He would never—"

Jericho interrupted, "Here we fucking go. Back to her same old shit."

"Back off, Jer," Tick defended, though her voice was small and unsure. It seemed Tick was even wavering in her support of her friend.

Darcy huffed, "It's not as though we can just decide not to give it to him. If he doesn't get what he wants, we are all as good as dead. If we're all dead, we can forget about finding the information on Harper."

There was a collective inhale of breath as the two Mods waited for

CHAPTER 10

Jesse to respond. He had suddenly gone pale, and Darcy wondered if that thought had completely left his mind until now.

"He wouldn't have given the information over anyway," Jericho argued, looking just as vicious as he had before their night in the alley. Darcy figured the days with Jericho as an ally, as short-lived as they had been, were over.

"Are you calling him a liar?" Darcy asked, though in her heart she knew she couldn't trust her father the way she had before she left. There was something about this mission—and the important details her father had left out—that didn't sit right with her.

Jericho narrowed his gaze. "Look me in the eye and tell me you trust him."

Darcy opened her mouth to spit fire at him, but nothing came forward. She knew just as well as he did that her father had something up his sleeve with Element Five, but she couldn't come outright and say it. If she admitted to the feelings welling up in her throat, she would be committing her biggest betrayal in the form of treason. She would finally be turning her back for good on the life she once knew so well.

"That's what I fucking thought," he harrumphed triumphantly.

Tick interjected, "That still doesn't give us the answer as to what the fuck we're going to do. We have to get the answers about Harper, but we know that this shit cannot get back to the Elite."

"The answer's obvious," Jesse spoke up, hiding his emotions behind a mask Darcy hadn't seen since the afternoon they had first crossed the Border. "We take the Element and run. We've run before, we can do it again."

"But, Jesse," Tick began. "Harper . . ."

"This is bigger than her, Tick. We all know it. As badly as I want to find her, we aren't gonna be able to do that if we're toast. We have to get this Element Five shit out of the hands of the wrong people and figure out a way to destroy it."

Jericho groaned, "That's another fucking thing. How the fuck are we supposed to figure out how to destroy this shit? The fucking key?" He said the last part sarcastically, throwing an arm out into the open space between himself and Darcy, who was sitting across from him. She had all but forgotten about her bestowed title. She wasn't sure what the Mod in the alley had meant when he said she was the key, but she was terrified to find out.

Jesse scoffed, "How much of that can we really believe? I mean, the guy was nuttier than a fucking cashew."

"He's legit," Tick defended, sounding haughty. "All the dirt I could find on him checks. He was injected with some kind of experimental drug, and suddenly, he can see the future. All of his predictions have come true—a one-hundred-percent success rate. You can't get much more legit than that."

Darcy curled her arms around herself and slunk back into the chair. Hearing more of the atrocities her people had caused made her reason waver. She wasn't so sure that bringing the element home to her father was a great idea. Darcy had heard firsthand what her people were capable of in order to maintain power, and she wasn't sure she trusted the outcome.

"That leads to another predicament," Darcy finally whispered. "Someone else is tracking us. They knew we were meeting last night, and they might very well be watching us now."

The small group was silent, save for the buzz of Tick's electronic eye as it scanned the room from wall to wall, as though it were looking for bugs. She quietly asked, "Darce, do you think . . . I mean, is there even the smallest chance that it could be Charles?"

All eyes were on her once again. She shrugged one shoulder to her ear and bit her lower lip. "I suppose it's possible," she began. "I just don't know how he would have gotten to us so quickly. It doesn't seem logical that he would have been able to figure out what we were up to last night so quickly."

"What about spies?" Jericho supplied, less venom in his voice.

Darcy nodded. "That seems more likely, but again, that would mean that my father is already aware of the information we have. That makes our next moves all the more important. If he knows that we know about Element Five, he'll be watching us even more closely now."

"There's no proof it was even him, though." Tick sighed, running a frustrated hand through her hair. "It could literally be anyone at this point. We could have someone from Faction 8 on our tail, or even worse, some unknown enemy."

CHAPTER 10

The thought of having more eyes watching their every move made Darcy's skin crawl. She didn't particularly enjoy the thought of her father watching her, but imagining an unknown predator lurking in the shadows made her feel even more exposed. Things seemed to be getting more and more murky as time continued.

"Regardless of whoever is watching us, we have to move through the Border tomorrow," Darcy informed the group. She had assumed Jesse already told them, but she wanted to be perfectly clear in their current situation. They could afford no more delays.

"Jer," Jesse said, "Give me an estimate on how long it should take us to get through to Faction 8."

Jericho stared into space for just a few seconds before returning to the group surrounding him. "If we pass through Faction 5 in the morning, we should be on track to make it to through to Faction 8 in three days."

Tick had pulled her laptop onto her lap and began typing away while Jericho was speaking. Darcy watched as she moved fluidly with only one hand as though losing the ability to work with two had no effect whatsoever on her skill. "Once we get into Faction 8," she started, continuing her efforts, "it should only take us about four hours to get to the lab. It says here that the wedding will be hosted at the Blake Estate—on the same stretch of land as Darien Blake's actual mansion—thirty minutes from the lab."

Jesse nodded, the wheels in his head turning over and over as he thought through their options. Darcy felt a pang of sadness for him in that moment. They were asking him to give up his search for Harper while simultaneously being the North Star in their search for answers—Darcy was ashamed of herself.

"We can play this off for three more days at least," Jericho said to no one in particular. "If we stick to the schedule and have no more hiccups, we should be able to keep this shit up for three more days."

Darcy gulped. "What happens after the three days are over? I can go to the wedding and you all can steal Element Five, but then where do we go from there? My father could detonate the failsafe at any time if he thinks we're being deceitful."

"Which would end Jesse," Tick grumbled as she continued her typing. "How long do you think it would take your father to notice we're heading in the wrong direction after we destroy this shit."

"Woah, woah!" Jericho interrupted. "Let's figure out how the fuck we're gonna destroy it first."

Tick sighed. "Looking into it, my love. Patience is a virtue."

"Yeah, a virtue I don't fucking have."

"Clearly," Tick teased with a smile. Darcy was happy to see a shift in the mood of their group but didn't fail to notice the weight of the unknown still hanging heavy above them all. They all knew that Darcy was the key to whatever it took to destroy this substance, but she didn't know what she possessed that somehow made her special in this regard. The way the Mod had gazed at her was as though she was reverent. It had thrilled her a little—this idea of being special in some way—but it also scared her. Was something wrong with her? Was he wrong about her?

Jesse cleared his throat quickly. "One thing we do know, is that these trackers have to come out sooner or later. If Papa Newton smells a rat, no doubt I'll be cooked. Jer, you think you can get these fuckers out?"

Darcy balked at the back of Jesse's head and looked to meet the steady faces of her comrades. Apparently she was the only one appalled at the idea of Jericho yanking this tracker from her spine. She had no doubt that the whole operation would be a crude one, leaving plenty room for a scar. "I could always keep mine in place," she offered, her voice shaking slightly with nerves.

"Are you planning on going home? Because that's the only way that tracker stays in," Tick reminded, shock clear in her giant green eye shining with emotion. Darcy opened her mouth to answer when she was interrupted by Jesse.

"Of course, she's going home, Tick," he admonished. "She can't stay with us forever. When this is all said and done, we'll run and she'll go home to Daddy and Captain Boring."

Darcy's jaw dropped to the floor, her face red. "I will make that decision for myself, thank you," Darcy ground out between her teeth.

Jesse turned to her once again, anger and defiance clear in his gaze. "No way you're going with us, Darcy. We wouldn't last a day out there with you. Everyone in all the Factions will be after our asses when they find out what we did. You'll stand out like a sore thumb, and we'll be caught in no time.

CHAPTER 10

We can't risk it."

"It would be easy enough to change my appearance."

"Some hair dye and a shopping spree aren't going to be enough. You've said it before, Chuck's not stupid. He'll find you and drag you back to hell kicking and screaming. Someone will have to pay for what we're doing, and if he finds you . . ."

"So, what then?" she practically yelled, popping out of her chair. "I go with him willingly and suffer the same fate? You know as well as I do that my father will not rest until he has what he wants."

"He'll have you, and I'll bet anything he'll see that as an advantage to finding us. You can give him bad information and keep him off of our tail long enough for us to get away. I'll take the heat for destroying Element Five, Jer and Tick can go retire somewhere warm, and Papa Newton can spend his days searching for a ghost."

"And what if he finds you? What then?"

Tick soothed, "Darcy—"

"No, Tick!" she shouted back, her tone running away from her. "I will not be ordered back to my life after everything we've been through. I am not some petulant child that can be hidden away when convenient. I am the one that is taking the risk. I am the one that is destroying this thing. At the very least, I should have a say in where I go when this is all said and done."

"Jess—"

"Fuck off, Jer," Jesse growled, standing over Darcy with his painted arms crossed over his chest. She could see the fiery anger in his eyes flashing like flames over her. "Let me deal with this."

"There's nothing to deal with, Jesse. I am deciding what my future holds—no one else."

Jesse scoffed, "That's rich coming from you. Aren't you still engaged? What about that little detail? Won't Captain Wonder Bread be waiting for you to come back and seal the deal?"

She shot daggers at him, stepping forward and poking her hand against his chest. "I am only engaged because society requires it. Without society, I am a free woman."

"Say what you mean, Darcy. It's not society, it's your fucking father

THE KEY

that requires it. You've been the model daughter for the last twenty-three years—now you're just going to join the Mods and be a part of our life? Un-fucking likely. You can't just change who you are in a week just because the freedom feels a little too good. Shit doesn't work that way."

"Is that so hard to believe? That I'm able to change so quickly? Look at everything I've already done to defy his thrall. I thought you said I was brave."

"Just because you're brave doesn't mean you're dedicated. We've been in this for a decade, you decided to take a vacation here—there's a difference. You belong back with your family, with your husband."

"He is not my husband," she shot back, sticking her finger roughly against his chest again. Her cheeks were flaming, and the squeak that left her lips when he grabbed a hold of her wrist roughly caught her by surprise. The action made her blood pressure rise to alarming rates. Her heart stammered wildly in her chest like a rabbit caught in a trap, but not out of fear. The growl he gave her along with his narrowed gaze sent electricity shooting down her spine. She found herself wetting her lips, the pressure in her belly melting to a sticky pool of desire. She wasn't proud of how her body reacted, but she wasn't surprised. Even the slightest touch from him could send her completely into overdrive. "And I will make the decisions about where I belong. Maybe I'll go find someone to claim me. It sounds to me like there are Mods out there that wouldn't mind the chance."

He pulled her roughly against his chest, his eyes steady but his chest rising and falling in time with her puffing breaths. "Watch yourself, Darcy," he warned, his lips pulled back in a possessive snarl. "You're playing with fire here."

"You two!" Tick intervened, muscling between them. "Separate now!"

They finally broke apart, the spell he had cast around them broken, and Darcy remembered that there were other humans in the room watching the entire thing unfold. She was humble enough to be embarrassed by their display and used her dark curls to hide her face from the lurking eyes of the man still seated on the couch. She was sure he had a thing or two to say about their little outburst, but she wasn't prepared to hear it.

"Now," Tick began again, huffing and pushing her hair away from her eyes with her good hand. "We're clearly not getting anywhere with this

CHAPTER 10

conversation right now. We know we have three days to get to Faction 8. That's three days for us to decide what to do. For now, Darcy and I are going back to sleep. When we wake up, we'll need something to eat. You two can make yourselves useful by making some food and planning our trip in the morning. If you need us, you can just wait." And with that, Tick pulled Darcy's arm and stomped their way back to the bedroom.

CHAPTER 11

Darcy and Tick spent hours curled beneath the thick comforter of Darcy's bed. Darcy had stripped herself of the sundress and replaced it with her sleep shorts and her old T-shirt. She had gripped Jesse's shirt in her fist, almost throwing it over her head, but her anger still bubbled deep in her gut and she tossed it over the back of one of the chairs. She wasn't sure where they stood currently, considering he kept her at arm's distance on the best of days, but it felt good to rebel against him, even slightly. She was tired of men trying to run her life. She was ready to make her own decisions.

Once her head hit the pillow, she closed her eyes and that was it. She could hear the small snores coming from Tick's side of the bed as she woke to flip to her other side, but she couldn't force herself to wake up more than that. There was nothing left for them to do that day, and if they both wanted to spend it resting, they had every right to rejuvenate their minds and bodies. It felt good to sleep without the pressure of all of their expectations looming over her head. They were still there, lying in wait for her to decide to come back to consciousness, but the freedom she felt in leaving them for a few hours was intoxicating.

"Darce," she heard a female whisper as she fidgeted below the blankets. "Darcy, are you awake?"

She groaned and swatted at the perpetrator against her peace. "I'm still sleeping."

Tick gave a giggle, and she felt the bed dip right next to her elbow. The smell of coffee wafted in front of her nose, and Darcy's body responded. Her eyes popped open, and her mouth curved into a smile. "Is that imported Faction 12 coffee?" Darcy asked, her voice thick from sleep.

Tick nodded. "It absolutely is." She curled her feet beneath her and took a sip before continuing, "Your fella must be feeling pretty shitty about the way you two left things. He brought us an entire buffet."

Shock hit Darcy square in the chest as she sat fully up to observe the trays of food that were spread along the table before the bed. Every breakfast food imaginable had been prepared and presented for Darcy and Tick's consumption. She couldn't believe her eyes—or the fact that she hadn't heard any sound of this being brought to them. "Jesse did all this?"

"I'm sure Jericho tried to help, but God love him, that man doesn't know a spatula from a spade. He's not so talented in the kitchen."

Darcy found herself grinning as both women pulled themselves from the bed and walked over to the spread. Fruit, eggs, toast, pancakes, bacon, sausage, waffles—all of it prepared to perfection and mingled with the aroma of coffee, warming her heart.

"I can't believe they had all of this stocked in the apartment."

"They didn't," Tick answered, taking another sip of her drink. "Jesse called in a favor . . . or so he told me."

"A favor?"

"He's got connections all over the Factions. The drug business is good business."

Darcy moved forward and grabbed a piece of crisp bacon. She bit of a chunk and chewed thoughtfully. She didn't think that Jesse was that sorry about their fight, but maybe sorrier about Tick and all she had been through. The poor woman had been almost melted into a puddle, burned in a bar, brought into every fight in the apartment, and forced to be the voice of reason between the feuding couple.

"Tick," Darcy began. "I owe you an apology."

"For what?"

"You have been forced into so many situations where Jesse and I or Jericho and I have been at odds, and it isn't fair. You've had your fair share of trauma and it isn't right for me to keep dumping on you."

CHAPTER 11

"Dumping on me?" she practically shouted as she handed the woman a mug for her coffee. "Is that what you think you've been doing?"

Darcy felt the hot creep of embarrassment lick up her neck to her cheeks. "Well, of course, it isn't your job to keep us from fighting all the time."

"That's what friends do." She cocked her head to the side and observed Darcy curiously. "As long as we have you, I will do my best to fight your battles with you."

Darcy grinned like she had just won the lottery and wrapped an arm around her friend's neck. She wasn't sure what she had done to have such a loyal ally, but she was glad for it. Darcy had a hollow feeling in her gut at the thought of leaving Tick. There would never be one quite like her, and she suspected her life would feel incomplete without the Mod.

The women sat quietly in their feast, talking about Darcy's life before she had left it all behind. They talked about her mother—the poor woman rarely left her room at all anymore—her siblings, and Adam. Darcy had explained how she had met Adam and the arrangement of their marriage. She had divulged the secret of their sex life—the fact that there practically was no sex life to speak of. It all felt very taboo and very, very freeing. She had never had the opportunity to be fully herself with anyone else. Tick remained the picture of serenity as they chatted in the quiet light of the afternoon sun. Darcy had thought that Tick might look at least a little scandalized at their topics of choice, but it seemed the woman felt it was an everyday occurrence to discuss the goings on in the bedrooms of her friends. And who knew, maybe it was commonplace in the world of the Mods to divulge such indecencies.

"So, it's all just for show? The marriage, I mean?" Tick asked as she crunched into a fresh strawberry.

Darcy shrugged and nodded slowly. "Sort of. It's more to secure a leader for our Faction once my father leaves his place of power. Krista's husband will lead Faction 1 and Adam will lead Faction 2, and we will be a force to be rivaled with in the North."

"What about Shane?"

"Shane," Darcy began and sighed. "He's a little more complicated. My father keeps him as a very close advisor and a military leader. He would like for Shane to marry the son of the Faction 3 leader, but Shane is such a valuable asset to our team, he's not ready to give him up quite yet. If Shane were to marry the son of Faction 3, he would leave our Faction to be at his husband's side until his father-in-law left power. That's too long for my father to wait without him."

Tick nodded and looked as though she was trying to digest all of this information. "Doesn't Shane have anything to say about all of this? If anyone has the power to rebel against Daddy Warbucks, Shane would be the one I'd put my money on."

Darcy smiled and shook her head sadly. "Shane is just as invested in our success as a family and as a Faction as my father is. He also has the ability to see whomever he likes until the date of his nuptials, so he's not too concerned with the impending loss of freedom. The rules for the men of our world are far less strict."

Tick made an unladylike harrumphing sound and complained, "Sexist Faction bullshit."

"I couldn't agree more."

"So none of you have had a say in who you end up with? It's just blind faith in your father."

Darcy replied, "Not so much blind faith as blind—"

"Obedience," Jesse supplied from the doorway. Both women startled and looked to see him with his arms crossed, staring them down from his position against the jam. "Can I have a minute, Tick?"

"Take the hour," Tick responded, pulling herself from her chair and kissing Darcy lightly on the forehead. "It sounds like our girl needs it," she added, and patted him on the chest before exiting the room.

Jesse moved himself from the doorway and shut the door without a word. Darcy waited silently for him to slowly turn and face her. He watched her as a predator watches its prey—waiting for the right time to pounce—and she swallowed thickly at the sight. He was lethal in every sense of the word, every muscle in his body completely controlled to strike until the moment he deemed it necessary.

"Jesse—" Darcy began but was interrupted by the slow shaking of his head. He broke their steady eye contact and pushed himself from the wall, his arms still crossed over his chest. "Jesse, I . . ."

"Not now," he instructed as he finally came close enough to lean down

CHAPTER 11

to her. She knew if she reached out and touched him, she would turn to a trembling pile of ash. Desire lit every flame in his blue eyes, and Darcy could feel it reflected in her own dark gaze.

Jesse leaned forward slowly and placed inked hands on either side of the chair she sat in. He leaned his head forward so they were practically nose to nose. She sucked in a deep breath, pulling his spicy scent in with it, the tang of him flooding her brain with ecstasy. She pressed her back more fully into the cushion behind her to try and create some much needed distance between them. Her body ached to reach out and touch him, feel his warmth against her. Her heart thumped like a jack rabbit in her chest, her entire body pulsing with a want so strong she felt it vibrating under her skin. It was pure magic, the way his body called to hers, and she was helpless respond.

"I don't ever want to lose you, Darcy." The words stung her like the popping embers of the fire between them. "But if I have to lose you, I'd rather do it to him than to death."

Darcy sighed. "Jesse, I'm not going to die. Can't you see that?"

"But you don't know that. You can't look me in the eye and guarantee that whatever this key bullshit is isn't going to lead to you taking a nose-dive right into hell."

"You're right, I can't, but I'll do everything I can to stay alive—and I have Tick and you and Jericho...."

"We can't help you with this," he replied, pulling her face closer to his by the back of her neck. Her lips grazed against his in a torturous dance and they both shuddered at the contact. "You saw what it did to Tick. This shit is too much for us to mess with."

Darcy rebuked, "But you'll be there for me."

"At least consider going back home."

"I can't go back there, Jesse, not after everything I've experienced since I left. It would be a fate worse than death to send me back to my father and Adam. I will shrivel up and cave in, no life left."

At the sound of his rival's name, Jesse grimaced and shook his head. She knew he didn't like the thought of her going back to him, but he had no idea the real depth of her despair when she considered it. Darcy knew if she went back to that man, her life would be nothing short of an empty shell of the possibility of what should have been. She would compare every millisecond there to what her life would have been like if she had stayed. She would live a life of regret, and Darcy had seen what it could do to a person. She had a taste of a true connection with the man before her, and she wasn't ready to give it up just yet.

Jesse replied, "If you go back, there's a better chance for the rest of us to make it out alive. There's less reason for other Factions to want us dead. Chuck isn't going to want to spill the beans on what he had us do—or that he even knows us—so it'll be a covert operation on his part. We'll be fried in a second if he tells other Factions we kidnapped you. Every fucker this side of the Atlantic will be scouring for you. We wouldn't stand a chance."

Darcy felt the grip of certainty steal her breath as tears pricked at the corners of her eyes. She knew he was right. She was going to have to go back—if only to save the people she loved—but the idea of incurring such a fate made her stomach roll and panic sizzle in her veins. "I'll consider it only because you asked me to, but that doesn't mean I'm agreeing to go back."

Jesse pulled back, and Darcy watched as something like relief swept over his expression. She wished she could feel the same, but all she managed was a slow burning sadness at the thought of the rest of her life rolling out before her like an angry storm. She wanted to tell Jesse that he was wrong and that they would be fine, but she knew he had made up his mind on the matter. Darcy might be able to sway Tick to her side, but she knew Jesse was a lost cause.

"Jesus, baby, you know how to pull on the old heartstrings," he grumbled at her as he rubbed the pad of his thumb across her cheek. "I swear you could bring an entire country to their knees with just a look."

She snorted in disbelief and ran her fingers up into his hair. "Overthrowing a country would probably be easier than persuading you to see my side."

He gave her a full smile then, tickling the edges of her collarbone with vigor. She gave a full laugh and allowed him to continue his onslaught with glee. "Watch yourself, Ms. Newton, I'll bend you over my knee if you're not more careful," he joked as his fingers danced along her ribs.

She wiggled in the chair laughing like a hyena. "Don't make promises

CHAPTER 11

you can't keep," she stuttered between giggles. Something in his eyes changed, and he stopped his playful tickling. Darcy sat upright and felt her face flame at her words. She knew they had been flirting, but had she crossed a line?

Jesse leaned forward suddenly and stole a kiss from her lips, pressing his tongue between her teeth as he dove in. She gasped at his sudden intrusion, but the balm his kiss laid over her soul was like magic. Darcy was helpless to deny the man anything he wanted, and that included the things she so desperately wanted as well.

He pulled back and watched her face—red blooms starting to form over her cheekbones—and grinned at her. He kissed along her jaw until he reached her ear, whispering, "We have three days left. I'm done wasting time." He pulled on the lobe gently with his teeth, sending a shockwave of pleasure from her ear to her toes. Darcy sucked in a sharp breath through her teeth as her back arched into his chest. He took the opportunity to grip her breast over her shirt; the slide of the rough fabric against the sensitive flesh made her cry out. She heard him groan at the sound and felt the thick head of his cock press into the inside of her thigh. She was wound so tightly she was afraid the dam might burst before he was able to move them to a more comfortable position.

His hands moved quickly, sliding up her sides, taking her shirt with them. "Jesse," she whined at the contact.

"Goddamn, baby," he crooned against her ear before he lifted her shirt over her head and pressed his palm against her bare breast. "I love the way you say my name."

A shiver drove itself up Darcy's spine as he used his finger and thumb to toy gently over her nipple again and again. He was pushing her faster and faster toward a boiling point she had never reached, and she was terrified of the results when she arrived there.

"No one has ever made me feel this good," she gasped out as his mouth found her other breast. She wrapped her legs up and around his waist, begging for more. He wrapped his fingers under her thighs and pulled her up with him as he stood—her nipple popping roughly between his teeth. Darcy was still wrapped around him like a vice, and his cock pressed right against her soaking core.

Jesse began walking, but instead of moving toward the bed, he only turned and deposited her on the table where Darcy had gathered her breakfast with Tick just moments ago. "No one's ever gonna make you feel this good again, you understand?" Jesse demanded as he pressed more fully against her overstimulated skin.

"Gah," she cried out, and gripped at his T-shirt. She belatedly nodded her head as she noticed he was watching her, waiting for her to respond. "No one else."

"Only me," he demanded again, pulling his own shirt over his head.

"Only you," she panted out, running her hands over his inked chest and abs. Her mouth watered at the sight, her roaming hands inadequate to sate the burning lust within her. Darcy leaned forward and placed open-mouthed kisses against the colors dancing on his chest and shoulders. She had wanted to experience the salty tang of his skin against her tongue for what felt like ages, and now she had her chance. She nipped at the vines on his neck, and he gripped the back of her head by her hair—not to stop her but to press her on.

Darcy had never been so bold. She had never felt so comfortable with another that she could explore their body on her own whims. Adam had always made her feel inadequate or inappropriate for trying to experience something new in the bedroom. He had told her he liked it best when she was quiet and left him to do the work. Now here she was—painted flesh between her teeth as she grazed the great green vines—wanton and needy and completely a wreck but looked upon as nothing short of beautiful by the man before her.

"Fucking tease," Jesse growled as he finally pulled her head back and plunged his tongue deep into her mouth once again. He wasn't kissing her so much as he was claiming her—branding every molecule of her body as his—and she wished she could hate it, but she trembled with the thrill of it.

Darcy pulled back and sucked in a deep breath, just enough space between them for Jesse to continue his torture on her breasts. His tongue and fingers worked in time to press her ever closer to the edge she had been racing toward. Her fingers raked over the small scars on his back, pulling his cock closer to where she wanted him most. He pulled one last time against her breast before leaning back and tucking his fingers into the

CHAPTER 11

waistband of her shorts. Jesse paused to look at her—both of them completely wrecked and unable to stop—waiting for her to deny him access. Instead, Darcy used her hands to lift herself briefly off of the table so he could push the shorts off of her ass and down onto the floor.

She was almost completely bare before him now, her lace underwear the only fabric between her skin and his hungry stare. She reveled in the reflection of lust burning up his eyes. He licked his lips like a man starved, and it sent her heart thumping in her throat. Jesse gripped the back of her hair roughly again and began biting at her lower lip, renewed in his effort to drive her wild.

Darcy rolled her hips against his jean-clad form and moaned at the hard ridge pushing in so closely to where she wanted him to be. She needed the friction and the thick pulse to sate the desire pulsing deep inside of her. He growled in response and pressed against her more fully. She felt herself shudder in response and let out an otherworldly cry of pleasure.

"Jesse, please," she begged against the rough hairs on his cheek. His fingers pressed deeply into her ribs at her plea, and he bit harshly against her neck.

He ground out, "Ask and you shall receive." His fingers tucked into the waistband of her panties, and she rolled back on her sit bones to give him more full access to her. Her fingers shook with anticipation, red blotches dotting her chest. She pushed an errant curl away from her eyes, and he gave her a toe-curling half-smirk as he dipped one single finger between her folds. She bent back onto her elbows—the skin of her arms flattening the pancakes behind her—as he swirled his finger lightly back and forth between the overstimulated skin.

"Jesse," she cried out as he continued to evade her attempts to amplify her own pleasure. Jesse thrust his hips forward at the sound of her voice and took a deep breath in. Darcy had plenty of experience with sex being as quick and painful as possible, and no experience whatsoever with whatever spell Jesse had currently cast on her.

"I'll take care of you, baby," he promised on a shaking breath. "Just give me some time to play."

She whined and bit her lower lip as he continued his torturous pursuit. He watched her face intently as his finger grazed ever so lightly against her clit. She bucked her hips forward, moaning her approval. She tucked her lower lip between her teeth as he circled over it again, applying just the right amount of pressure. Her thighs began to tremble around his waist, and her breath was leaving her in jerky moans.

Jesse's fingers traveled further south, exploring at their own volition. Darcy thought her chest might explode from the pressure building with every second he spent between her thighs. His eyes met hers—his pupils blown wide and his lips swollen from her gnashing teeth—as he slipped one digit slowly inside of her. Darcy's eyes rolled back, his thumb connecting once again with the sensitive bundle of nerves, and her jaw went slack.

"Jesus," Jesse moaned out, and leaned his opposite palm against the table for balance. "You're a fucking dream, sweetheart—so fucking tight." She sucked in a sharp breath at his words that seemed to only take her higher.

"Jess," she whined, rolling her hips against the finger that still hadn't moved. He stuttered out a growl of excitement and began pumping into her slowly.

She felt the pressure growing in her belly, her muscles tightening and expanding as though she didn't fit properly in her own skin. Darcy was gasping and gripping at his shoulders, her tongue laving at the side of his neck, desperate for some sort of relief. She tucked her hands down between them and attempted to unbutton the jeans that covered his own hips. She needed to feel him inside of her. If a single finger could bring her this much pleasure, she could only imagine what his cock would be able to do.

He whispered against her cheek, "There'll be time for me to get mine, sweetheart." His voice had gone soft, and the rough edge had hidden itself behind the affection, if only for the moment. "This is about you. You like that, baby?"

Her head jerked unevenly as she nodded and whimpered against his lips. He slowly moved his wrist, and a second finger joined the first. "Ah," she cried against his feverish skin, the pulsing in her pushing into her bones. His thumb worked more quickly against her clit, the pressure he applied driving her into a new high. "Jesse, I-I . . . Something is—" She tried to warn him, tried to make him understand, but he cut her off with a sloppy kiss of teeth and tongues weaving until she could no longer tell where he ended and she began.

He growled, "Let it go, Darcy." And she did.

CHAPTER 11

Her entire universe exploded on a guttural cry. Wave after wave of pleasure crashed against her, the heat from her body radiating out and exploding like stars in the universe they had created between them. Her limbs shook with the sheer power of her carnal satisfaction. Her breathing had all but stopped, her heart crashing like thunder in her ears, and her eyes had rolled completely back into her head.

Darcy had never felt so completely whole in her entire life. The fire of lust and something deeper than simple affection still burned inside of her, but there was an added layer of satisfaction that no man had ever been able to give her. She had always thought that sex was a chore—something to endure for the sake of your husband—but now she knew the truth. With the right person, sex could be the most sensational act of devotion one could give, and she had finally experienced it.

Jesse chuckled and removed his hand from within her. Darcy whimpered at the sensation of loss but felt his opposite hand smooth against the skin of her bare thigh. His hands were warm and calloused, creating goosebumps in their wake on her smooth skin. He grumbled, "If this is what it's gonna be like every time with you, I'm a bigger jackass than I gave myself credit for."

Darcy opened one eye languidly and did her best to give him a glare. "Why is that?"

"There's no fucking way I'm going to be able to let you leave. I have never seen anyone look as fucking beautiful as you do right now."

She flushed deep red from the roots of her hair to the tips of her toes. If she had the ability to move any of her limbs, she would smack him square in the chest simply out of embarrassment. But, instead, she closed her eyes once again and smiled triumphantly, rolling her head against the waffles beneath her. "You'll forget about me soon enough. There'll be other women to occupy your time, and I'll be nothing more than a woman you once knew."

She waited for his witty retort, but nothing came. Jesse's hands gripped beneath her chin and roused her from her half-dozed stupor. Darcy opened her eyes quickly and blinked at the serious scowl on his face. "It's only ever going to be you," he admitted, watching her chocolate gaze intently. "No one is even going to come close, sweetheart."

She smiled brightly at his admission. She knew deep within her soul that there wouldn't be another like him for her either.

CHAPTER 12

Darcy and Jesse had spent the next two days immersed in planning the heist that would change their lives forever. They had passed through the borders smoothly, but there was still a lingering sense of anxiety that hung over them. Darcy had secretly wanted to continue what she and Jesse had started in the confines of their room—the thought of exploring Jesse's body too distracting for polite company—but she also knew they needed to come up with a plan for when they arrived in Faction 8, and plan they did. Every available second of travel and stay was dedicated to planning. Tick had sat for hours with her laptop perched on her lap—no matter how many times Jericho had griped about her resting—and worked every possible avenue. Jesse plotted and schemed, throwing out all the instructions and skills needed to complete the mission. All three were in agreement that they needed to acquire more guns and ammunition before their mission began, but that was the only real snafu so far.

That, and the fact that Darcy felt queasy at the mere thought of leaving them forever.

She knew it needed to happen to keep them safe, but every time one of them mentioned that particular detail of their plan, Darcy felt herself cringe. She knew the moment would come sooner rather than later, but she wasn't ready to give up the sweet moments she and Jesse had shared between the planning—a graze of fingers against bare skin, a kiss at the corner of lips as he shuffled himself into their shared bed in the early hours of the morning. These small moments made her heart sing. They made her realize that it didn't matter where they were or who they were, she would choose Jesse in every lifetime they had together. They were meant to be.

But that wasn't enough for the group to change their minds. It was decided that Jesse would drive Darcy to the wedding, and he and the others would go to procure Element Five as her father had planned originally, Jericho removing Jesse's tracker in the process. If they stayed the course and stuck to the original plan, it would give the three Mods time to escape and dispose of the dangerous chemical before Charles knew anything was amiss. But none of that required Darcy. She was to go back to her normal life and pretend as though she knew nothing of the plot to deceive her father. She would keep the rouse going for as long as she could to buy them more time. She would walk back to their shared quarters and spend the night on her own. She wouldn't contact her father until late the next morning to report that Jesse had not returned with the element. That would give them a solid twelve hours to get themselves into the slums and hopefully over the Border before anyone began looking for them.

The plan was set, the details ironed out, and all that was left to do was to get there. They had made it to the last leg of their journey. Her father had gone suspiciously quiet and hadn't required any real updates from her. Darcy suspected that he was giving her the space she required to prepare for the task ahead. In reality, she was dragging her feet along the side of regret, hoping and praying that there would be some reason Jesse found for her to stay along with them. She had tried over and over to convince them that they may need her assistance for something, but they had all discredited her attempts.

"I'm stopping here," Jesse announced to the passengers as they came upon a refueling station. "We all need a break."

That was the truth. No one had said a word in about an hour, and Darcy could practically taste the tension surrounding them. They were a little under an hour away from the Faction 8 Border, and Darcy was nervous. They were all nervous. Something about their final leg of the long journey seemed to make them all anxious.

"Good," Jericho agreed. "My ass fell asleep about twenty minutes ago."

CHAPTER 12

Tick offered, "Want me to rub it?"

"Gross!" Darcy whined, and grabbed her umbrella from beneath the seat, passing it up to Jesse, as was tradition. A storm had rolled through not too long after they had entered the Faction 7 Border, and it had hung on through the night.

"You want to talk about gross!" Jericho began. "Don't even get me started on the sounds I heard coming from your room a couple of nights ago."

Darcy's cheeks turned crimson in a flash, and she saw Jesse shoot Jericho a wolfish grin from his position beside him. "What can I say, I know how to take care of my woman."

Darcy shot forward and slapped his shoulder in annoyance, though he wasn't wrong. Tick snickered beside her friend and bumped her shoulder in camaraderie. Darcy wasn't sure what her life would be like after these next twenty-four hours, but she knew that she would be a different woman living it. The old Darcy would have been mortified and angry by Jericho and Jesse's banter, but now she saw it for what it was—an act of love.

Tick placed the glasses over her eyes with practiced ease and opened the umbrella as Jericho opened the door. Darcy was aware of the cameras as she exited the vehicle and felt the hot press of Jesse's fingers against the exposed skin of her inner wrist. Darcy shivered from head to toe—lust igniting like a flame in her belly—and worked to keep the need she felt tucked behind a hard mask. It was almost impossible to hide her feelings toward Jesse when he was close to her, but the moment he touched her, all bets were off. They had shared only the barest physical contact between them since the afternoon Jesse had showed her what true affection looked like—planning had taken the forefront of everyone's minds—so the lightest of touches from him sent her into a trembling mess of hot need.

"Keep your hands to yourself," she admonished playfully, her voice staying low enough for only him to hear.

He grumbled close to her ear, "That dress is coming off the minute we get where we're going. No more waiting."

A thrill ran up her spine as she made brief eye contact with the man just behind her, diligently holding her umbrella. She could see his pupils completely blown wide, and the shit-eating grin he threw her way let her know he wasn't messing around. He felt it just as keenly as she did. Feeling bold, she reached back and tucked a finger ever so slightly into the front waistband of his slacks, pulling gently and releasing just as quickly as she had started.

Jesse let out a low rumble from his chest and grabbed Darcy's tricep from behind. He used her arm to steer her into a small alcove and used the enormous umbrella to cover them both. Jericho had no doubt escorted Tick to the women's restroom, and they were far enough away that they were safe from his prying eyes. The cameras were a different story entirely. Darcy prayed that no one would be watching them too closely. They had been lucky so far, and she was afraid to push it.

As afraid as she was, she couldn't deny the thrall Jesse had over her. He pressed into her space and she pressed back. There was never a time that her body didn't immediately respond to his. She had worn this particular dress with him in mind. It was a light-blue organza, flowing in all directions down to just above her knees. The sleeves stopped just below her elbows and wrapped around her front, giving quite the view of her neck and collarbones. She knew how enticing these particular pieces of her body were to Jesse, and he did not disappoint. His lips found the ever sensitive space where her neck met her shoulder and nipped.

"You're driving me insane, sweetheart," he rumbled against her skin. She felt goosebumps fan out over her arms as she reached up to grip his waist under his jacket. He looked absolutely mouthwatering in his now-typical all-black uniform. The reds and greens popped even brighter from under his collar, and the black letters across his knuckles stood bold against the obsidian background.

Darcy breathed, "You're not the only one."

He grinned and placed a searing kiss across her lips quickly. "I wasn't kidding. The minute we're behind closed doors tonight, you're mine."

She nodded her head, licking her buzzing lips with anticipation. She hoped he kept up his end of the deal this time. She wasn't sure she could handle living the rest of her life without knowing what it would be like to have Jesse in the most intimate way one could have another. She opened her mouth to whisper her assent against his waiting mouth when his phone suddenly began ringing between them. Jesse let out a hardy sigh and checked the ID on the screen. He screwed up his nose for just a second

CHAPTER 12

before lifting a finger to Darcy's eye line and walking away answering, "What do you want?"

Darcy would be lying if she said she wasn't curious about who was on the other end of the line, but she made sure to give Jesse his privacy. He had taken some business calls while they were on the road, but most of them were quickly resolved and left open-ended, knowing full well that he wouldn't be back to take care of his clients.

She waited only a few seconds longer before walking into the restroom, where she found Tick frantically typing on her own device. "If we were a newspaper stand, we'd be set for life," she said from her seated position against the sink.

"Huh?" Darcy asked, cocking her eyebrow and seriously wondering if the woman were having some sort of stroke.

"We've got issues, Darce," Tick answered, not looking up from her screen. "A mountain of fucking issues."

"I don't like the sound of that."

"Yeah, well, hang on to your ass because it gets worse." She stood suddenly and brought the rickety excuse for a laptop before Darcy's deep-brown eyes. "See that?"

Tick was pointing to the bottom of the screen below rows and rows of zeros and ones that somehow made the email appear before Darcy. "Yeah?"

"See what it says?"

Darcy scanned the screen quickly:

> *All fruit products will need to be shipped overseas in an air-tight container using only our services. We will expect the product to arrive at its destination before the spring season. Questions regarding this shipment should be brought to me directly. I trust your discretion in this matter.*
> *Regards,*
> *Edwin*

Darcy looked to her friend again, struggling to see what the woman was so worried about. "What do we care about some fruit being shipped overseas?"

Tick sighed heavily and rolled her eyes all the way back into her skull.

"Sometimes I hate that you're an Elite. It's all code. This was all sent from DymoCorp."

Darcy continued, "They have their hands in a lot of dealings around the world. They are probably working on a sustainable—"

"From Edwin Ellis? I think he's got bigger fish to fry than some sustainable fruit shipment."

"Maybe—"

"To Darien Blake?"

This stopped Darcy in her tracks. Darien Blake—the leader of Faction 8, her father's biggest rival, and the catalyst of this entire journey—had no reason to be interested in a shipment of fruit. Edwin Ellis and Darien Blake were hiding something, and the thought of what that something could possibly be made Darcy's blood drain from her face. This only meant trouble for the ones she loved most.

Darcy finally whispered, "You think they're talking about Element Five?"

Tick nodded, a smile crossing her lips briefly. "*Ding, ding, ding!* We have a winner."

"You think they're moving it?"

Tick shrugged but answered, "If my decipher is correct—which it always is—it sounds like they're moving it tonight."

"Tonight? That's not enough time for us to get what we need or to change our plan."

"But if we don't move, then we'll miss our chance."

"Where would they be moving it? Do you think Edwin sold it to Blake?"

"I'll look into it," Tick replied, but she put her laptop back into her oversized purse. "But, I think our biggest issue right now is figuring out when they're shipping this shit and how we're going to get our hands on it before Blake does."

Darcy started her response when a knock sounded on the door. Both women jumped like a bomb had detonated, and Darcy placed a hand over her thumping heart. They made brief eye contact before another harsh thud rapped against the door, most likely Jericho fighting a migraine and ready to be back on the road as soon as possible. Tick moved past Darcy and opened the door. Three Martyrs stood before them, and the woman in front held a gun between Tick's eyes. Darcy let out a yelp of surprise as

CHAPTER 12

Tick stumbled back into the room, seeming just as shocked as Darcy.

"Surprise!" the female Martyr holding the gun cheered as though she were at a birthday party. Suddenly, her hand flew out, and the hard edge of the butt of the gun struck Tick across the temple, causing her to collapse before she could even reach her hand up to defend herself. The woman stepped over Tick's limp form, and two men followed. All three were dressed from head to toe in black leather, necklaces clanking together with each movement, bringing Darcy's attention to the bright white fate she was about to incur. Swaths of black paint smeared across each of the Martyrs' eyes and over the bridge of their noses in a battle uniform now distinctly familiar to Darcy. She was sure she was the only Elite that had ever encountered the Martyrs so many times and lived to tell the tale. She was hoping she had enough luck to grant her one more escape.

The reminder of just how dangerous these beasts were had Darcy quickly backpedaling into the room, throwing anything and everything she could find at the two male Martyrs that had started advancing on her. She tipped furniture and let fly anything she could get her hands on, including a small crystal lamp that cost more than the SUV sitting outside waiting for her. She was squawking, "Jesse! Jericho! Help!" over and over as she made it deeper into the room. The three Martyrs laughed at her attempts to stop them, not even approaching her with urgency. The two men were dodging her clumsy attempts to keep them at bay as if she were a toddler throwing toys in the middle of a tantrum.

"They're a little tied up at the moment. Looks like you're all on your own, Elite," the woman sneered as Darcy continued to flail her way into some sort of safe haven. She wasn't familiar enough with the space to know if there was a back room or another way out, but she knew the front door was not an option. The size of the gun the woman held—and the fact that now all three of her protectors were unconscious or worse—told Darcy that her chances of making it out of this encounter alive were almost zero. Her only shot was to find some sort of back entrance to escape through.

Darcy ran into a small space next to the toilet stalls and looked around for a knob or handle. Her shaking fingers frantically pulled chemicals off of the wall and tipped shelving units as she looked for some way out. With her back to the room, she heard the slow approaching footsteps of boots on the luxurious oak flooring. Panic seized her heart and she began yelling, her own terror getting the best of her; sweat dripped profusely down her temples, causing her curls to stick to her forehead. Her frantically shaking fingers finally brushed a seam in the wall. It felt as though someone had painted over a door or a small entrance to a storage space. If she could pull her way into the space, she would be able to hide and maybe escape.

The shelving units she had pulled down in her frantic search were being pulled back and thrown into the hallway by the giant goons that had been chasing her. Darcy felt her way along the crack before finally finding a handle that had long since rusted and had started to decay. Darcy gave a hard pull and heard a sullen creak come from behind the old door. Adrenaline pumped as she yanked harder and harder on the door. She could feel the looming presence of her fate closing in as the bodies of the men came closer. There was only one wire rack left between her and their meaty fists. She pulled as hard as her arms could bear, bracing her leg against the wall beside the door to use as leverage to open the rusted thing.

Finally, the door sprang free, sending Darcy careening backward hard enough to hit her head on the floor. Dust and debris rained down over her as musty air hit her square in the face. She could see sunlight peering in between old wooden boards as she sat up and wiped the dust from her eyes. The wire rack beside her disappeared as she brought herself to her feet. She sprang forward toward the now-open doorway, but it wasn't enough.

Two meaty claws grabbed hard to her arms and pulled her back away from her freedom. She screamed, kicking her feet in the air as her heels dragged across the floor. Pure agony ripped itself from her heart and out of her mouth. She clawed and punched and kicked as hard as she could, all of her frustration and anger finding its purchase in the wild swinging of her limbs.

"Let me go! Put me down!" she screamed, sweat pouring down her back as her limbs rattled. She continued her onslaught of assaults, though it barely seemed to register with the two enormous men dragging her backward between them. She tried to find a foothold, but the slick bottoms of her sandals only slid against the cool wood beneath them. She had wished she could fling them from her feet. She would have a better chance of freeing herself if they were off.

CHAPTER 12

One of the men pulled Darcy harshly against him and grumbled hotly against Darcy's ear, "The more you fight, the harder this is gonna to be for you."

"Please," she sobbed as they dragged her back across overturned furniture, the fight draining out of her with his words. She was making no difference in stopping them from reaching their destination than she would have made standing still. They finally made it back to where the woman stood in the doorway, leaning against the doorjamb. She was inspecting the barrel of her gun as though the entire scenario before her bored her.

"I'll give you whatever you want." Darcy sighed as the tears dripped off of her chin and landed against her breastbone. "Please, just leave them be." Her voice was thick and her limbs were tired.

The quiet white reflection of teeth in Darcy's peripheral vision almost sent her back into hysterics. It was as though she was surrounded by them. Great, giant molars were taunting her from around the necks of her soon-to-be-murderers. She wondered if Jesse would mourn her the way he mourned his sister. Or would he want to avenge her death? Become a martyr of the Martyrs? She knew Jericho would feel relieved by her absence. She had only complicated things for him.

The Martyr woman responded jovially, "Oh, sweet girl, they aren't part of the deal," she motioned to Tick's lifeless form on the ground, and Darcy's heart flew into a rage so deep and guttural she felt it in her bones. "Just you."

"Deal?"

She stated simply, "Everyone has a price. You just happen to be the exchange in goods."

"I'll match it!" Darcy suddenly shouted as they exited the restroom. She saw several motorcycles and an old rundown sedan waiting for them beside the ransacked SUV. This was the second SUV they would go through in a week. "I'll beat it! My father is the wealthiest man in all of the Factions! He'll give you whatever you desire."

Now that they were out in the gray afternoon rain, Darcy felt a renewal in her efforts to flee. If she could get herself free from these people, she could run to safety. She wasn't as fast as they were, but all she would need to do is to get the attention of someone on the road. Someone would have to be coming for them by now. These places were filled to the brim with security cameras. How had no one come to their aide thus far?

Darcy let her body go limp, the men groaning as they took on the extra weight. The backs of her sandals dragged along the harsh edges of the asphalt. She was hoping that one of them would catch on something big enough for her to pull her way free.

The woman simply scoffed, "I don't care who your daddy is. I made a deal, and I'm sticking to it. You ought to be thanking your lucky stars that I'm willing to make a deal. Most Martyrs would kill an Elite soon as talk to them. I just happen to be a little smarter than that."

Darcy's shoe caught on a rock. She practically screamed with joy. She felt the tug at her leg and knew the Martyrs carrying her would feel the drag soon. She readied herself and yanked her arms as quickly as she could out of their grasp. They hadn't been ready for the motion, so she was able to slide free from their grip quite easily and began sprinting toward the road. It wasn't a far run to where the road was, but it was also not a main road. This station was on the outskirts of the land, nowhere near the highway and nowhere near anyone that didn't belong here. She just hoped security was almost to them.

The thundering footsteps of the Martyrs were not far behind her as she took to the road. There was no sign of anyone in either direction, but Darcy kept on. Someone had to find her eventually. The two heavy sets of footsteps of her captors seemed to be trailing farther and farther behind, but a lighter set of footfalls was only gaining on her. She knew better than to look back, but the heavy breaths of her female assailant were pressing hot against the back of Darcy's skull, and she knew she couldn't beat her. She had never been fast racing against other humans, so thinking she could outrun a Mod was almost laughable.

The woman reached out and clobbered Darcy on the back, sending her spiraling down to the side of the road. Darcy's cheek, arms, and knee all burned as her skin scraped hard against the surface. She rolled quickly to see the woman standing over her. Darcy leaned back on her bleeding elbows and launched a sandaled foot up into the other woman's nose. Blood poured heavily from her assailant's nostrils as she let out a shrill cry of pain.

CHAPTER 12

Darcy used this distraction to pull herself upright—her dress in complete shreds of cloth—and started to run again. By this time, the two men had caught up with her and gripped her arms, twisting her around to face forward. The Martyr woman had murder in her eyes as she lifted her gun to Darcy. She placed the barrel hard against Darcy's temple and let loose a guttural cry of anger. Spit flew from her lips and splattered thickly on Darcy's sweat-and-blood-soaked cheek.

"How dare you!" the woman screamed in Darcy's face, and pressed the gun harder to the hot flesh of her face. "I should fucking end you! Fuck the consequences and fuck the reward! No one makes a fool of me!"

"Then do it," Darcy dared from between clenched teeth. Darcy had never been more serious than she was in this moment. She would rather this Mod end her life with the gun in her hand than to be turned over to a fate she couldn't imagine. "Then fucking do it."

The woman screeched again, the rage seeming too much for her to bare. She pulled back the hammer and pressed her finger to the trigger before one of the men said, "Arson, wait!" The woman hesitated but didn't look from Darcy. "If you end her here and now, you'll have two entire Factions all over your ass. If you deliver her, she'll be dead and we can live on with the reward money. She's not worth it."

"You just want your money."

"That's true," he admitted but didn't let her go. "But so do you."

Arson opened her mouth to give a response, but then snapped her jaw shut again. Darcy waited with her heart in her mouth for what felt like an eternity before the other woman decided to release the hammer and placed the gun at her side again. Fresh blood still glistened along her upper lip and down her chin, but the woman did nothing to wipe it away. This moment reminded Darcy of one of her conversations with Jesse. Arson was just as much a human as she was, but it didn't seem that way. How could a human hunt another for profit? What was the reward for ending the life of another so easily? Darcy couldn't fathom it.

"I hope they make you suffer," Arson snarled as she raised the gun once again only to smack Darcy on the side of the head with it. A white hot pain smeared across Darcy's consciousness right before everything went black.

CHAPTER 13

When Darcy came to, she wasn't sure where she had expected to be, but a warehouse was not on the short list that had filled her mind. The cool, damp air smelled musty and old but had a certain lightness to it that told her they were in an open space. Her head throbbed and her stomach rolled as she slowly blinked her eyes open. Darcy felt her cheek smart and winced in pain, causing the wet pain at her right temple to flare even brighter. She felt the cold dampness of blood streaming from her head down her neck and over her exposed shoulder from where Arson had attacked her. She replayed the events at the rest stop over and over as she started to gain her bearings. Darcy wondered if her friends knew where she was, if they were coming to find her. If they were even able to come find her.

She suspected Tick was in as much pain as she was, but she wasn't sure how the other two had faired. Jesse couldn't feel pain, which would have made him quite the opponent to take down. It would have taken near death—if not death itself—to stop him from fighting back. Jericho had only been at half best with the weather, which didn't give Darcy much hope that he had survived either. Lord knew the man didn't know when to quit, especially if he thought Tick was in danger.

If they were dead, she wished she were too.

Darcy finally lifted her head and took in her surroundings. There wasn't much to behold beyond what she had imagined a mostly empty warehouse would look like. She was tied to an old folding chair in the center of the room. There was a large garage door about forty feet from where she was sitting, and an oil stained cement floor beneath her. There was a set of rickety steal steps that led up to a small office space at the side of the space, and some steal walkways that had long since rusted over crisscrossed above her head. The ceilings were enormously high; the roof some sort of metal sheeting that annoyingly amplified Arson's footsteps as she paced beside where Darcy sat.

"Where the hell is he? This shouldn't be taking this long!" Arson pouted as she continued to pace with a phone resting in her outstretched palm. Every few seconds, she would glance down and check the screen again, looking for something and coming up short.

The two enormous men that had captured Darcy were flanking her, guns at the ready in the event that she would try another escape. Darcy was surprised she wasn't a nervous wreck of tears and pleading now she was conscious, but her survival instinct must have kicked in unknowingly and she felt herself alert and looking for the next best option for getting out of there. She asked in Arson's general direction, "Waiting for someone?"

Arson only sneered at her, pausing briefly in her manic pacing to deliver a swift backhand to Darcy's already raw cheekbone. Darcy tasted blood on the inside of her lip, and bile rose as her stomach threatened to empty its contents all over the concrete floor. She wondered if this was what it felt like to have a concussion.

"I would take that as an emphatic yes," Darcy continued, though her words sounded slurred even to her own ears. She really started to believe that maybe her run-in with the gun back at the station left her with permanent damage. She didn't have the experience that her other teammates did to know for sure. "It might help your odds if we were somewhere less— how do I put this gently—disgusting."

"Jesus," Arson breathed, and pushed her hand through her long dark hair. "I don't know how those Mods put up with you for so long. They're probably glad I took you off of their hands."

Indignation shot through Darcy's gut as she shook her head vehemently and snarled, "You're only mad because you were beat by an Elite

CHAPTER 13

and needed these two to bring me in. Had it been up to you alone, we both know you would have failed."

"Didn't you learn your lesson back in Faction 7, Elite? You'll never beat me. I have years of training, and all you have is a pretty face. Well, at least, it used to be pretty."

Back in Faction 7? Where were we? Darcy thought to herself through the shock of Arson's words. She had assumed they were where they had left off, but it seemed they were farther from her friends than she thought. She suddenly remembered the chip in her head. Her father must be aware of her location by now. Fear replaced her anger as she wondered if her father had assumed they failed and enacted the failsafe in Jesse's brain. If the Martyrs hadn't killed Jesse, her father would have been the final nail in his coffin without a doubt.

"We're not in Faction 7?" she asked, trying and failing to keep the fear out of her voice. The reality of her situation had set in, and she felt the sharp stinging of fear prick at her arms and ears.

Arson smiled coyly, recognizing that she had the upper hand at last. "What's it matter to you? It's not like you'll see the outside of this warehouse after tonight. I'm not sure what the old man wants from you, but if I had to guess, I'd say he isn't looking to keep you hanging around."

Arson was unwittingly giving her clues the more she spoke. Darcy was just hoping she could keep the woman gabbing enough to get some real information. "Do you know who I am?" Darcy started again, ignoring the woman's last comment. She waited as Arson paused and gave a small nod of her head. "Then you must know who my father is and what he is capable of. When he finds me, he's going to make you pay dearly for your crimes—he'll have your head for this no matter how little you were involved. You'll wish you had never been born by the time he's finished with you."

Arson let out a bark of laughter, accompanied by the chuckles of her male companions. "I wouldn't be so worried about my head if I were you. The way I saw you snuggled up with that Mod back there at the station, my guess is your ass is the one in trouble, not mine."

Darcy felt red hot embarrassment creep up her spine and averted her eyes to the cold floor. She had known better than to be out in public so obviously ignoring the rules of society, but she had been so swept up in the moment that she had forgotten how easily they could be spotted. She had known better and she should have done better, for both of them. If she could go back, she didn't think she would have changed anything—given her current circumstances—but she might have tried to keep their affair quieter, less messy. She didn't want him implicated in any more of her offenses than she had already bestowed upon him.

Arson continued, "Oh, what? Cat got your tongue now?"

Darcy sent her a scathing glare just as the garage door lifted and they were all blinded by a pair of headlights so bright that Darcy had to shut her eyes to keep her brain from feeling like it might explode at any moment. She had guessed that whomever they were waiting on would have eventually come for her, but she had naively hoped that maybe they had stood up her companion. She could handle Arson—she was even beginning to like her a little—but this new, unknown threat was something her poor frazzled nerves couldn't grasp. In the last five days, she had been through more traumatic experiences than she had in her entire life, and her nerves had officially had it. She felt herself starting to tear at the seams.

Arson breathed, "Finally," and Darcy heard rustling as Arson started moving toward the vehicle and in front of Darcy. She continued to squeeze her eyes closed against the offending light and the pounding thud of her brain against her skull when the wheels stopped turning over the concrete floor. The fear she had felt stinging earlier now became an aching buzz as the sound of doors slamming began to echo off of the hollow walls around her. Darcy counted as they closed: one, two, three. There were at least three new people entering the arena, and she didn't like her odds.

"Anchor!" a male voice greeted excitedly, only mere feet from where Darcy sat. "Great work! She's in a little worse shape than I had hoped she'd be, but no matter. She's here and that's all I needed from you! Excellent!"

Arson grumbled, "The name's Arson." Darcy held in a hysterical chuckle but couldn't stop the laugh from reaching her hunched shoulders. Arson continued, "Where's my money?"

"All in good time, my darling, all in good time," the same voice continued. "Fellas, could we kill the lights? It seems our guest of honor is struggling to join the party."

There was a mechanical click as the car—and the headlights—shut off.

CHAPTER 13

Darcy lifted her head and reluctantly blinked her eyes open. Once again, she was not sure what she had expected to see when she opened them, but this was so far beyond what she had imagined that she thought she might be hallucinating. The man before her beamed as he walked closer to her view. She sat upright in the chair and shook her head several times to try and clear away the fog was taking over. This could not be real. He could not be here.

Darien Blake had paid Martyrs to have her kidnapped.

His bright white teeth stood in complete contrast to his silky caramel skin. His eyes were a deep brown—just a shade shy of black—and his head had been shaved bald. His beard was a salt-and-pepper color but still had enough dark in it to make him look years younger than he was. She knew for a fact this man before her was just a few years shy of her father, but he didn't have a crease on his face that made him look a day older than forty. He was an attractive man in his burgundy three-piece suit and black shirt and tie, accompanied by black suede shoes. He was mere inches from her face in an empty warehouse that had been abandoned long before she was even born—acting as though this were the most natural thing in the world.

"Darcy," he breathed out against her skin, and smiled even brighter. "I am so pleased to see you. Do you know who I am?"

Darcy nodded and whispered, "Yes, Mr. Blake."

"Excellent!" He clapped and stood back to his full height. He seemed just as pleased as he could possibly be about all of this, while Darcy was left dumbfounded and more confused than she had ever been in her life.

Arson spoke up again, "We had a deal. Where's my—"

"All in good time, my darling!" Blake reassured as he snapped his fingers at his men. "Fetch me a chair! Ms. Newton and I have a lot to discuss, and I fear looming over her is not the way to approach this."

His men began bustling around the space, searching for a chair no doubt, as he turned in a circle, one arm tucked beneath the opposite elbow and his chin resting on his fist, as if thinking things through. Darcy was unsure of what they would need to discuss—minus the minor fact that she had just been on a mission to steal the thing Blake very well may have been trying to procure from one of the top labs in all the Factions—or why he wanted to see her at all.

Arson stepped into his path. "I want my money."

"Yes," he said a little more impatiently, his armor cracking only slightly. "And you will have it once I have ensured that my product is delivered in the way I ordered it to be."

He stepped around Arson just as the men appeared with a folding chair for him to sit on. One man brushed the dust from the seat as the other stood directly behind him and searched the area as though he was waiting for a silent attack. "Have these men removed," Blake ordered, motioning to Arson's men. "They're not of our company, and I will not do business with them present."

Blake's men approached the two men and started to shoo them away. Arson stepped before them and put her palms up to Blake's entourage. She shouted, "Woah, hey now! We had a deal, Blake! They're with me, and they're not going anywhere until the deal is done!"

Blake rubbed his temple as though this minor nuisance was causing him distress. "Then let us be done."

"That's what I've been saying! Give us our—"

"Dispose of them," he ordered dully, and suddenly shots were ringing out. Darcy remembered a time not so long ago when a similar sound had her screaming on the side of the highway, her body pressed against Jesse's and her heart in his hands. Now, she jumped in the chair and ducked her head, trying to take cover. The terror that had once took control of her seemed to have run dry, and she was left with only the fear for her own safety.

Darcy hadn't heard the bodies fall among the gunfire, but the sickening sound of their dragging corpses against the cold ground made her turn her head and finally be sick.

"Oh," Blake gasped as she heaved onto the floor beside her. "You're not all right at all. It's just as well that we were rid of her. These Mods—so ghastly. It makes me sick to even think of them. Don't you agree?" He smiled at her on the last question as though they were discussing the weather over brunch instead of the life of a human that had just been snuffed out with the snap of his fingers.

Darcy ignored his question and asked, "Why did you bring me here?"

He smiled coyly at her, his teeth shining brightly under the dim lighting.

CHAPTER 13

"That's the question, isn't it, Darcy. Why did I bring you here?" He rubbed the salt-and-pepper smattering his jaw and pretended to ponder over his own words. "Why don't you tell me?"

The air left her lungs in one great whoosh, and her stomach dropped down to her heels. She had suspected that he had known her actual motives for being in the Faction, but now that she had seen his true nature, she feared his knowledge could be deadly.

"I-I . . ." she stuttered, trying to remember anything except for the truth. "I'm here for your daughter's wedding."

Darien gave a quiet chuckle and crossed one ankle over his knee, his pants riding up slightly to reveal burgundy socks to match his suit. "Now, Darcy, you don't think I actually believe all that rot, do you? We're both adults; we know the ways of the world. Why don't you tell me the real reason you're here?"

She swallowed hard and tried to pull free from her rope binding. "Why did you bring me here?" she demanded again, her voice edging the line of hysteria. Darcy's breath was coming too quick for her to catch up with; her head was beginning to swim as her vision clouded.

Blake gasped. "Oh, my dear." He snapped his fingers toward one of his goons and they stepped toward her. "You're far worse off than I imagined. We'll need to speed things up if we're going to get down to it."

The giant man stepped behind Darcy and loosened the rope. Her arms tugged free and fell uselessly to her side. Her head dipped slightly, and blood dripped from her lower lip onto the stained fabric of her once beautiful dress. She had remembered putting it on this morning and thinking about how much Jesse would like the color on her—how it reminded her of his eyes. She had hoped to see him light with all of the excitement she had felt when she saw him.

Tears flushed her eyes as a small sob escaped her broken lips. "Where are my friends?"

Blake ticked his tongue against his teeth and replied, "I would imagine by now, they're long gone. If they weren't able to flee into hiding, I'm quite sure your father has taken care of them by now. He wouldn't want any loose ends getting in the way of his plan. If I know Charles, he's already scheming and plotting his next course of action." He rubbed his hands together excitedly before his eyes, then clapped them together twice in quick succession. "The thrill of a worthy adversary never disappoints."

Through her tears, Darcy asked, "So you knew the entire time? You knew we were coming?"

"Of course, I knew! I've been tracking your father for years. There is nothing that man does or says that is a secret from me, no matter how cunning he may fancy himself."

Darcy was stunned. She had thought her father was an impenetrable fortress, but it seemed there were holes in his organization even he was blind to. "How?"

"Oh, dear sweet, Darcy. There is nothing that I don't know. I am the most powerful man in all of the Factions, and no one is the wiser. I have spies in every organization that is worth its salt—I have for years. But, your father's is the one that interests me the most."

"Because he's your biggest rival," Darcy guessed, her tears drying for the moment as she focused solely on keeping her eyes open. They suddenly felt so heavy, and the persistent ringing in her ears was making it hard to concentrate on the man in front of her. She had hoped death would find her, but she wasn't so sure her injuries were enough to take her out. She would meet her end by the man in front of her, and she hoped he would make it quick.

"Because of you, Darcy." His tone had gone dreamy, and it was reminiscent of the voice that she had heard in an alley just before the man had turned to goo. The sound had her lifting her head again, staring at the madman beaming back at her. He was wearing the same awed expression that the Mod in the alley had, and her stomach twisted. The look had been endearing on her long-gone confidant, but on Blake, it felt slimy against her raw skin.

"Why me?" she asked, hoping his reasoning was something far less terrifying than the fact that she was the key. She didn't want to be the key anymore. She wished she could rid herself of the title and flee from her fate.

Blake scoffed, "Because you're the bastard daughter of a Mod, and I need you to finish what your father and I started."

Darcy shook her head. And shook it again. Huh? She couldn't have heard him correctly. She wasn't a bastard. Her father had been around her

CHAPTER 13

entire life—granted, he had never been involved in her upbringing, but he had always been in the vicinity of her life. If anything, her mother had been the one that had been absent from her life. The woman had hardly left her room. Darcy had never interacted with Mods before her newfound companions—not even her housing staff. So, she concluded, he must be confusing her with someone else.

"I—" she started, and huffed out a confused breath. "You must have me mistaken."

Darien Blake gave her a million-watt smile, his smirk barely concealing his excitement. "You don't know," he breathed out, and chuckled so loudly it echoed off of the hollow walls. "She never told you."

"Told me?"

"About your birth father."

"My father is Charles—"

Darien interjected, "Your siblings' father is Charles Newton. Your father was named Samuel Bishop, and he was a modified human."

The room started spinning. Darcy was gasping for breath, trying to wrap her head around what he was saying. Maybe he was confused, or maybe she was confused. She must not have heard him properly—her head injury was starting to confuse reality and fantasy. Darcy wondered if she had brain damage and that was why she was hearing things. That must be it. She must have some sort of damage.

She denied, "No, you must—I mean, that's not possible."

Blake crossed his legs and folded his hands over his knee as though he was about to divulge one of the greatest stories he could imagine. "Sweet girl, you hold the strongest power this world has ever seen within you, and you don't even know it." He cleared his throat and straightened his back slightly. "Almost twenty-four years ago, the scandal of the century happened in Faction 2. The leader of Faction 2 had caught his wife in an affair with a Mod. The Mod had been hired to the house as a driver. Soon after he was hired, his wife had started an affair with the thing. It was disgusting—atrocious really. We were all scandalized. Of course, there was no proof—it was all being spread through the gossip pages—but we all know those stories are based on some truth.

"Once the rumors started, there was no stopping them. Pictures began to surface of your mother and the chauffeur together. Nothing horribly lewd, but just the sight of them together made us all sick. It was truly horrifying. It was rumored that Charles had the being killed and thrown into the incinerator. None of us saw any more pictures of the man, and none of us heard another word about it. Things returned to normal until nine months later, when a baby girl was born."

The floor dropped from under Darcy and she gasped. This couldn't be real. He had to be lying to manipulate her for whatever means he thought her useful for. "You're lying," she whispered, barely loud enough for her own ears to catch. She couldn't take one more thing; she might explode.

Blake's tone turned sympathetic as he said, "Unfortunately for you, I am not. Have you ever wondered why you look so different from your siblings? Why your father has always preferred them to you? The significant age difference in you all?" Of course, Darcy had considered all of these factors for most of her life, but she had never given them much validity. She had thought they were merely the musings of a misunderstood teen. But now, the stark differences between them all seemed so obvious. She had to have known on some level that she had never fit quite right with the others.

Darien continued, "The media spun the birth of the baby as something Charles and Nina had planned to show their strength in their marriage. The rest of us all knew this was a ploy to hide the truth, no matter how loudly your father tried to deny it. As time went on, we had all started to forget the vile background of your birth, though the whispers continued whenever you or your mother would appear at events. There was always an underlying contempt the Elite held for you and your mother. Her sins, unfortunately, sealed your fate among us.

"Your mother eventually hid herself away—locked up like a princess in a tower. I'm sure she fancied herself a princess as much as the rest of us despised her. I would imagine she couldn't stand the sight of you: the constant reminder of her transgressions." He shuttered dramatically. "I cannot imagine the pain of her humiliation. Once she was out of the picture, Charles did everything he could to keep you away. He sold you to the highest bidder once you turned of age and sent you on a fool's errand that would most likely end in your death. I'm sure he's squealing with glee right now at the thought of your demise."

CHAPTER 13

Darcy felt sick again. If there had been anything left in her stomach, it would have risen by now. She wanted to deny everything he was saying—poke holes in his tale until all of the air filtered out—but it all made too much sense. She had lived most of her life cowering in the shadow of her father and older siblings, never really able to make them see her worth. Darcy was all dark and rough edges where her siblings were light and sharp. She had always dismissed their differences and her own fears as nothing more than the intrusive thoughts of an insecure child, but now they had some truth to them. Why had she always been hidden away? Why hadn't her father trusted her? Why did he send her here when he had never given her a second glance?

"Does that mean . . .? Am I . . .?" She couldn't bring herself to finish the thought. If her biological father was a Mod, did that make her somehow . . .?

"Thus bringing us to why I need you at all," Blake continued. "Your father was not like most of the modified humans that have settled in your part of the world. He was biologically engineered to be a weapon, not physically. Chemicals were added to his very DNA to make him almost toxic to us humans. It was an incredible feat for science, but unfortunately, it never worked the way they had planned. His reactions were too strong, or he would need specific DNA strands to strike. It was far too complex, and the scientists behind it abandoned their quest.

"When the Second Civil War ended, he did what every other Mod did and went to the gutter where he belonged. He worked for Charles and had an indecent affair with your mother, thus creating you. We had all heard the rumor that Charles had killed him, but the truth was, your mother tipped him off and he escaped before he could incur his fate. He had disappeared into thin air. Charles searched for him for years, but it was all to no avail—not surprising, considering the bumbling stooge he is." Darien smirked at his insult, and Darcy continued to struggle with the idea that this man felt so far superior to her father that he scoffed at the mere thought of him.

"What does this have to do with Element Five?" Darcy asked, giving up the ruse that she was an innocent. Clearly, Darien Blake had more knowledge than Darcy could fathom and pretending otherwise would only put her behind the eight ball.

Darien smiled fully and adjusted himself in the steal chair. "The years went by, and we had all but forgotten about your mother's transgression and the poor bastard child she bared. That was until the mining started. Out here in Faction 8, there are mountains and valleys to mine for all their worth, and mine we did. We dug farther than anyone had gone before. Our technology after the Second Civil had advanced so far that we were finding new ways of using the resources this planet had been trying to give us for millions of years.

"Almost three years to the day, we struck gold. Our miners found something so new and so unique, they didn't know what to do with it. It was powerful in its raw form but unpredictable. It was useless to me unless I could find a way to stabilize the matter and give it a specific target. I enlisted the help of my dear friend Edwin Ellis and his team of scientists to analyze the Mod DNA available to us from the database used during the war in order to find the key to our success. Call it fate, call it dumb luck, but I think this universe has a funny sense of humor. The key to stabilizing this beautiful gem was through your father's modified DNA. We could use his modified blood to harness the power of the element and provide a target for its attack."

Darcy's breath shook as she whispered, "You have my father?" She was terrified of the answer. On the one hand, she wanted nothing more than to find the man that held the answers she never knew she needed, but on the other hand, she wasn't so sure she ever wanted to meet him. Meeting him would make this all too real for her.

Blake suddenly looked sullen as he shook his head. "I had your father for the last two years. It had taken us months of working around the clock and endless resources to finally track him down and bring him in. Admittedly, he was not a willing participant in our study. He was a stubborn one!" His voice sounded almost amused as he slapped his knee and let out a bark of laughter. "I'm guessing that's where you get it from."

"What happened to him?" she asked, not missing the past tense he continued to use when speaking about the man. She suspected he was dead, but a small, almost imperceptible part of her wanted him to be missing. If he was still missing, he would be able to fill the spaces within her that now felt vacant and worn.

CHAPTER 13

"He had made several attempts to escape my clutches. He had even made it off of the property more than once! But, in the end, he decided his own fate, and he felt that not being in this world was preferable to being under our hospitality. He drained himself of his blood, making it all useless to our efforts. I thought our mission was over—all of the progress we had made ruined! Honestly, my sweet girl, I was depressed—such an ugly time in my past, I'll admit. I had fallen sick with despair and had locked myself away. My reason for being on this Earth had been destroyed, and I found the will to continue on almost unbearable. I couldn't stand the thought of being on the same planet at those things for one more day.

"The scientists back in the lab continued to work day and night to find a solution to our current problem. We had made a short supply of weapons, but nothing near what we would need to make the impact that I would need to make. It could maybe level a small slum, but that was not nearly enough for every slum across the Factions. They tried everything to salvage the blood of your father, but he had done his homework and rendered his blood useless. So, we were back to square one—such a pity."

His downtrodden voice could have made Darcy sick. She was so tired—and tired of his ramblings—and wanted all of this to be over. Darcy wasn't sure if she wanted to be unconscious or if she just wanted to be back with Jesse and Tick—hell, she would even take Jericho at this point—but she knew her mind and body were on the verge of shutting down. Everything felt fuzzy and blurry around the edges. It was like a vast pool of nothingness waiting for her just over the horizon if she could only reach it.

Darcy slurred, "So then you found me?"

Blake's smile was bright enough to light the entire warehouse. "Exactly! Such a smart girl! I had an epiphany one morning. I saw your engagement announcement in the paper and knew you would be the key to what I needed. If you were truly this Mod's daughter, you would have his DNA—or a version of it—running through your veins. It should be easy enough to doctor you up and use you for my own purposes and, I would assume, your goals as well. I have never met an Elite that didn't find the very presence of those Mods anything less than abhorrent—well, save for your poor, ill mother."

Darien Blake clearly didn't know her very well. She gave a smirk in his direction, finally feeling as though she had the upper hand for a change. It felt good to be back in control. "I hate to break it to you, Mr. Blake, but you and I clearly don't share the same goals. I won't be a part of your mission to eliminate the Mods."

Darien seemed shocked, but not deterred in the least. "That really is too bad. I was hoping that Charles had instilled in you the same beliefs we had all been raised on. But"—he clapped his hands loudly once and leaned back on his small chair—"no matter. Just like your father, you'll be a fine match, and I have the means of keeping you exactly where I want you: with me."

"And what if I say no?"

"I will send your severed head to Charles Newton in a box." He sounded more deadly than he had in all their conversation—the false smile dropping from his face and his eyes turning as cold as ice.

Darcy scoffed, "You've already told me he wouldn't care, and with the information you've shared with me, I don't think that sounds like a terrible idea."

Seeming almost impressed by her words, Blake snapped his fingers twice—his smile returning as though it had never left—and one of his men stepped forward and handed him a phone. "I hadn't thought you would choose this route, but I did have a second plan in place just in case you decided to play hard to get." The phone blinked to life, showing a scene playing out before her, and the sounds of Tick struggling filled the room.

"Get your hands off of me, you filthy son of a bitch! Where's Darcy?" Jesse yelled over Tick's grunting.

Jericho chimed in, "You better hope to God I don't get out of here, because when I do, I'm gonna set your asses on fire. I'm gonna burn you motherfuckers to the ground!"

"Jesse!" Darcy screamed, her energy reviving and tears springing to her eyes and falling down her cheeks. "Tick! Jer!"

"Darcy!" all three yelled back, squinting at the screen to better see her face. She stood suddenly and tried to run to them, but her legs gave out beneath her and she collapsed to the hard ground. "Darcy, no!" Tick screamed as Jesse gave an unintelligible yelp.

"All right, men," Blake ordered into the phone screen. "Darcy has decided she would rather die than work for me—which I still do not

CHAPTER 13

understand—so you can dispose of her companions."

"Wait!" Darcy wailed, and began clawing herself forward across the disgusting floor. "Wait! I'll come with you! Let them be! I'll do whatever you ask!"

Darien Blake's slimy smile slithered back across his cheeks. Darcy was sobbing again, pleading with every ounce of energy she had left in her. Shining with the delight of a child on Christmas morning, Blake's dark eyes watched her grovel. She felt hopeless. She could hear the screams over the speaker on the phone in front of her but was powerless to stop whatever fate Blake had decided for them.

"Oh, Darcy," Blake hummed, slowly standing. He prowled toward her like a jungle cat stalking its prey. He knelt before her and lightly grasped her chin in his soft hand. "I'm so happy you've decided to see things my way." He kissed her forehead gently, like a father to his daughter, and stood slowly before turning to his men. "Keep the Mods at our off-shore facility. As willing as Darcy is to work with us now, I'm quite sure that fire will reignite just like it had in her father. I feel we may need to keep our aces tucked close in our pockets."

One of the men nodded quickly and gave the instructions to the phone where she could hear her friends crying out to her. She had lost. She went into this journey believing that this would be her chance at proving herself, but she had failed. She didn't care about pleasing Charles any more, but the fact remained that she was more lost now than she had been a week ago.

"Don't look so downtrodden, my love," Blake instructed, buttoning the jacket of his suit and smoothing his hands down the front lapel. "The adventure has only begun! Tomorrow will be your wedding day!"

Darcy shook her head, too exhausted to muster the confusion she should be feeling. "Who will I be marrying?" she asked, knowing better than to fight his words at this point. He had proven that he knew far more than she, and it was useless to resist his words.

Blake gave a shocked chuckle and placed a delicate hand over his heart. He informed, "Why, you'll be marrying me, of course."

"You? You have a wife."

He scoffed at her and waved a hand in her direction. "She was easy enough to get rid of. Nothing my men at home couldn't handle once I had you in my grasp. She is gone, and tomorrow, you will take her place."

Darcy felt as though she was sinking into the floor beneath her. She had thought that this moment could not get any worse, but it seemed the depth of her imagination was seriously lacking. Around every corner was a new and more terrifying low for her to reach. "I thought you wanted to experiment on me, not marry me. You don't need a wife to rule."

"Right you are!" Blake chirped, and pointed a finger at her. "Such a smart one, you are. You might just be my favorite wife yet! I do not need a wife to rule my Faction, but I will need you as my wife in order to rule your Faction. Just the thought of seeing the look on Charles's face when our wedding is broadcast over to him." Darien tipped his head back and let loose a hardy laugh as though he couldn't imagine anything funnier. "All of his hopes and dreams will fly up in smoke the second we say our vows. It's just so poetic, I don't know if my dreamer's heart can take it!"

The pieces started to slowly fall into place for Darcy. If he married her, he would be next in line to control Faction 2. He would have the highest title and, therefore, rights to the Faction when Charles passed—that is, as long as no one questioned Darcy's lineage. "I'll tell them I'm not really his child."

"There's that fire again! That is precisely why I kept your friends tucked tightly away. If you so much as breathe a word of any of this to anyone, they'll all die by my hand. Well, all of them except for Homa—I'll send her right back to the waiting arms of her father, and he can deal with her transgressions however he sees fit. Though, if she were my child, I would take the other eye and spoon feed it to her—ungrateful little brat."

Darcy gulped and laid her head against the cool floor of the warehouse. There was no beating him. She would have to find a way out of this, but for tonight, she couldn't see past closing her eyes and drifting into unconsciousness. "You'll never get my father's approval. He'll divulge your true nature."

"Your father is dead. Remember that, my child." His voice had gone hard, as though even alluding to Charles as her father was a punishable crime. "Charles will approve our marriage if he would like to keep his own transgressions a secret from his people. If anyone finds out the true nature of your little adventure, Charles will be pulled from his throne and tried

CHAPTER 13

for treason against the Factions. He wouldn't risk his career for a child he never wanted. This will be a blessing to him."

"What about my friends? Where are you taking them?"

Blake clicked his tongue at her and wagged his finger as if she were a naughty child caught with her hand in the cookie jar. "That information is not for you to know, my love. From now on, your sole purpose is to stay in my good favor. As long as I am pleased, your friends will continue to stay alive."

That was all she really needed to hear. If they were alive, there was a chance she could get them all out of this. There had to be a way around this. But for now, she couldn't take anymore. She pressed her cheek more fully to the cool concrete beneath her and let her eyes fall closed.

CHAPTER 14

She felt a light rubbing against her elbow, and Darcy groaned at the contact. She was exhausted. All she had wanted was to sleep for the rest of her days—unless she woke to a miracle, there was no reason for her to open her heavy lids. The rubbing continued, harder this time, and accompanied by a sigh. Darcy was determined to ignore it. She saw no reason to acknowledge her new situation.

As it stood, Darcy was being roused whether she wanted to or not when the rubbing turning into a full body shake. She peeked one eye open to stare into the periwinkle walls surrounding her. She was in the middle of a luscious bed with billowing white blankets and comforters, lined with lace edges. The bed was lifted high on a pedestal with long wooden stairs leading up to the luxurious furniture. The shaking at her elbow continued as she turned her head.

"It's about time you decided to wake up, lazy bones," a small, frail voice admonished. The voice belonged to a small woman that had to be nearing the age of eighty. Her face was as dark as melted chocolate and resembled a sheet that had been left in the dryer too long. It was cracked around the edges and lined with creases around her eyes and mouth. Her cheeks sagged slightly with the weight of her years, and her dark eyes looked as though they had seen more than Darcy could imagine. The weariness within them told stories. Her body was small, and her back hunched with age—the small frame masking her clear strength.

"Who . . . ?" Darcy began to ask as the woman stripped the blankets from her body. Darcy was still wearing her bloodstained dress, caked with dirt and grime from the events of the night before. No longer did the fabric shine with a blue tint, but instead was a murky gray that had been ripped and tattered. She reached a hand up and felt around her face and head. The only evidence of her night of abuse was a smallish circular knot at her temple. Darcy was shocked that her head wasn't throbbing or her face swollen beyond recognition. "What . . . ?"

The woman sighed, annoyed. "I am Laurie. You are in Faction 8, and today is your wedding day. You've slept the day away, and now I am behind schedule if I want to have you ready in time for the binding. Come on, lazy bones, let's get you out of this bed."

The words "wedding day" had bounced around in Darcy's skull like a bullet, rendering her motionless in her attempt to leave the bed. "Wedding day?" she whispered, the words constricting her throat like a vice.

"Is there an echo in here?" the woman replied, having none of Darcy's astonishment. "You're marrying Darien Blake, the most powerful man in the world in a little under"—she checked the small golden watch on her thin wrist and let out a low whistle—"two hours, which gives me no time to have you ready the way that I should. Get up! Come on! The food's over there; eat quickly."

She grasped Darcy by the elbow in a surprisingly strong grip and hefted her from the bed. Darcy's legs wobbled as she was dragged down the large steps and placed on a crimson couch. There was a wide array of lunch items—small finger sandwiches, fruit, cheese, tea, coffee, and other confections—and it all made Darcy's stomach turn. A similar image flashed across her mind of a spread not as delicate but much more thoughtful. That had been the last time she had been truly happy. It was a moment of bliss she would be forced to carry with her for the foreseeable future. The thought was almost too much to bear.

Her heart longed for Jesse. It astounded her that she had gone most of her life without him, but it had only taken him five short days to sink so far into her skin, she felt like she couldn't breathe without him. Where was he? Was he okay? How was she going to get out of this without him?

CHAPTER 14

He was the one that seemed to always have the answers. He and Tick. She needed them both. They were the lights that always seemed to guide her in the right direction. Now, she felt like a ship lost at sea.

"Eat," the old woman demanded as she pushed her way into an adjoining room and began filling an opulent tub with water and perfumes from different golden bottles. "I don't have time to waste."

Darcy croaked, "I'm not hungry." Her voice sounded strange to her own ears. It was hollow, echoing off of her empty heart.

"Even better," the woman—Laurie—agreed. "Now, get in here and get your teeth brushed."

Darcy obeyed the order, if not a little slowly as she felt like a fawn learning to walk for the first time. She held on to every available surface she could as she moseyed her way into the equally large bathroom. Darcy slowly made her way over to a mirror that took up the entire wall behind the tub, where Laurie was still busying herself with her potions and concoctions.

Darcy stared in horror at what looked back at her. Her face may not have been swollen any longer, but her skin was almost entirely purple. Her face looked as though she had been kicked by a mule. Her eyes were an astonishing shade of black, and her cheekbones stood out in a splash of deep red ringed in blue. Her hair was tangled with debris from her night of terror—rocks and dirt clumping in her curls. If she wasn't staring it right in the face, she might almost believe that it all had been nothing more than a nightmare.

"What happened?" Darcy asked, replaying scenes from a memory she was convinced could not have been reality.

"You came in here early this morning looking like hell warmed over," the woman griped as she readied her soaps and placed damp towels in a warmer opposite the tub. Darcy noticed this seemed to be a practiced routine for the old woman and wondered how many times she had been forced into the procedure in her long years. Darcy also wondered how a woman—not a Mod as far as she could tell—had come to have such a career. It was beyond bizarre to see a woman waiting on an Elite and not a Mod. "Some men dragged you in there and dumped you in that bed. I just about had a heart attack when they told me you were going to be Leader Blake's new wife. I would never question his motives, but seeing you in such a state, I had to wonder if the man was thinking clearly.

"He came to my quarters early this morning and told me to prepare for the wedding today. You can imagine how busy I've been making the preparations, but when the most powerful man in world tells you to do something, you get your hindquarters in gear and fulfill his wishes."

Laurie worked her way back to Darcy and motioned for her to spit and rinse. Darcy did both, feeling a little lightheaded as she raised her head back to face the woman in the mirror. Laurie wasted no time stripping Darcy of her filthy dress and undergarments. Darcy sucked in an embarrassed breath as her cheeks turned to rubies. Laurie didn't seem fazed in the least by her nakedness, as though, for her, seeing a woman at her most vulnerable was common practice.

To Darcy's relief, Laurie ushered her into the steaming bathwater. As devastated and horrified as Darcy felt about her current circumstances, the water felt like a balm to her soul. She sunk deep into the water and let out an approving sigh. If everything in the world was wrong, this was the only moment that felt right. The water immediately began to turn a brownish color with the dirt and blood dissolving from her skin.

"Enjoying that, are you?" Laurie asked, giving her a discontented huff.

Darcy sighed. "Yes,"

"Well, get used to it because we're going to be here for a while. I've never in all of my days seen a woman in such disrepair."

Darcy turned slightly to look at the old woman just as she dumped hot water down her face and shoulders. Darcy spluttered and coughed as Laurie dumped another round of water over her bare skin. The scalding heat felt like heaven, but Darcy wished she could get a word out. She finally had her opportunity when Laurie began scrubbing a strong-smelling soap into her scalp. Her cracked nails scratched roughly against her skin, and she winced.

"Do you know how I came to be this way?" Darcy asked, wondering what the woman was privy to.

Laurie replied, "That's not for me to know. I only do as I am asked; I don't ask questions."

"Your boss," Darcy began, feeling anger rise high in her chest and throat, "had me attacked and—"

CHAPTER 14

"That's enough of that!" the old woman boomed, and dumped water over Darcy's head again. "You will not speak ill of Leader Blake in this house. You may be his wife in an hour, but for now, you're one of his subjects. You'll act accordingly."

Darcy opened her mouth to reply again, and the woman dumped another bucket of water on her. Darcy now wished she had access to a shower. This woman was not going to be an ally for her, that much was clear. Darcy knew it was traditional to have the bride pampered by her staff before her wedding, but Darcy wished for solitude. She needed to find a way out of this place and back with the people she loved.

It occurred to her that her friends didn't even know the truth about her. She was still struggling to process all of the information she had been told the night before. Darcy wasn't a Newton—Darcy wasn't even really human. She wasn't really a Mod either, though. She hadn't known she was modified—but she wasn't modified; she had been born into it. All of it was confusing, and she wasn't sure how she felt about any of it. She longed to speak to her mother—something she hadn't done in years—if only to get the answers to finding out who her real father was and how she had kept this from her for so long.

Would her friends even want her anymore?

That thought made her hold her breath for a beat. She knew how Jericho felt about the Elite, but how would he feel about a half-Elite, half-Mod person? Would he welcome her as one of their own, or see this as a reason to ostracize her further? Would Jesse still want her? Would he be accepting of her new position or skeptical of her? Somehow, she knew Tick wouldn't mind her differences. Tick had always loved and accepted her for exactly who she was, and the blood running through her veins would make no difference to Tick. She could about guarantee it. But the others, she wasn't so sure of.

"Where will the wedding be held?" Darcy asked numbly. She wasn't sure she could bring herself to endure more pain. Her heart was shattered beyond repair.

Laurie shook her head as she took a sponge out from below the tub and began scrubbing Darcy's shoulders. "Here, of course. Your wedding will need to be done quickly so you can be presented properly at Ms. Sasha's wedding later this evening."

Sasha's wedding.

Of course, that would still be happening. Darcy had all but forgotten that was tonight. She wondered what the other Elite would think of her being married to Blake. There would be talk and speculation, of course, but with Darcy's new knowledge of her own status among the Elite, she wondered what they might think of this travesty marrying one of the most powerful men in the world. They would all have to know something bigger was happening. Would one of them step in? Would they question the validity of it and save her from Blake? She didn't think any of them would be brave enough.

What about the bruises? What about her appearance? Surely, they wouldn't be able to ignore the face of a woman that had clearly been forced into this against her will. If nothing else, would Shane come forward? Would he be brave enough to save his illegitimate sister?

Laurie huffed at her as she scrubbed roughly against her skin. "Don't act so put out. There are women all over the Factions that would kill to be where you are today. You have been handpicked to be the wife of the leader of Faction 8. You will be married to one of the most powerful men in the world—taken care of for life. You'll never have to worry again."

Darcy huffed behind her tears at the naivety of the woman next to her. If she only knew what had actually brought Darcy there today. The bruise that was taking up the majority of Darcy's face should have been this woman's first clue to the true nature of her upcoming nuptials. It was not a happy one, that was for sure, but maybe this woman was overlooking that piece to make herself feel better about her own hand in all of this.

"Did you do this for his previous wife?" Darcy asked, her voice thick with tears. "Get her ready to endure her fate?"

"I've done this for all Leader Blake's wives," she answered as she began scrubbing the other arm. "I have been here for Leader Blake since his rise to power. He has been nothing but good to me all of these years. No matter who Leader Blake might be to his wives, he is not that man to me, and I cannot hate him for their transgressions."

"So you know?" Darcy whispered, shocked by her words. "You know what happened to the other women?"

Laurie stopped her incessant scrubbing and looked Darcy in the eye, the

CHAPTER 14

woman showing the first signs of sympathy since their relationship began. "I am not in control of their actions. Infidelity is punishable by death. They sealed their own fate."

There was a quavering in her voice that spoke louder than her words. She knew. How could she have lived here for so long and not know? He had been through more wives in his short ten-year reign than Darcy had ever known another to have.

Tears suddenly welled in Darcy's eyes as the woman dumped bucket after bucket of smelling oils over her head. Once Darcy was able to breathe, she looked at the woman. There was a spark—not quite sympathy but something adjacent to it—in the old woman's eyes as she gazed at the bare girl before her.

"I-I," Darcy stuttered, "I don't want to be here. He's forcing me to be here. Help me." Her voice had taken a hysterical cadence all of a sudden as she gripped the woman's shoulders in her talons. "Help me find a way out of here. He would never know it was you! I can protect you—"

Laurie slapped Darcy across the cheek hard in quick succession until her hysteria died away. The woman looked just as crazed and desperate as Darcy felt. She gripped Darcy hard enough to bruise her—not that anyone would know any different with all of the other bruises marring her body. "You will do this for us." Her dark eyes were wild, and her dark skin cracked around her eyes. "You will make the sacrifice that only you can make to save our race. We are all depending on you, you spineless, selfish little girl. You're so fortunate that he would choose you above everyone else. Save us all, Darcy, and you will receive your reward."

It struck Darcy as odd that this small woman would know so many of Blake's secrets, and that she would be a willing participant in the genocide of millions of people around the world. Darcy mentally chastised herself for even thinking otherwise. Of course, she would be a willing participant in his games: she had been with him since the start of it all. There wasn't a single Mod to be found on the premises—that Darcy could tell, anyway—which would seem odd to anyone unaware of Blake's psychotic prejudices.

Darcy muttered, "What did they do with her . . . his previous wife?"

She wasn't sure why she was even asking. It wasn't as though she would receive the same treatment—she was nothing more than a means to an end for Blake. Her only hope for survival was that he needed her alive to rule over Faction 2, at least until her father died, and then he would be free to do with her as he pleased. The thought turned her stomach. She was thankful that she hadn't eaten anything that day. It would have all come up by now, anyway.

"That doesn't concern you, love," Laurie chirped, as though she hadn't just physically assaulted her. "Now, come out of that tub before you wrinkle. It's time to put your ceremonial gown and headdress. We can't be late for your big day."

The woman seemed as delighted as she could—sporting an ever present scowl—as she lifted a towel and averted her eyes for Darcy to step out. Darcy left the porcelain on shaky legs and wrapped herself in the plush comfort of the fabric before her. The towel reminded her of the hundreds she had encountered throughout her life, but none felt as much like a prison cell as this one did.

Laurie escorted her across the room to a changing screen. The dress was hanging in delicate waves down the opaque screen before her. It was a light chiffon fabric, the bright blossoming color of blood fresh from the slaughter. It could have been a simple gown, easily overlooked with its modest neckline and long, sheer sleeves, but the color demanded the eye. It commanded the attention of everyone around it simply by being. It was as fierce and dangerous as the man that had demanded she wear it. She knew she would be easily picked from a crowd in this, no chance of escaping for the bright-red beacon. Something like hope deflated in Darcy's chest. He would not make this easy for her—he had more than proven that in their early morning tete-a-tete, but she had hoped she could find a hole in his armor.

Laurie huffed, "I'll give you some privacy to put the gown on, but once you're done, you'll have to come around so I can do your hair and place the headdress."

Darcy simply nodded, tears springing suddenly to her eyes again. It was all too real. She was here—physically she could feel herself in the room—but she felt like she was a million miles away. Darcy could have convinced herself that this was some sort of twisted dream she was having if it was not for the feeling of the light fabric scratching against her skin as she pulled it down over her head.

CHAPTER 14

It fit like a dream, and Darcy hated every second of it.

The feel of the fabric swishing against her bare knees was almost enough to make her crumble. The wail she had been holding back all morning began to bubble at the hollow in her throat again. She could take a beating from Laurie, but she wasn't sure her spirit could take the weight of her final act of personal betrayal. Darcy was doing this to save them, but how much of herself could she give before she lost herself completely? Would she be too far gone to save them?

Darcy knew she would need to get out of this trap quickly before he could completely destroy her. She had known from the moment he had unveiled his plan that this was all going to be very painful for her, but she needed to stay strong for the people she loved. Even if they didn't accept her for who she was now, she would save them from Blake.

"Are you finished yet?" Laurie demanded as she rounded the corner and took in Darcy hunched form. "Why," she breathed out, clasping her hands before her and almost looking starstruck, "I think you've looked better in this gown than any before you."

That was enough to send Darcy over the edge. She began retching, though there was nothing more to come up. She was wearing a dead woman's dress—no, not a dead woman, dead *women*. Their ghosts seemed to close in around her like the fabric of her dress, suffocating her and making it almost impossible to breathe. Darcy's vision began to swim, and she prayed this would be enough to put her out again. She needed a break. She couldn't do it anymore.

"None of that!" Laurie scolded, and gripped Darcy's shoulders in her hands again. "We'll have none of that today. I have enough to worry about without you falling unconscious again. You're acting as though you haven't had enough sleep! You've slept more than anyone I've ever seen, young lady."

Darcy wanted to argue with her. She wanted to scream in her face and tell her she couldn't take it anymore. Instead, she sobbed, "I just want to go home. Please, let me go home."

"You are home. The sooner you recognize that, the sooner we can all move on."

Laurie practically lifted Darcy off of her feet and pushed her into the chair before the mirror in the bedroom. Darcy sat numbly as the woman tacked pin after pin of hair to her head. She felt like a doll, being poked and prodded, but she couldn't feel a thing. Her brain wouldn't let her feel anything. Darcy had gone into full survival mode. She thought of Tick—all of those months spent in torture, losing her eye and almost all of her abilities—and how she had made it through that hell. Darcy could make it through this. Her torture had only begun, and she had lives to save.

"There," Laurie said softly, and stepped back from the mirror.

Darcy looked at her reflection and almost didn't recognize her own face. Her hair was braided and tied in intricate patterns; Laurie had laced diamonds and pearls between the folds and down across her face in a mock veil. This must be the customary headdress for the Elite women of this Faction. She had never been to a Faction 8 wedding before, but now she was getting a firsthand look at it all.

"Now, to cover those nasty bruises. We can't have Leader Blake seeing you in such a state."

Darcy almost chuckled at the woman. She had to know he had already seen her; in fact, it was by his order that these bruises were administered. He hadn't been overly pleased to see that she had been so beaten down—and now she knew why—but he hadn't been devastated to see her in such a state. Darcy wondered if the man could feel anything at all for anyone besides himself. She doubted it. She had watched him kill in cold blood—he had talked about his previous wife as though she were nothing more than an insect that needed to be exterminated. He didn't see any of them as people, Mod or not.

Laurie focused in on Darcy's face and neck, using paints and concealers to cover every color of bruise she could reach. Her eyebrows were screwed together in a scowl as she worked from cheek to cheek, stepping back every so often to admire her own work or adjust a color pallet. Darcy noticed that it didn't seem to be the first time Laurie had needed to cover blood and bruises. She could only imagine the abuse his other wives had to endure before he finally let them rest.

Laurie finally stepped back and sighed heavily. "You're ready."

Darcy didn't blink. She didn't move. Laurie rolled her eyes in annoyance, as though she expected Darcy to thank her or be overcome by how

CHAPTER 14

wonderful she now looked, before moving to the heavy oak door. She opened it, leaned her head out, and came back in. Two enormous men followed Laurie into the room and stood like redwoods beside her.

"Come with us," one of the men said, not looking at her, but Darcy knew the demand was meant for her. Neither man looked down at her, as though they had done this millions of times, but Darcy didn't mind. She didn't want to be looked at. She wanted to disappear.

She sat there silently for a moment longer before standing slowly. She turned and began walking between the men: one leading the way ahead of her, and one following closely enough behind her that he could grab her if she tried to flee. They were smart to position themselves in such a way. Darcy's only thought as they moved down the luxurious corridor was how many windows and exits she could find. The entire hallway was lined in windows—she could see the voluptuous back gardens that stretched for miles—but every door was shut tightly as she moved past them. She could probably climb out a window, but it would take her time and she would need a good amount of privacy to do so. That was not something she could accomplish with her current company. She also needed to secure the location of her three companions before her escape. She needed them to be safe before she could ensure her own safety.

"Here," the man said as they all stopped in front of the door that led into her final destination. She felt shaky and queasy all over again. Her nerves jumped on end as though a live wire had touched her arm. One of the redwoods opened the door before her and pressed a hard hand against her back, forcing her to move forward instead of turning back.

Her feet stuttered as she walked slowly into the room. Blake was smiling at her brightly, much the same way he had the previous night in the warehouse. She hadn't seen him since then, and the sight of him made her stomach turn. She was not ready. She couldn't do this. Her entire being was screaming at her to turn and run from this monster. He was a kidnapper—a murderer—and he was now going to be her husband. The thought made her pause in her short steps toward him. Her mind whirled with thoughts of escaping—of flinging herself out of one of the windows, injuries be damned.

There was a mousy man standing directly next to Blake. He was short, with floppy brown hair and enormous thin-rimmed glasses that kept sliding down his narrow nose. He used a thin finger to pressed them back up and sweep the light sheen of sweat on his forehead. Darcy wondered what Blake had over this man to get him to come to his home and perform this ceremony without the presence of the proper ceremonial artifacts. Darcy was honestly unsure of how any of this was going to be legal. It was only the three of them and the armed guards at the doors and windows; none of the legally binding personnel were present and no documentation that she could see.

Blake looked down at his watch and sighed a little impatiently. "Darcy, my darling, we need to hasten this process if we're going to make it to the other wedding on time."

His daughter's wedding was in less than an hour. He would present Darcy to the thousands of people from all over the Factions as his wife at this event. The gossip pages would have her face displayed in every household in less than an hour. The world would know that she had given in and let this tyrant steal her away. She wondered what Charles would think. He had to know that she was not doing this willingly. But, if Blake's words were anything to trust, she imagined that he wouldn't care for her safety. He would only care for the status of his mission, which had successfully been thwarted.

The trackers.

She wasn't sure where the thought had come from, but she was suddenly terrified that her father would active the failsafe of Jesse's tracker. There would be no saving him from his prison if he was already gone. She reached a hand back and rubbed at the scar at the base of her neck. It didn't feel as though Blake had touched it. She prayed that her father had been smart enough to leave the chip in place for her companion. *Please, let him be smart enough.*

Blake huffed again and pointed a meaningful glare at one of his henchmen. The man behind Darcy stepped forward and grabbed her bicep roughly, dragging her to stand before her betrothed. Blake sighed in relief and straightened his raspberry-colored tie. The small man seemed to be vibrating with nervous energy as he shuffled from foot to foot, juggling the large book cradled in his arms. Darcy watched as he juggled the book

CHAPTER 14

over to his opposite arm and used his free hand to press his glasses back between his eyes.

"That's more like it." Blake sighed again and looked to the small man standing between them. "Please begin, Tim."

Tim looked at her—with worry tracing every line of his face—before gulping and looking down in his book. Darcy could see the beads of sweat rolling from his temples as he looked down to the pages. "I, chief peace officer of Faction 8, Tim Waller, am present today to legally bind Leader Darien Blake to Ms. Darcy Newton. In this binding, Ms. Newton will act as wife in all of her duties and responsibilities, as bestowed upon her by Leader Blake, without question. It will be her duty, and hers alone, to ensure the happiness and peace of her husband henceforth. Ms. Newton will perform any and all acts requested by her husband without argument. She is required by law to obey him and cease any relationships with anyone outside of her husband's approval. He is her master and her guardian.

"Leader Blake, do you take on the responsibility for this woman? Do you agree to guide her and endure the burden of training her as your wife in order for her to complete her wifely duties?"

"I agree," Blake chirped as soon as the words had left Tim's lips. The whole ceremony had always tasted bitter in Darcy's mouth, but the words directed to this man about her were like acid. She was being ordered to obey him. She was having to make a promise that she wasn't sure she could keep. She knew if she did this and turned her back on her marriage vows, she could be punished by death. But she also knew that if she denied him, he would drag her to the sewer and do what he wanted with her anyway, killing her friends in the process. It was a hopeless situation, and Darcy couldn't seem to find the exit.

"And do you, Darcy Newton, promise to listen, obey, and cater to all of this man's needs, no matter the price?" the man asked.

Her breath caught in her throat, tears welling high in her eyes. She wanted to scream at the top of her lungs—tell him she would rather eat glass than accept these terms—but she stopped herself.

"You're braver than they let you think."

She was brave. She had been brave her entire life. She had breathed fire and beat down her demons before, and she would do it again. Through all of the wallowing and self-doubt she had placed upon herself, she realized that she was in the best possible position to help her friends. To save them. She would find her allies and build her plan from the inside. She would endure whatever torturous fate Blake had in mind for her because she had to.

She wiped her tears and cleared her throat. "I promise," she answered, her voice stronger than it had been in days.

"I now recognize this union as bonded through the power given to me by the Factions."

And with that, her fate was sealed. Blake raced forward and sealed a kiss to her battered and bruised lips. He stepped back and sent her a superior smirk, his eyes glazed with excitement and power. The excitement radiated through the room as he quickly clapped his hands twice. She suspected if they had not needed to go to his daughter's wedding, he would have thrown her to the wolves this very second. He had beat her, and she belonged to him now. There was no stopping him from reaching his goals—or so he thought. Darcy smirked back at the man, feeling more hope and power than she had since she had met him.

Blake thought that he had won—what he didn't realize was that the game had only just begun.

Printed in the USA
CPSIA information can be obtained
at www.ICGtesting.com
LVHW051548240524
780934LV00002B/216